Oscar found himself wanting to put his arm around Kate, to shield her from the life blows she'd been taking.

Which brought him up short. What was he doing thinking about a woman that way? He had no business having tender feelings for anyone. What was wrong with him?

"I've got chores to do and then I need to get into the workroom. Orders are backing up with all the time I've been spending on other things." He let his daughter Liesl slide to the ground, but in spite of cautioning himself, his thoughts were still on Kate and his reaction to her.

He'd done more than he'd intended already, housing her, feeding her, even clothing her. That was neighborly, and that was also where he drew the line. He'd share his material possessions up to a point, but he would not share his heart. That belonged entirely to his dead wife.

He needed to be by himself to get his head ⌐ straight. Too much time spent with the wid⌐ Amaker was making him forget himself.

Erica Vetsch is a transplanted Kansan now residing in Minnesota. She loves history and romance and is blessed to be able to combine the two by writing historical romances. Whenever she's not immersed in fictional worlds, she's the company bookkeeper for the family lumber business, mother of two, wife to a man who is her total opposite and soul mate, and an avid museum patron.

Books by Erica Vetsch

Love Inspired Historical

His Prairie Sweetheart
The Bounty Hunter's Baby
A Child's Christmas Wish

ERICA VETSCH

A Child's Christmas Wish

HARLEQUIN® LOVE INSPIRED® HISTORICAL

Recycling programs for this product may not exist in your area.

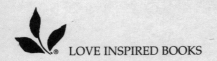

® LOVE INSPIRED BOOKS

ISBN-13: 978-0-373-42549-5

A Child's Christmas Wish

www.Harlequin.com

Printed in U.S.A.

Glory to God in the highest,
and on earth peace, good will toward men.
—*Luke* 2:14

For Heather Vetsch, whose love language
is gift giving, and who anticipates Christmas
better than anyone I know. Love you, dolly! —Mom

Acknowledgments:

My thanks to Adriana Gwyn
for her help with the German translations, and to
the Dodge County Historical Society for help with
the history of Berne and Mantorville, Minnesota.

Chapter One

Berne, Minnesota
November 1, 1875

"Lord, haven't we suffered enough?" Kate Amaker didn't say the words aloud, but they echoed in her head as Grossvater Martin urged the horses to hurry over the wooden bridge and up the slight rise to their farm drive. *"How much more can we take?"*

Ahead, a dull orange colored the night sky, illuminating the undersides of billowing gray clouds of smoke. Something on their farm was burning. Something big. What building was it? The barn? Thankfully, all the cows were out in the pasture tonight. The cheese house? An entire summer's worth of cheeses gone up in smoke? All their equipment…their livelihood?

Rattling over the bridge, they drew near, and Kate's heart sank. It was neither the barn nor the cheese house.

It was their home.

Kate put her arm around Grossmutter Inge and

gripped the edge of the wagon seat with her other hand. The horses responded to Grossvater's shouts by galloping up the hill, the wagon jouncing and slewing.

Johann and Grossvater had built the farmhouse together, replacing the three-roomed log cabin the family had lived in when they first arrived from Switzerland more than twenty years before. It was the house Johann had been so proud to bring his bride home to after their wedding almost two years before. The farmhouse was to shelter them through the coming Minnesota winter and welcome her baby in a few weeks. An ache started behind Kate's ribs, so heavy she couldn't take a deep breath.

Flames shot from every window and licked out under the eaves. Smoke bellied out in puffs and twists and tendrils, drawn up against the stars.

Grossvater brought the wagon to a halt well back from the fire. The horses snorted and stamped, and Kate sat in frozen horror on the wagon seat as the merciless flames engulfed the house.

Grossmutter clutched Kate's arm, her mouth open but not making a sound. Tears tracked down her cheeks, catching the light of the fire and glittering as they followed the wrinkles and seams of her lined face.

Kate turned back to the fire, knowing it was far too advanced to stop. Already the shingles were beginning to smoke. Soon, the flames would engulf the roof. Nothing could be saved. She huddled in her late husband's woolen coat, too shocked to grieve.

Shouts caught her attention, and the sounds of horses and wagon wheels on the road. Neighbors, coming home from the same church service where the Amakers had been worshipping and giving thanks to God for this year's harvest, drawn by the flames.

They drove into the farmyard in their wagons and buggies, but once they spied the three Amakers, no one dashed about trying to rescue anyone or save anything. No one tried to put out the fire. It was too late, and everyone knew it. Instead, they sat, faces illuminated by the angry blaze, silent, like Kate and Grossmutter and Grossvater.

What was there to say?

After a time, someone reached up to assist Grossmutter to the ground, and then reached up again for Kate, putting his hands under her arms. Numbly, she braced herself on the man's shoulders and found herself looking into the eyes of their closest neighbor, Oscar Rabb.

He took great care swinging her to the ground, and she felt the solidness of his muscles under his thick, black coat, steady and strong. The moment she was on her feet, he let go, stepping back. His broad-brimmed hat shaded his eyes, but the glow from the fire touched his cheeks and beard. He watched her, as if he thought he might need to catch her if she fainted.

She hadn't realized how big he was. Not just tall, but solid. She'd only seen him before from a distance as he worked in his fields, never this near. He had been an acquaintance of Johann's, but not a close friend. He was something of a recluse, a widower with a little girl, she believed.

The glass broke in the upstairs windows and fire shot out, voracious, consuming everything in its path. A hard lump formed in Kate's throat. All their things, all their memories.

"There was no one in the house?" Oscar asked. He stood facing the fire, his hands in his coat pockets, his breath making frosty puffs in the night air.

Kate shook her head. "No. We were in town. At church."

She turned away and put her arm around Grossmutter, who wept softly. When the fire began to encroach on the grass, neighbors brought buckets from the trough, dousing the flames lest they race toward the barn.

The heat was intense, smoke billowed toward them, stinging eyes and lungs. Grossvater led the team farther from the fire, and Kate guided Grossmutter back to stand beside the wagon.

"Oh, Katie, dear." Mrs. Hale bustled over. The proprietress of the only mercantile in town, along with her soft-spoken husband, Mrs. Hale had her finger in every possible piece of gossip pie. "So terrible." She fluttered and patted Kate's arm, an "isn't it awful" delight in her eyes. No doubt she'd be giving first-hand accounts to everyone who came into the store for the next week.

Kate nodded, unable to speak.

"We saw the flames clear from town and just had to come to see if we could help. Your poor house. God's blessing no one was inside." Mrs. Hale's hat, festooned with flowers and feathers, bobbed in the orange glow. "Did you leave a candle lit? Or a fire in the fireplace? That's how these things start, you know. I'm always so careful. I never leave the house without checking that I've put out all the lamps. Imagine how difficult it would be for us, and for the whole town, really, if we lost our house and the store. Hale's Mercantile is so vital to the town, after all. Why, folks would have to go clear to Mantorville for their purchases." She leaned in. "Are you sure you put out all the lamps?" Casting a glance Grossmutter's way, she whispered, "Old folks can be so forgetful, can't they?"

Anger burned in Kate's chest, hot as the house fire. Mrs. Hale was such a busybody that by tomorrow she would have it spread around that the Amakers had no one to blame but themselves for the fire, since they were so careless. "How it started isn't important, and I'm sure it had nothing to do with my family's age. Accidents happen, fires happen, and assigning blame or starting rumors won't help."

Mrs. Hale's brows, carefully plucked and arched, rose. Her lips puckered, and she put on her most long-suffering look. "You're distraught, Katie, dear. No doubt that's the reason for your harsh tone."

"Kate."

"Excuse me?"

"My name is Kate, not Katie. Kate or Mrs. Amaker." She eased Mrs. Hale's hand off her arm.

"Well." Mrs. Hale straightened, her chin going up. "I see Mrs. Quilling over there. I'll just go ask about her lumbago. *She* appreciates my concern." She lifted her hem and strode away, and Kate's heart fell. Why had she risen to Mrs. Hale's bait when she knew from experience that it did no good?

She tucked her hands into her coat pockets, pressing her palms against her stomach, feeling the hard roundness and the reassuring kick of her unborn baby.

The baby that now had no place to lay its head when it arrived.

It was all gone. Their clothes and food stores, books, blankets, furniture. All gone.

What were they going to do now?

The Amaker place was a total loss.

Oscar Rabb turned away from the blaze and went to his wagon to check on his daughter, Liesl. The four-year-old lay wrapped in a quilt, sleeping in the wagon box on a mound of straw. Rolf, his Bernese mountain dog, lay beside her. When Oscar drew near the wagon, the big animal raised his black-and-white head, his tail swishing the straw. Seeing that his daughter was safe, Oscar leaned against the wagon box to watch the fire. Rolf rose, shook himself and sidled over to put his head on Oscar's arm, begging to be petted.

The poor Amakers. The old couple and the young woman. He hadn't had much to do with them for a while. Then again, he hadn't had much to do with anyone but Liesl for the past two years. To his knowledge, he'd never met the younger woman, though he'd seen her from time to time. Pretty enough, he supposed, in a wholesome way. He remembered hearing that Johann Amaker had gotten hitched, but at the time Oscar had been too deep in his own grief to want to celebrate someone else's marriage.

But tonight, when he'd looked out his front window and seen the orange glow, he had scooped Liesl out of her bed, wrapped her in a blanket and raced out to hitch up his team. All the way to the neighboring farm, he'd feared that the Amakers were trapped by the fire. When he'd arrived at the blazing house at almost the same time as Martin's wagon had raced into the farmyard, he'd been weakened with relief. A house could be rebuilt, but a life lost was gone forever. Seeing them safe, he'd almost turned around and gone home, but something had made him stay.

"Tough time of year for this to happen," George Frankel said, stuffing his hands in his pockets and rocking on his boots. George had a farm a quarter mile to the south and a houseful of children, twelve at the last count. He was an easygoing—some said lazy—fellow who always had big plans but never seemed to accomplish any of them. He liked to chew the fat, and Oscar avoided him whenever possible.

"Any time of year is a tough time for this to happen." Oscar stroked his dog's broad black-and-white head. "It's good they weren't home." The flames were no longer roaring. Instead, they crackled and popped like a campfire. The wind carried most of the smoke to the north, away from where the handful of people milled and shuffled, but occasionally a gust would drift toward them, stinging eyes and clogging throats.

"Course, if they were home, it probably wouldn't have happened. They could've put it out before it spread." George shrugged, sneezed and dug in his pocket for a huge, wrinkled handkerchief.

Or they might have been in bed and trapped by the fire or overcome with smoke. George had a way of speaking his thoughts that assumed there was no other way of looking at things than his, and he loved to argue. Oscar wondered how soon he could get away. If he had known there was no danger to the family and that so many people would come, he would've stayed home.

Neighbors drifted by the Amakers, shaking Martin's hand, hugging the old woman and the younger one…what was her name? Kathy? No, that wasn't it. But something like that.

She was small—shorter than his wife had been—with dark brown hair. What had surprised him as he'd lifted her down from the wagon was that her eyes were blue. The clear blue of a summer sky. He wasn't used to looking into blue eyes. Gaelle's eyes had been brown, brown like Liesl's, brown like his.

Mrs. Hale, the shopkeeper's wife, bustled around, talking nineteen to the dozen. Another person Oscar avoided if he could. She was a do-gooder, but she never seemed to act out of true kindness. More like she wanted everyone to know she was doing good, as if someone was keeping a scorecard and she wanted to make sure she got full credit for her charity. Whatever she was saying to the younger Mrs. Amaker wasn't going down too well.

Good for young Mrs. Amaker. Someone should stand up to the old biddy's interfering ways.

"The question is, what are they going to do now?" George blew his nose, honking like a southbound goose. "I'd have them to my place, but we're cheek-by-jowl now."

And you have never gotten around to adding onto your house, though you've talked about it for ages… half a dozen kids ago.

Per Schmidt edged over, his whitish-blond hair bright in the glow of the fire. "I vish I could take zem in, but zere is no room at my house. My brother und his family haf come from de Old Country to live vid me und Gretel." His accent was so thick Oscar wished he'd just go ahead and speak German, which was as commonly heard in Berne, Minnesota, as English. But Per was proud of his English, proud to be an American now.

Martin Amaker, a tall, spare man, looked stooped and sort of caved in upon himself. He drew off his hat and ran his gnarled hand through his thin, white hair, staring at the destruction where his home used to be.

Oscar felt for the old man. With winter coming, two women dependent upon him and his house gone up in a shower of sparks, he had to be feeling bludgeoned. Oscar patted his hip pocket, feeling the small lump of his wallet. Hopefully the community would take up a collection so Oscar could contribute. He didn't want to just walk up and offer Martin money. That would be unbearable for both of them. No, a collection would be best. Oscar didn't mind giving money toward a good cause, mostly because it was anonymous and simple.

Another buggy rolled into the yard, the snazzy chestnut pulling it stomping and blowing, tossing her head. Ah, here was just the man to start passing the hat. The preacher levered his bulk out of the buggy, setting the conveyance to rocking. His tiny wife took his hand, looking like a child next to her giant of a husband. They both went right to the Amakers, heads bent in empathy.

They spoke, and Mr. Amaker shook his head, shrugging. Pastor Tipford scanned the crowd of neighbors who were already filtering toward their wagons, and his eyes came to rest on Oscar. An uncomfortable feeling skittered across Oscar's chest. Pastor Tipford visited Oscar regularly, trying to get him to come back to church, trying to get him involved in the community again. But Oscar wasn't ready for that. He still felt too raw inside to endure the company of well-meaning church folk.

He motioned for Oscar to come over.

"Looks like the pastor wants you." George sniffed again. "Rotten cold I've got. Passed it around the house like candy, we did. Every last kid sneezing and coughing and dripping. Not even the baby escaped."

Oscar stepped back. The last thing he wanted was to pick up George's cold and risk passing it on to Liesl.

Pastor Tipford motioned again.

"You better see vat he vants." Per hitched up his pants. "I vill be going now. Nothing to do here anyway. The house is gone." He went to his wagon, and climbed aboard. "*Gute Nacht*... I mean, good night."

Oscar checked on Liesl once more, told the dog to stay and waited for Per's wagon to roll past him and down the drive before heading toward Pastor Tipford and the Amakers. He braced himself for the sorrow in their eyes, tucking his hands into his coat pockets, taking a deep breath. Other people's grief always made his own more acute.

"Ah, just the man we need." Pastor Tipford clapped him on the shoulder, a hefty blow.

"Pastor." He nodded. "Mr. Amaker, I'm sorry about your house. I wish we could have saved it."

Martin Amaker looked at him, but he didn't really seem to see. His eyes behind his spectacles were unfocused and blank.

Shock.

The elder Mrs. Amaker trembled, twisting her fingers in the fringe of her shawl. The knot on the kerchief under her chin wobbled. The pastor's wife hugged her again, rubbing her arms as if trying to restore warmth.

But it was the younger Mrs. Amaker that drew Oscar's attention. She stood a little apart, her face golden in the reflection of the lowering flames. Her eyes were wide, and she huddled into the coat that was too large for her. It looked like a man's garment. Her dead husband's perhaps?

They had that in common, he realized. The loss of a spouse. He could understand her desire to keep her husband's memory close. She must really be missing him now.

God, you exact too high a price. What did she do to deserve this? First her husband and now her home? For that matter, what did I do to deserve to lose Gaelle? Or Liesl her mother?

"Oscar, the Amakers need a place to stay for the night." Pastor Tipford spoke in his most "let's all be reasonable" tone. "Your place would be perfect. You have the room, and you're right next door, so tending to the chores tomorrow would be simpler for everyone."

His place?

No.

He hadn't offered hospitality in years. Not since...

Everyone looked at the pastor. "The Frankels are too crowded, and anyway, there's been sickness there. And the parsonage is tiny," he pointed out. "You can help out, can't you, Oscar?"

Mrs. Tipford spoke up. "Of course he will. And I'm sure Liesl will love having some company." She gave Mrs. Amaker another reassuring squeeze. "It's all going to be all right, my dear. You can rebuild a house.

We're just thankful that no lives were lost. Now, it's late, and it's chilly, and there's nothing more we can do here. Everything will look better in the morning." She turned Mrs. Amaker toward the wagon, still whispering in her ear.

Without so much as a nod from him that it was all right. Women could be like that…tornadoes in petticoats, pushing the world around to suit themselves, and in such a nice way that men hardly protested.

But Oscar *was* going to protest. His home wasn't open for visitors, even for a night. There had to be another option, something that didn't involve strangers invading his peace.

"Come along, Kate," Mrs. Tipford called over her shoulder. "You shouldn't be out in this night air any longer."

Kate. So that was young Mrs. Amaker's name. Pretty name.

She reached up with both hands to tuck stray tendrils of hair off her face and her coat fell open.

Oscar felt as if he'd been punched in the gut.

She was pregnant.

He turned away, but the image was seared on his brain, and he was jerked right back to the center of his own grief. He'd lost his wife in childbirth two years ago come this Christmas. Having a woman in the family way around his house, even for one night, was going to rip open all the old wounds.

He couldn't do it. He wouldn't do it. Pastor Tipford would have to find someone else.

A hand touched his arm. He looked down into Kate Amaker's face. Her cheeks were gently rounded and looked so soft. How long had it been since he'd stood this close to a woman? Oscar sucked in a breath and smelled lavender mixed with wood smoke.

"Thank you." She bit her lip for a moment, her eyes looking suspiciously moist.

His muscles tensed. He hated to see any woman cry, even Liesl. It made him feel so helpless.

"It's kind of you to put us up. I don't know what we would do, where else we would go." She blinked hard, lifting her chin, her shoulders rising and falling as she breathed rapidly, staring at the glowing embers. "I… it's just…gone." Her pretty eyes met his once more.

And just like that, Oscar had houseguests.

Chapter Two

Everything…gone. Kate could hardly wrap her mind around the fact. Her clothes reeked of smoke, and if she closed her eyes, she could still see the merciless flames, the showers of skyward-rushing sparks, hear the crackle and roar. It was so hard to believe.

Away from the fire, the night was black and cold, the moon barely a sliver and the stars remote. The wagon rattled up the drive toward Oscar Rabb's house, and Kate kept her arm around Grossmutter. Neither had said a word since climbing onto the high seat. What was there to say? Words weren't enough to describe her sense of loss.

Oscar's house sat atop a small hill, facing south. Two-storied, white clapboard, with lots of windows. A porch stretched along the front. The overall design was more compact and less flamboyant than the house Johann had built, but the porch was similar. How many evenings had Kate and Grossmutter sat on the porch shelling peas, snapping beans, while Grossvater and Johann had sat on the steps, talking over the day's work, planning for the future? A hard lump formed in Kate's throat.

Oscar Rabb's house, porch notwithstanding, looked dark and forbidding with not a single light shining from any of the windows.

Ahead of them, Oscar drove his wagon down the slope behind the house toward his barn. Kate knew Oscar hadn't wanted to offer hospitality, that he'd been on the verge of refusing, but he had been too well-mannered. And Mrs. Tipford had practically co-erced him into it. Well, they didn't want to have to accept hospitality, either, but what else was there? Pastor Tipford had been right. Oscar's place was the logical, if reluctantly given, choice.

Grossvater directed the horses, Schwarz *und* Grau—Black and Gray—after Oscar's wagon, draw-ing up in front of the immense red barn with its gam-brel roof and sliding doors.

A large dog leaped from the bed of Oscar's wagon, his tail a bushy plume and his breast glowing white in the darkness. Every bone ached as Kate forced her-self to stand and climb down over the wagon wheel. The dog came over, friendly and sniffing, nudging her hand with his broad head for a pat.

"Rolf, come." Oscar snapped his fingers, and the big dog bounded to his side. "He can be a nuisance sometimes."

Kate and Grossmutter stood out of the way as the horses were unhitched and turned out into a small pen. Oscar forked some hay over the fence and then went to his wagon. He scooped up a blanket-wrapped bundle, holding it to his shoulder. Kate spied small, stocking-clad feet peeping from under the hem of the blanket.

This must be Oscar's daughter. Liesl, wasn't it? Kate's mind was so muddled she hadn't even thought to wonder where the child had been during the fire.

"This way." Oscar led the way up the curved path to the back of the house. "Watch your step."

"You go ahead. I'll follow." Kate let Grossvater take Grossmutter's arm and fell in behind them, lifting her skirt and the hem of Johann's heavy coat, weary beyond words. All she wanted was a quiet, warm bed, some place to curl up and sleep…to forget what had happened for a while.

They gained the porch, and Oscar held the door open. "I'll light a lamp."

He laid his daughter down on a bench beside the door and rattled the matchbox on the wall. A *scritch*, and light flared, illuminating his face. He touched the match to the wick of a glass kerosene lamp on the table and replaced the chimney. Light hovered around the table and picked out objects around the edges of the large room.

He'd brought them into the kitchen rather than through the front door, but the room seemed to have a dual purpose, one end for cooking and eating, while the other, through open pocket doors, appeared to be the sitting room. Chairs and a settee grouped around a massive fireplace. In the kitchen, beautiful wooden furniture filled the room—a sideboard, a bench, a table and chairs, all decorated with intricate carving. Oscar Rabb must be better off than most of the farmers around Berne if he could afford such fine furnishings.

The dog's nails clicked on the hardwood floor as he went to his water dish, lapping noisily and scattering droplets when he raised his head.

Upon closer inspection, the large room was…rather untidy. Not filthy, but definitely cluttered. Boots and shoes were piled by the door, and it appeared someone had taken apart some harness on the table. Straps and buckles and bits lay everywhere. At least there weren't dirty dishes, but Kate could tell it had been a long time since the room had received a thorough scrubbing.

Battered children's books and blocks lay on the rug in front of the settee, a rocking horse stood in one corner and what looked like a pinafore hung from his ear. A stack of newspapers stood beside a large wooden rocker. Was that where Oscar sat each night, reading while Liesl played? She categorized what she saw without really caring, observing only, too tired to do much else.

Oscar shifted his weight, shoving his hands into his pockets. "Bedrooms are upstairs. I can carry some water up for you as soon as I get Liesl settled. I imagine you want to wash some of the smoke off."

Kate wrinkled her nose. Her coat—Johann's coat— reeked of the fire, and she knew her hair did, too. She'd love a hot bath, but she'd settle for a cold basin of water and a bit of soap.

Their host shucked his black, wool coat and tossed it over the back of a chair. He lifted his daughter into his arms, cradling her head against his chest. Kate spied glossy, dark hair, and rounded, sleep-flushed cheeks. Long lashes, limp hands, a pale nightgown. Her heart constricted. There was something so sweet about a sleeping child, especially one held in a parent's embrace. Her hand went to her own baby, sleeping there under her heart.

"If you'll get the lamp?" Oscar looked at Kate and inclined his head.

She lifted the glass lamp and followed him toward the staircase. Grossmutter and Grossvater followed behind. At the top of the stairs, a hallway bisected the house. Four doors, evenly spaced, two on each side of the carpeted runner, and a window let a small amount of light in at the far end.

"You can sleep in here. And the older folks across the hall. Liesl's room is next to yours, and mine's across from hers." Oscar opened the first door on the right. A stale, closed-up smell rolled out. Starlight hovered near the windows, and the lamp lit only half the room as she stepped inside. The bare mattress on the bedstead had been rolled up and tied, and a sheet draped over what looked to be a chair. "There's sheets in the bureau. Sorry the bed isn't made."

He really hadn't been expecting company. Kate pushed a stray lock of hair off her forehead, forcing down a weary sigh. "It's fine. We'll take care of things." She set the lamp on the bureau, found another lamp there and lit it for her in-laws. "Get your daughter settled back into bed. We're sorry to inconvenience you like this." She was barely hanging on, willing herself not to cry. How soon could she be alone?

Grossvater took the second lamp. "Come, Inge. We will get some rest. As Mrs. Tipford said, perhaps things will look better in the morning. Thank you, Oscar, for a place to stay tonight." He put his arm around his wife and led her across the hall.

Oscar stood in the doorway, frowning. He lifted Liesl a bit higher in his arms, appeared about to say something and then shrugged. Finally, he turned away. "I'll be back with that water."

Kate left her coat on. She was chilly, though she wasn't sure if it was because the house was cold or from shock.

The rope binding the mattress roll was rough on her hands, but the knots came loose easily enough. With a couple of tugs, the feather-tick flopped open. She nudged it square on the bed frame. Searching the bureau—another hand-carved beauty—she found a set of sheets and a pair of pillows in the deep drawers.

Across the hall, she heard some rustling and bumping. Peeking through her door, she saw Grossvater spreading a sheet across a wide bed while Grossmutter slid a pillow into a case. They were speaking to each other in German, soft, gentle tones. Kate smiled as Grossvater called his wife "*liebchen*." There was so much love and affection in his tone it made Kate's heart hurt. In spite of all they had lost, they still had each other.

Boots sounded in the hall, and Kate returned to making up her bed. She had just finished spreading the top sheet smooth when there was a tap at her open door.

"I brought you some blankets." Oscar stood in the doorway, a bucket dangling from one arm, the other full of quilts.

"Thank you." She came to take them, careful not to touch him. The sharp tang of cedar drifted up. The blankets had been in a chest somewhere. "I'll share them across the hall."

Coming back from leaving more than half the blankets with her in-laws, she found Oscar flinging open a patchwork quilt over the bed. He'd poured water into the pitcher on the washstand, and he'd raised the wick on the lamp.

He drew the covering sheet off the chair, setting the rocker in motion as he wadded the muslin up. Standing there in the glow of the lamp, he waited, watching her.

What did he want? She drew her coat around herself. "Thank you. I hope we won't be too much of a bother. I'm sure we'll get something sorted out tomorrow." Though what, she couldn't imagine right now. "We'll need to be up early to tend the cows. If you wouldn't mind knocking on my door when you wake up?"

He nodded. "I'll say good night, then." He crossed the room and closed the door behind himself.

Kate opened her coat and let the heavy garment slip down her arms. Laying it over the rocker, she reached up and began unpinning her long, brown hair. It tumbled in waves about her shoulders. She had no brush, so she finger-combed the locks, separating them into strands and forming them into a less-than-elegant braid. Pouring water from the pitcher into the basin, her lips trembled. The water was warm. He must've drawn it from the reservoir on the stove. That was thoughtful of him.

Looking into the mirror, she grimaced. Soot streaked her cheeks, and her eyes were red from smoke and unshed tears. She looked as if she'd been dragged through a knothole backward. What a sight.

Dipping the corner of a towel into the water, she

scrubbed at her hands and face and neck. Patting herself dry, she considered her options for the night. No nightgown. Only a smoky dress with a let-out waist. Wrinkling her nose, she shed her dress and decided to sleep in her chemise and petticoat. She hurried to spread her clothing out over the footboard of the bed, hoping they would air overnight.

After all, they were the only clothing items she owned now.

Sliding under the covers, she curled up, wrapping her arms around her unborn baby. Loneliness swept over her, loss and sorrow crashing into her chest. She reached for the second pillow, burying her face in the feathery softness, letting the tears she'd been holding back flow.

The baby rolled and kicked, bumping against her hand, warm and safe in her belly. Which was just as well, since she had no home for him or her at the moment.

Oscar closed the damper on the stove, checking that the fire was well-banked and letting Rolf out for one last run before he climbed the stairs to his bedroom. The clock on the mantel said it was already tomorrow, and he needed to be up early. Familiar with his house in the dark, he didn't bother with a lamp.

His boots sounded loud on the stairs, and he wished he had remembered to take them off in the kitchen. Liesl, once asleep, could slumber through a brass band marching through her bedroom, but his houseguests probably didn't sleep that soundly.

Light snoring came from the old couple's room. He was glad someone was getting some rest. They were in the room his wife had reserved for her parents when they came down to visit from Saint Paul. Those infrequent visits had always made Oscar uncomfortable. His in-laws had wanted their daughter to marry someone from town, a doctor or banker or lawyer, someone who could provide an easy life for her in the city in which she was born. But she had married him instead, a farmer and woodworker. It had been on one of his trips to the city to deliver his hand-carved furniture that he'd met Gaelle. One look and he'd been a goner. Three happy years of marriage, one daughter and a baby on the way…and now nearly two years of emptiness…except for Liesl. If he hadn't had that little girl to look after, he didn't know what he would've done.

He shook his head, letting go of the banister to start toward his own room. A sound to his right made him pause. The muffled sound of a woman crying. It seeped under the door and into his chest.

The widow.

Helplessness wrapped around him, and his own grief, never far below the surface, rose up to engulf him. He shifted his weight and a floorboard creaked.

The crying stopped, and he walked down the hall, feeling guilty at intruding upon her sorrow. Grief was a private thing, and it must be wrestled one-on-one. He knew from experience. Well-meaning outsiders weren't welcome.

He peeked into Liesl's room one last time to make sure she was still under the covers. His daughter often slept like a windmill, throwing aside blankets and pillows and apt to be sideways in the bed before dawn. A sound sleeper, but an active one.

For once, her head lay on the pillow, the blankets tucked to her chin where he'd placed them upon their return to the farmhouse. Her journey out into the night air didn't seem to have done her any harm. Of course, she'd been well wrapped up and had Rolf curled up beside her, sharing his warmth. The dog followed him into the room and flopped onto the rug beside her bed, his tail softly thumping the floor. Oscar smiled and smoothed Liesl's nut-brown hair, his hand engulfing her little head. She looked just like her mother and chattered like a chickadee from dawn till dusk. He'd do just about anything for her.

He shut her door and entered his own room. The weak moon had long set, and faint starlight was the only illumination, but there wasn't much to worry about knocking into in here. A single bed, washstand, and armoire, all made by him, were the only furnishings.

He eased his suspenders off his shoulders, loosening his shirt where it had been pinned by his braces. Letting the suspenders fall against his thighs, he poured water into his washbasin. Washing quickly, Oscar got ready for bed.

Once in bed, he couldn't sleep. Stacking his hands under his head, he looked up at the ceiling and thought about the Amakers. He'd known Johann for years. They'd gone to school together, loaned one another horses and equipment when in need, been members of the same congregation, but they weren't close friends. Oscar wasn't particularly social, and since his wife's death, he'd stayed to himself even more.

Still, it bothered him that Johann's widow was crying down the hall, alone and grieving.

And pregnant.

Every time he thought about that, it was like a fist to his gut. He didn't want to be responsible, even in a small way, for an expectant mother. Too much could go wrong. He'd have to find another place for the Amakers soon. Maybe even tomorrow. By tomorrow afternoon, he was sure a collection would've been taken up, and maybe they could rent a place in town until a new house could be built.

He rolled to his side and willed his eyes to shut and his mind to stop thinking about the woman across the hall.

It seemed he'd only been asleep for a minute when something patted his face. He squinted through his lashes, pretending to still be asleep as the light of a new dawn peeped through the window. Liesl stood beside his bed, her hair tousled, cheeks still flushed from sleep.

"Daddy, the sun is waking up."

She said the same thing every morning. She'd always been an early riser, and he'd been forced to teach her that she couldn't get out of her bed until the sun was up. So she waited, every morning, and at the first sign of dawn, she was in here urging him to get up and start his day. He lay still, eyes closed, playing the game.

"Da-a-a-dddyyy!" She patted his whiskers again. "You're playing 'possum.'"

He grinned, reached for her with a growl and grabbed her, wrapping a knitted afghan around her. "Brr, it's too chilly to be standing there in your nightdress. Is it time to milk the chickens?" He rubbed his beard against her neck, careful not to scratch too hard.

She giggled and squirmed, kneeing him in the belly as she twisted in his grasp. "Silly Daddy, you don't milk chickens." Liesl took his face between her little hands, something she did when she wanted him to pay particular attention to her. "Daddy, I had a dream last night."

Which was nothing new. Liesl was an imaginative child who had dreams, both night and daydreams, that were vivid in color and detail.

"What did you dream this time, punkin? That you were a princess?"

Her brown eyes grew round. "How did you know?"

He gave her a squeeze, tucking her head under his chin for a moment. "It might be because we read the princess story again before bedtime last night."

Liesl giggled and shoved herself upright. Her hair wisped around her face, and she smeared it back with both hands. "I did dream I was a princess, and you were there, and we had a picnic, and I had a pink dress, and there were beautiful white horses and sunshine and cake."

"So, it's a pink dress now, is it? Yesterday it was blue. I thought blue was your favorite color." He sat up and wrapped the blanket around her again, scooting up to rest his back against the headboard.

"I like all the colors, but today I like pink best." She fingered the stitches edging the blanket. "Pink, with blue flowers? For Christmas?"

He laughed. "Pink with blue flowers. Got it." Somewhere along the way, she'd latched on to the idea of presents for Christmas. He must've mentioned it to her once. That's all it took with Liesl. Say something that interested her, and she grabbed it with both hands and ran with it. But he'd told her she could only expect one thing for Christmas, so she must be very sure what she decided upon. As a result, the wish changed every day.

He chucked her under the chin. "There's something I need to tell you. We have visitors."

Her little brows arched. "Where?" She looked around the room as if expecting them to pop out from behind the door.

Laughing, he dropped a kiss on her head. "They're sleeping down the hall. Last night their house caught on fire, and they didn't have anywhere else to sleep, so they came home with us."

"A fire in a house?" Worry clouded her brown eyes. "What house?"

Pressing his forehead to hers, he wished he didn't have to expose her to such harsh realities as house fires. "They are the Amakers, who live next door."

"With the brown cows?" she asked.

"Yes, with the brown cows." The Amaker pastures bordered Oscar's land, and from the top of the hill, he and Liesl could look down and see the herd of Brown Swiss as they wended their way to the milking barn each evening. Speaking of which, he needed to get up and wake his guests as Kate had asked last night. There were chores to do, cows to milk and decisions to be made.

"Scamper back to your bed, Poppet, and I'll be in to help you get dressed in a minute."

"I can do it myself, Daddy." She gave him a look that reminded him of her mother. Bossy, but sweet about it.

"I know, but I like to help." And she still needed

him, even if she didn't think so, if only to fasten her dress up the back and button her little high-topped shoes.

He dressed quickly, ran his fingers through his unruly hair and went to Liesl's room. She sat in the middle of her bed, leafing through one of the story-books they read each night. She stopped on the picture of the princess. "See, pink."

"I see." He gathered her clothing. It was time to do laundry…again. It seemed he barely had the last washing put away before it was time to get out the tubs again. He would be the first to admit he wasn't much of a housekeeper. The farm took so much of his time, the housework usually got a lick and a promise until he couldn't ignore it any longer. "Well, it's going to be a green dress today because that's what's clean."

"I can do it, Daddy." Liesl was growing more independent by the day, always wanting to be a bigger girl than she was. Oscar would do anything to hold back time, because he had firsthand knowledge of how fleeting it was, but that was something you couldn't explain to a four-year-old.

He handed her the items one by one and she put them on. When it was time for her stockings, he got them started around her toes and heel and she pulled them up. Then the dress. She turned and showed him her back to do up the buttons. He laid her long, straight hair over her shoulder and fitted buttons to holes. Then her pinafore over the top, with a bow in the back.

"Time to do hair." Oscar reached for her hairbrush on the bedside table.

"I don't like doing hair. It tugs." Liesl handed him the hairbrush, a scowl on her face.

"Can I help?"

The question had both Oscar and Liesl turning to the door.

Kate Amaker, dressed and ready for the day.

Oscar sucked in a breath, his heart knocking against his ribs, staring at her rounded middle that the voluminous coat had covered last night. He was no judge, but was she ready to deliver soon?

Liesl looked their guest over, and Oscar waited. The little girl could be quite definite in her likes and dislikes.

Evidently, Mrs. Amaker fell into the "likes" category, for Liesl smiled and handed her the hairbrush.

"What happened to your tummy?" She pointed at Mrs. Amaker's middle.

A flush crept up her cheeks, and Oscar cleared his throat. "Liesl, that's not polite."

His daughter looked up at him with puzzled brown eyes. "Why, Daddy?"

"It's all right." Mrs. Amaker smiled, her face kind. "I'm going to have a baby. He's growing in my tummy right now, and when the time is right, he'll be born."

Liesl's face lit up. "A baby. In your tummy? When will the time be right? Today?"

Mrs. Amaker laughed. "No, sweetling. Not for a couple of months. Around Christmas."

Oscar's gut clenched. He'd lost his wife and second child around Christmas.

Liesl had a different reaction. She clapped her

hands, bouncing on her toes. "That's it, Daddy. That's what I wish for this Christmas. A baby. Can I have a baby for Christmas?"

Chapter Three

Kate took the hairbrush from Oscar and sat on the side of the bed, not meeting his eyes. The poor man looked stricken. She should change the subject. "You have lovely hair." She smiled at Liesl. "I love to brush and braid hair. Is it all right if I help you?"

Liesl, eyes round, nodded and turned, backing up until she rested against Kate's knees. Oscar stood, jamming his hands into his pants' pockets, looming, a frown on his bearded face. Kate wondered if she'd overstepped by offering to brush and braid Liesl's hair, but it was too late to recall her offer.

"Are you a princess?" Liesl asked, breathless.

Kate laughed. "No, darlin', but bless you for asking." She wanted to hug the little sprite. "You're Liesl, right? My name is Kate."

Drawing the brush through Liesl's hair, Kate remembered her mama doing the same thing for her. "Do you have ribbons for your braids, or do you use thread? My mama used to use thread for every day, and ribbons on Sunday for church." Liesl's hair fell almost to her waist, thick and glossy brown. It would be easy to braid.

"Daddy uses these." She held up two strips of soft leather. "He calls it whang leather. He made it from a deer."

Leather to tie up a little girl's hair. Still, it probably worked well. She parted Liesl's hair and quickly fashioned two braids, wrapping the leather around the ends and tying it. "There you go. You look sweet."

"Thank you. Daddy says I am pretty like my mama, but it's how I act that is important."

"Your daddy is right." She caught "Daddy's" eye and smiled.

"Can we go eat breakfast now?" Liesl hopped on her toes.

"Absolutely. Right after we turn down your covers to air the bed. Shall we do it together?" Kate pushed herself up awkwardly, and before she got upright, Oscar was there at her elbow, helping her. His hand was warm on her arm, and she was grateful for his assistance. "Thank you. It's getting harder to maneuver these days."

He stepped back, his eyes wary, and she laughed. "Don't look so worried. I told Liesl the truth. I have a couple of months yet. Until Christmas."

He didn't laugh with her.

Breakfast was an ordeal. Kate had little appetite in the mornings these days, and especially not for oatmeal so sticky it clung to the roof of her mouth and tasted of damp newspaper. Grossmutter would have made a coffee cake for breakfast today, using her sourdough starter from the crock that always sat on the shelf behind the stove. Now the shelf, the crock and the stove were gone.

Their host and the maker of the meal shoveled the gooey mass into his mouth as if stoking a furnace. His daughter sat on a high chair, her little boots kicking a rung as she poked and stirred her oatmeal, taking little bites and watching the strangers at her table. Uncertain, but clearly curious.

As for Oscar Rabb… Someone had put a burr on his shirttail. He must have morning moods, because from the moment she'd offered to help with his daughter's hair, he'd been wary and gruff, as if having them there put him out considerably and he couldn't wait for them to leave.

Inge and Martin ate quietly, still looking exhausted and facing a difficult day. How could Kate help them through it when she felt as if she was barely hanging on herself? And yet, she must. Johann would expect it, and they needed her. And she loved them as if they were her own grandparents. Having lost her family soon after her wedding, Johann's grandparents were all the family she had left now.

"I am finished." She put her spoon down, her bowl still more than half full. "We had better get going soon. The cows will be waiting at the barn door."

"Oscar," Grossvater said. "I would like to leave Inge here, if that is all right? Kate and I can tend the cows and the cheeses. Perhaps Inge can help with the little one." He nodded toward Liesl.

The little girl's eyes grew rounder, and she looked to her father. "Actually…" He let his spoon clatter into his empty bowl. "I was thinking that you should all stay here. I can milk your cows for you today."

Kate blinked. He'd been grouchy all morning, and now he was volunteering to milk ten cows all by himself? Cows that weren't even his? He'd been reluctant from the first to have them in his house, and now he was offering to give them even more help?

"That's very kind of you, Mr. Rabb." Kate scooted her chair back and went to stand behind her family, putting her hands on their shoulders. "But we don't want to be any more of a burden to you than we already have been. We must see to our own chores, and we must decide where we are to go."

Inge stood and began clearing the table. "Nonsense, Martin. We will all go. We need to see what can be salvaged of the house, if anything, and there is plenty of work to do this morning. I am old, but I am not useless." She gave her husband a determined look, and he shook his head, smiling and patting her hand.

"I only wanted to spare you the unpleasantness for a while. If you are sure, we will all go."

Liesl hopped off her chair and scampered toward the door, lifting a contraption of wood and straps and toting it to her father. "Me, too, Daddy?"

He took the odd item and rubbed her head with his large hand. "You, too, Poppet, but we'll take the wagon over and use this later."

"Can she ride in our wagon with us?" Liesl pointed to Kate.

Kate stopped buttoning her coat—still smelling of smoke—in surprise. "Me?"

Liesl nodded. "I like you. You're pretty. Are you sure you aren't a princess? You look like the princess in my book." She turned to Grossmutter. "Did you know she has a baby in her tummy? Daddy's going to get me a baby for Christmas. He said I should ask for the one thing that I want most, and he would get it for me."

Grossmutter smiled. "Do you mean a doll baby?"

Liesl shook her head, her braids sliding on her shoulders. "No, I have a doll baby. I want a real baby. Like Miss Kate's." She crossed her arms, a determined look in her little brown eyes. "I like Miss Kate."

Kate laughed, smoothing her unruly hair and glancing down at her masculine coat, ordinary farm dress and burgeoning middle. "Bless you, child. I like you, too." Her father had his hands full with this one. Just how was he going to dissuade her from her wish of a real baby for Christmas?

Oscar's frown took some of the pleasure out of the little girl's compliment. "Mrs. Amaker probably wants to ride with her family. Don't pester her."

Which Kate took to mean he didn't want her riding with him and his daughter. Liesl's mouth set in a stubborn line, but she didn't argue with her father.

So they arrived at the Amaker farm in two wagons. Kate took one look at the burned-out shell of a house, the half-toppled chimney and the wisps of smoke still drifting from the piles of ashes, and covered her mouth with trembling fingers.

It definitely did not look better in the morning light.

Grossvater pulled the wagon to a stop and sat with the reins loose in his hands, resting his forearms on his thighs. "We must thank God that we were not at home when this happened, that none of us was lost in this fire."

He wrapped the lines around the brake handle and climbed down, reaching up to help Grossmutter. Kate began to descend the other side of the wagon, but before she could step on the high wheel, Oscar was there, reaching up for her and lifting her gently to the ground. He looked sober and wary.

"You should be careful. You wouldn't want to fall." He stepped back. Liesl waited in his wagon, but the dog had jumped down, already nosing around the edges of the devastation.

"Come, Kate," Grossvater said, holding out his hand. "We need to pray."

She rounded the wagon and joined the old couple. She needed to hear Grossvater pray, to lean on the strength of his faith, because hers was feeling mighty small this morning. Tucking her hand into his work-worn, age-spotted clasp, she sucked in a deep breath and bowed her head. A smile touched her lips as Liesl's hand slipped into hers.

"Our Father, we give You thanks for this day and that we are here to praise You. We thank You that we still have our cows and our barns and our land. Our hearts are heavy, but we are trusting in You. You are sovereign. You are good. You have a plan to bring good out of something we see as a tragedy today. We are weak, and we need Your strength.

"We give You thanks for Oscar Rabb and Liesl, and for their hospitality. We ask that You bless them and help us to be a blessing to them as they have been to us.

"Please give us the peace that is beyond our earthly understanding. Make Your will plain to us. We are trusting You to provide. *Dein Wille geschehe.*"

Liesl tugged on Kate's hand and whispered loudly, "What does that mean?"

Kate bent as far as her rounded belly would allow. "It means 'Your will be done.' Sort of like 'Amen.'"

"Oh, amen, then." She grinned, then sobered. "It's sad about your house. Are you going to live with us now?"

Oscar made a noise that wasn't really a word but wasn't exactly a grunt, either. Kate shook her head. "No, sweetling. We aren't going to live with you. Your father was kind enough to offer us a place for the night until we could decide what to do."

Inge put her arm through Martin's. "This is our home. We will rebuild."

Kate looked at Grossvater over the old woman's head, noting the strain in his eyes. Where would the money to rebuild come from?

Martin patted his wife's hand. "For now, we need to milk the cows. They are setting up their chorus."

Down by the barn, the herd of ten Brown Swiss bovines stood near the door, and from time to time a plaintive moo sounded. At the gate on the other side of the barn, four crossbred heifer calves nosed one another, tails swishing, ready for breakfast.

"Climb aboard, Poppet." Oscar shouldered his way into the contraption Liesl had brought to him in the house, and it arranged itself into a sort of pack. He crouched, and the little girl grasped the straps and threaded her legs into the correct places, facing backward and sitting in a little webbed seat on her father's back. Oscar stood carefully and looked over his shoulder. "All set?"

"Yep." Her small boots swung, and she grinned.

Kate stared.

Oscar shrugged, gently, so as not to unseat Liesl. "She's been riding in this since she was two. I couldn't leave her alone in the house while I worked, so I made this."

Grossvater let the cows into the barn, and creatures of habit that they were, they each went to their own stall. Kate took her milking stool from its peg on the wall, and Grossmutter gathered the buckets they had cleaned and put away before going to church last night. While Grossvater fed the cows, Kate started at the far end with the milking.

All the cows were named after Swiss cantons and towns—Grossvater's choice. Saint Gallens, Zug, Geneva, Lucerne, Berne... Kate knew each one well. The barn smelled of hay and cows and milk and dust. Light came in the high windows and the open door at the end, and she rested her cheek against Jura's warm side, falling into the steady milking rhythm, hearing the milk zing into the bucket, the tone changing as the level rose. Soon, Grossvater began milking the cows on the other side of the aisle, and farther down, she heard Liesl's voice, chatting with her father as he, too, milked cows.

Grossmutter patted Kate on the shoulder. "I will go to the cheese house and brush and turn the cheeses."

"We won't be long here. We'll put the milk in the springhouse. I won't worry about cooking another batch of cheese today." Kate finished with Jura and picked up the heavy bucket of warm, foamy milk.

She took it down the barn to where clean, empty milk cans sat on the handcart Grossvater used to take milk down to the springhouse. The cows were giving less milk now. In high summer, ea... cow gave several gallons of milk every day, and Kate made a new batch of cheese every couple of days throughout the summer. But now they gave less than half the summer amount, and she could store the milk for a few days before making a batch of cheese.

"Let me do that. You shouldn't be toting such heavy things." Oscar took the bucket, lifting it easily and pouring it into the open can.

Liesl twisted over his shoulder and waved. "Daddy, can I get down?"

"Not just yet, Poppet. Wait until we're done in the barn."

"Mr. Rabb, I appreciate your help, but I'm not helpless." Kate took the bucket to go to the next cow.

"No, you're not helpless, but you are in a delicate way." His face reddened a bit, and Kate's warmed.

"The work must be done." Not that she had always been the milkmaid. Making cheese was one thing, but barn work another. Johann hadn't liked her in the barn doing what he considered a man's chores. He had always been the herdsman, but after his death, Kate had needed to do more work about the farm. Grossvater couldn't do it alone.

She'd been feeling overwhelmed with the farm work already. In a couple of months, after the baby was born, how would she be able to get everything done? At least the baby was coming in the winter, when farm work slowed down, but Martin and Inge weren't getting any younger, and there would be another mouth to feed. Would they be able to keep up with all that the farm required? And how could they get the money together to rebuild the house? Everything was so costly, and their savings were meager. Last spring, Johann had spent a fair amount of their savings buying a Brown Swiss bull to improve his herd.

It was that bull that had caused the accident that had cost Johann his life.

Now the bull was gone and so was the money.

Kate's shoulders bowed under the burden, and she tried hard to hold on to Grossvater's faith-filled prayer.

God, help me find a way.

Oscar let Liesl climb out of the carrier. "Stay where I can see you, and don't go near where the fire was."

"Yes, Daddy." She went to the gate where the calves had their heads down munching the hay Martin Amaker had forked over the fence. Rolf, her shadow, went with her, tail wagging gently, eyes alert.

A wagon rolled into the yard, and Per Schmidt climbed down from the high seat. *"Guten Morgen."* He surveyed the charred remains of the house, sweeping his hat off his head when the Amaker ladies came out of the barn toward him.

"Morning." Oscar began a slow circuit of the burned-out area, but he could see nothing in the ashes to salvage. Bits of bent metal, puddles of melted glass, bricks fallen from the chimney, but nothing worth saving.

"Dere is not much left." Per followed him. "Vat are dey going to do? Do dey haff family to help?"

He didn't know. Oscar glanced over to check on Liesl and found that Kate had helped her climb the gate to look over at the calves. Kate stood behind the little girl, holding her safely, their heads together.

Which reminded him of how easily she'd brushed and braided Liesl's hair this morning—a task he usually struggled with—and how seeing the two of them together like that had been a kick to his middle. He'd been surprised at how quickly Liesl had warmed to having strangers in the house and to Kate in particular.

And now Liesl wanted a baby for a Christmas present. He wasn't really worried about this, because she changed her mind every day. Tomorrow she would want a doll pram or a kitten or new hair ribbons.

"I saw Prediger Tipford coming down the road. He vill be here soon."

Oscar hoped so. Surely by now Pastor Tipford had come up with a plan for the Amakers, a better place for them to stay until they could rebuild.

Martin Amaker came out of the barn slowly pulling the milk cart. Oscar nodded to Per and went down the path.

"Let me help." He took the handle of the cart. "To the springhouse?"

"Yes. Thank you, son. Milking is heavy work, is it not?" Martin tugged a handkerchief out of his pocket and wiped his brow. "Though I must confess, everything seems heavier today."

Oscar made short work of storing the milk. The springhouse, built over a diverted part of Millikan Creek, was damp and cold. A row of milk cans stood along the back wall, and Oscar added the two from the cart.

He tried to imagine Martin and Kate doing the

heavy work of the farm all alone for the past six months. Guilt hit him. Johann had been gone for half a year now, and what had Oscar done to help his neighbors? Nothing. But he had his own farm to look after, and a child, and a house. He was nearly overwhelmed at times himself.

At least he could salve his conscience that he had offered them hospitality last night. A paltry bit of comfort, but it was something.

Pastor Tipford and his wife drove into the farmyard as Oscar returned the cart to the barn. Kate helped Liesl down from the fence, holding her hand as they walked up the slight slope to greet the newcomers.

Her other hand rested on the swell of her unborn child, and Oscar swallowed. Losing his wife in childbed had been a double blow. God had taken Gaelle and their second daughter on Christmas Eve almost two years ago. Even now, the grief could steal his breath.

"Ah, Oscar, I trust you got the Amakers settled last night, and you were all able to get some rest?" Pastor Tipford's voice filled the farmyard. He always spoke as if he were talking to someone in the back pew.

Mrs. Amaker nodded. "He was most kind."

The preacher's wife smiled at him. "Of course he was."

Oscar shoved his hands into his pockets. He wished they'd get on with the discussion. His own chores were waiting.

"Martin, Inge, we were able to spread the word of your situation last night when we returned to town, and a small collection was gathered." Pastor Tipford handed Martin a small sack. "Everyone wishes it were more." He shuffled his large feet.

Oscar frowned. He hadn't been asked to contribute yet. Not that he had much hard cash. Most of his money was tied up in the farm, the implements and the livestock. With the harvest, he had enough to pay his account at Hale's Mercantile and purchase basic supplies for the winter. He wouldn't have any more cash coming in until he could finish and sell the furniture he made during the winter months. Several orders had come in, but they weren't even started yet. But still, he would give a little something to the Amaker collection.

Martin Amaker took the purse from Pastor Tipford, his eyes suspiciously bright. Inge's lips trembled, and Kate stood with her hand cupping Liesl's head. "How can we thank everyone?" she asked.

"Don't you worry, child," Mrs. Tipford said. "Pastor has already thanked folks for you. Now, we need to get down to brass tacks. What are your plans?"

Martin shook his head. "We have had little time to discuss anything."

"Well, the Bakers have said that Kate can come stay with them, and the Freidmans have a guest room for the two of you."

Kate's eyebrows rose. "Be separated? And away from the farm?"

Oscar frowned. The Bakers lived in town, but the Freidmans lived on a farm at least five miles north of Berne. He didn't like the notion of the old couple that far from Kate, nor of Kate being on her own. And what about their livestock? Who would take care of the milking cows and calves?

"Child, no one we asked had room for all of you." Mrs. Tipford shook her head. "I wish the parsonage had an extra bedroom or two, but it's so small we almost have to go outside to change our minds." She laughed at her little joke. "As for the farm, Gregor Freidman has said he will drive Martin out to do the chores twice a day. He's retired now, so he has the time."

From what Oscar remembered about Gregor Freidman, he was even older than Martin Amaker and twice as frail. If they got an early snowfall, all too likely here in Minnesota, two old men shouldn't be on the road between here and town. It would be a twenty-mile round trip from one farm to the other.

Pastor Tipford rubbed his hands together. "Anyway, it is only for a few weeks, until you get another house built. Lots of folks will be willing to help with the work. It will be a community effort. I can drive you down to Mantorville to the sawmill to order the lumber today. They could probably have a couple wagonloads delivered tomorrow afternoon."

Martin and Inge shared a look, and Kate bit her lip.

"That's very kind of you, Pastor." Martin straightened his age-bent back. "But we…" He stopped, staring at the horizon for a moment. "We are not in a position to rebuild right now."

Rolf came to lean against Oscar's leg, and he reached down to pat the dog's head. He could sympathize with Martin. If he had lost his house, he wouldn't have had enough laid by to rebuild. Of course, he could get a loan at the bank to pay for lumber and hardware. He hated to buy on time, but sometimes you had to.

"Not rebuild?" Pastor's voice boomed.

Martin's voice seemed thin and frail. "Not right now."

They must be even harder up than Oscar thought. And now they were going to be separated from each other, living with different families in town?

Liesl reached up and took Kate's hand, her face scrunched, looking from one adult to another, not understanding what was happening. She was a sensitive little thing, quick to perceive moods, even ones she didn't understand.

Kate's other hand rested on the gentle mound of her unborn baby, and her face was as pale as the milk he'd just put in the springhouse. Oscar had the ridiculous urge to go to her, to put his arms around her and offer her some of his strength. He shook his head. Their problems weren't really his concern, were they? He had enough trouble of his own, which he took care of on his own.

"You don't have to decide anything right now. You are welcome to stay at my place until you can make other arrangements." Oscar almost bit his tongue, so surprised was he. Where had that come from? He'd just issued an invitation of indefinite duration? And not just to an old couple, but to an expectant widow?

"I'm sure it would only be for a couple of weeks at the most, right? Just until you sort things out."

Had he lost his mind?

And yet, he didn't find himself wanting to renege. What was wrong with him?

Chapter Four

When they returned to Oscar's house, Grossvater went with him to the barn, but Oscar shook his head at Kate's offer to help. "I don't need you to muck out stalls. If you stay in the house and mind Liesl, that will be enough."

He squatted beside his daughter. "You can show the ladies around the house, right?"

Liesl nodded, uncertainty wrinkling her brow. No doubt she went to the barn with him every morning.

"We'll be back soon." He brushed his knuckle down her cheek.

Kate watched the two men walking side by side down the slope to the barn, one white-haired and lean, the other strong and tall. How many times had she watched Johann and Grossvater like this, heading out for a day of farming together?

"What should we do now?" Liesl took Kate's hand.

"What do you usually do in the mornings?" Kate asked.

"Go to the barn with Daddy." Liesl shrugged. "That's a funny coat."

Kate smiled at the quick swap of topics. "It is, isn't it? That's because it belonged to my husband. It's kind of big, but when I wear it, it helps me remember him." She headed for the kitchen door, her stomach rumbling. "All that work made me hungry. How about we get a snack?"

Grossmutter was already in the kitchen, surveying the room, hands on hips. Kate knew that look.

"Liesl," Kate said, bending to the little girl. "I don't think we properly introduced you two. This is my *Grossmutter*. That means 'grandmother.' I am sure she won't mind if you call her that, since it seems like we will be staying with you for a few more days."

Grossmutter smiled, her lined face gentle as she put a work-worn hand on Liesl's head. *"Schätzchen."*

Liesl looked to Kate.

"That means 'sweetheart.'"

The child beamed. "She's nice. And so are you."

"I think we should have our snack, and then we can see about helping out around here. We might not be welcome in the barn, but we can make a difference in the house." Kate went to the cupboard. She felt the need to keep busy, to keep her thoughts at bay for a while. And to somehow repay a bit of Oscar Rabb's kindness.

She sliced a rather misshapen loaf of bread and spread it with butter.

"There's honey in the pot on the shelf." Liesl pointed. "I like honey on my bread."

So they had honey, too. Afterward, Grossmutter found a broom, and Kate wiped Liesl's chin and hands with a damp cloth.

"You and I can do the dishes, and you can tell me

where everything goes." Kate drew a chair up to the counter for the child and filled the washtub with warm water from the stove reservoir. Shaving a few soap chips off the cake beside the pump, she stirred them until suds formed and placed the breakfast dishes and snack plates into the water.

Liesl talked the entire time they washed and wiped dishes. "Daddy doesn't like doing dishes, so he waits until night time to clear up. He says he'd rather do a lot at once than have to do them a lot of times during the day."

Kate smiled, handing her a tin cup to dry. She wasn't overly fond of dishes herself.

"Daddy lets me help, but I can only dry the cups and spoons and forks. He does the plates himself. When I'm big enough, I'll do all the dishes all by myself. Daddy says he will be glad when that day comes."

Grossmutter opened the kitchen door and swept the dirt outside and off the porch. When she came in, she began sorting the boots and shoes beside the door into neat rows.

By the time the men had finished the barn chores and returned to the house, Kate had washed the kitchen windows with vinegar and water, scrubbing them with crumpled newspaper that Liesl had found for her, and Grossmutter had taken her broom to the cobwebs in the corners and along the crown moldings. Liesl had been given a damp cloth and the task of wiping down all the kitchen chairs, which had been moved into a row at the far end of the room. Kate had tied an empty flour sack around the little girl's waist to spare her pinafore. She looked adorable, concentrating on each rung and chair leg, chattering the whole while, surprisingly at ease with the women when it was clear she spent almost all her time with just her father.

"What are you doing?" Oscar filled the doorway.

"Daddy. I'm cleaning. Aren't I doing a good job?" Liesl held up the rag, her face alight. "Kate and Grossmutter are cleaning, too."

Kate looked up from her hands and knees where she was scrubbing the floor around the stove, and Grossmutter put a row of glasses back in the cupboard, having just wiped down the shelves.

"You are doing a beautiful job." He nodded to his daughter, but he didn't take his eyes off Kate as he came in and put his hand under her elbow, helping her to stand. "Could you come outside for a moment?"

His eyes were stern, his expression fierce. Though his grip on her arm was firm, it wasn't tight as he directed her to the porch.

"Where are you going, Daddy?"

"We'll be back soon, Poppet. Just keep on with what you're doing." He closed the door behind him.

Kate clasped her elbows, turning to face the sunshine. Overhead, a V of Canada geese honked and flapped, heading for warmer temperatures.

"What are you doing?" Oscar asked. "Scrubbing my floors?"

She looked up at him. He stood with one hand braced on a porch post, the other on the railing, looking out over his fields dormant now that the harvest was over. He wore a patched flannel shirt, the plaid faded from many washings, the sleeves rolled up to reveal strong forearms dusted with brown hair. Everything about him exuded masculinity and strength. And his jaw had a hint of stubbornness.

He also clearly had a bee in his bonnet about expectant mothers doing basic chores. What was she supposed to do? Wrap herself in a quilt and huddle in a rocking chair until her time came?

"You don't have to scrub my house. I know I'm no housekeeper, but my house isn't exactly a pigsty." He frowned, and she realized he wasn't upset about her working while in what he called "a delicate condition." Rather, they had offended him.

"Of course your home isn't a pigsty." She went to stand beside him. "I'm so sorry if we've overstepped. Grossmutter and I are keeping busy and, in a small way, trying to repay you for some of your kind hospitality."

Some of the tightness went out of his shoulders. "I'm not looking to get repaid. Anyway, you shouldn't be scrubbing floors. You should be sitting at that table with your family figuring out what you're going to do next, where you're going to go."

Because the sooner they were out of his house, the better. He hadn't wanted them to begin with, and he wanted them gone at the earliest possible moment. Her eyes stung, but she blinked hard, unwilling to cry.

"We'll do that now." She went back into the house, picked up the sudsy bucket and went outside, pitching the contents in a silvery arc onto the grass beside the steps. When she returned to the kitchen, she began placing the chairs around the table once more. Grossmutter and Grossvater stood at the dry sink, watching her with troubled eyes.

"Are we done?" Liesl asked, still holding her rag.

"For now. Why don't you go see your daddy? He's out on the porch."

"I want to stay with you and clean. I like cleaning." The child swiped the seat of the last chair with a flourish.

"I know you do, sweetling, but there are things we grown-ups have to talk about." Kate motioned to her family.

Liesl's eyes narrowed. "Things that little girls aren't supposed to hear?"

Kate had to smile at the child's perspicacity. "That's right, little miss. You go outside, and take Rolf with you. I'm sure he's ready for a run."

Liesl took her sweet time going out, letting Kate know she wasn't pleased with the end of the morning's activities, and Kate smothered a smile. Such a saucy little minx.

Lowering herself carefully into a chair, Kate clasped her hands on the shiny tabletop and looked at Grossvater. "What are we going to do? Can we rebuild the house? Even a smaller one?"

Grossvater took his wife's hand in his and shook his head. "There is not much money. Johann didn't tell you both because he didn't want you to worry, but he mortgaged the farm to build the new house. And the bull cost a great deal of money, I know. If we still had the bull, we could sell it to get some of the purchase price back, but..." His faded blue eyes were sad, remembering how he had needed to put down the expensive bull who had proven too mean to have on the farm. "We can pay off the loan as soon as we sell the cheeses, but there will not be anything left over. I will go to town tomorrow and talk to the banker, see if he will extend the mortgage and loan us enough to build at least a small house. And if I need to, I will look for a job."

Patting his hand, Grossmutter nodded. "We need to find a place to stay where we can be together. We cannot stay here forever. Herr Rabb has been generous, but it is clear he would prefer us to be gone from his house. We will need to find a place to rent, and that will cost money."

Kate twirled a strand of loose hair around her fingertip. "I'll go to town with you and see if I can get a job, perhaps at the mercantile." Though she would loathe working for Mrs. Hale, she would do it for these dear people. "Or perhaps at the bank or the café or the hotel. I'm good with figures, or I can cook or clean. At least for a couple of months."

Grossmutter pressed her lips together, eyes clouded. "There is one more thing we can do."

"What?" Kate asked.

"Martin, you should send a telegram to your brother. Perhaps he can help us."

Grossvater pinched the bridge of his nose. "Ask my brother for money?" He puckered as if he had tasted something sour. "I don't want to have to do that."

She sighed. "I know you do not, but you should at least write to him and tell him what has happened."

Kate smoothed her dress over her unborn baby, putting her palm against her side when the little one thumped and stretched. Grossvater's brother, Victor, ran a leather tanning company in Cincinnati, very successful if his letters were to be believed. He'd often chided Grossvater for becoming a farmer in what he called the backwaters of Minnesota, abandoning the family business to strike out on his own. There had been some rift between the brothers, something she never knew the details of, which made Grossvater asking for Victor's help even more unpalatable.

Kate spread her hands on the table. "We must also be careful not to impose upon Mr. Rabb more than we have to. I am afraid we might've hurt his feelings by cleaning his kitchen. He took offense, thinking our helping him was a judgment of his housekeeping skills."

"Oh, no, did you explain?" Grossmutter asked.

"I told him we were only trying to keep busy and to repay him for his hospitality, but that seemed to offend him further."

"He is a proud man, I think. He has asked for no help, not even with the little one, since his wife passed away," Grossvater said. "We must be careful, as you say. And we must find another place soon. Perhaps we should go to town today."

"That might be best." Kate rose. "I'll get my coat."

Oscar drove his wagon up Jackson Street in Berne, conscious of Kate Amaker beside him on the seat. Mr. Amaker sat on a board roped across the wagon box behind them.

"You didn't have to do this." Kate gripped her hands in her lap, cocooned in her husband's big coat that still carried the scent of smoke. "We could've driven in ourselves."

"It's no trouble. I needed to go to town, anyway." Odd as it was to be traveling with Kate and Martin, it felt odder still not to have Liesl with him. They were never apart. The ride had been much quieter without the four-year-old's constant questions and commentary.

Liesl hadn't even fussed about staying with Inge at the farm.

The ease with which his daughter had taken to the Amakers surprised him. And, if he was honest, made him a bit jealous. He had been her whole world for her entire life, but in less than a day, she had befriended their guests.

Berne was a small town of under a thousand residents. One store, one restaurant, one hotel, one church, one bank. The train had bypassed Berne by ten miles, going through Kasson to the south, stopping the town's growth and potential while still in its infancy. Still, he liked the little farm town, though since his wife's death, he came only when he needed to pick up supplies. He had a standing order at the mercantile every two weeks, and he was able to get in and out of town quickly without having to talk to many people.

Not this time, though, since it would take the Amakers a while to complete their business. "Where will you go first?"

Martin leaned forward. "I will go to the bank, and Kate can go to the store. We will hurry."

Oscar nodded and pulled up in front of the tiny brick building that housed the bank. He parked the wagon and leaped to the ground, reaching up for Kate. He took great care lifting her down, making sure she was steady on her feet before letting go. She didn't look at his face, busying herself with brushing her coat and smoothing her hair. He took her elbow.

"Don't worry about the time, Martin. I'll see Kate to the store. I have business there myself."

It had been almost two years since he had walked with a woman in town. Gaelle had gone with him every Saturday, rain or shine, enjoying getting off the farm and seeing people. Browsing the store, having tea at the restaurant, visiting her friends. She had been as chatty as Liesl, social and energetic. He hadn't known that he would miss those trips until they were gone.

The bell over the door jingled as Oscar opened it to allow Kate to go in first. He breathed deeply, inhaling the scents of vinegar, apples, leather and patent medicines. He'd give Mrs. Hale credit. The store was light, bright and well-organized. The shelves were all painted white, and the floor had been waxed to a high shine. Built on a corner, the store had wide windows allowing sunshine to stream in. She had arranged some of the wares in the windows, inviting browsing customers to come inside, and everything was clearly labeled in a fine script.

Mrs. Hale looked up from where she was writing in a ledger spread on the counter. "Oh, Mr. Rabb, I wasn't expecting you today." She slapped the book closed. "It will take me some time to assemble your order."

"That's fine. I need to add a few things, anyway." With three more people to feed, he'd need to increase his grocery list. A frisson of worry went through him. He was comfortably off, but hosting the Amakers for any length of time would be sure to put a dent in his finances.

Kate bit her lower lip, standing beside a table

full of bolts of calico. She trailed her hand over the top bolt, pink with tiny blue flowers. Oscar's mouth twitched. Liesl had asked for a pink dress. For Christmas. Before she'd asked for a baby, of all things.

If those were the only two choices, she'd be getting a dress, and that was that. Perhaps he could prevail upon Mrs. Tipford to sew one up for her. Getting clothes for Liesl was one of the hardest of his tasks as a father, but the pastor's wife had been helpful recently.

"Mrs. Hale," Kate said, stepping forward, fingers knotted. "I was wondering if you might need some help around the store. Perhaps through the Christmas season?"

Mrs. Hale had picked up a feather duster and was fluttering it over some perfume bottles on the shelf behind the counter, and she barely paused. "Katie, my dear," she said, glancing over her shoulder for a bare instant before turning away again. "I am not looking for any help, but even if I was…" She paused. "It isn't seemly for a woman in your condition to work outside the home. I'm sure you understand."

Oscar had noted that Kate's shoulders had gone rigid when Mrs. Hale called her Katie. Katie didn't suit her at all. It was a little girl's name, not a grown woman's, and from what he had observed, Kate Amaker was a grown woman, carrying her burdens with resolution. A widow, an expectant mother, caring for her elderly relatives, and now a disaster-survivor. No, Katie didn't suit her at all.

She flattened her hands on the gentle mound of her stomach, and she pressed her lips together, lifting her chin a fraction. "Mrs. Hale, this is a community of sensible farmers. I am sure no one would be offended by the sight of a widow earning her keep, even if she is going to have a baby."

"Regardless," Mrs. Hale said, brushing Kate's opinions aside, "I'm not in need of help, but if I was, I would want to hire someone who could work more than a few weeks. You're nearing your confinement, correct? No." She shook her head. "I'm afraid it wouldn't work. Now, Mr. Rabb, what can I get for you?" The storekeeper turned her shoulder to Kate as if the subject was forever closed.

Heat flared in his stomach along with a desire to jump to Kate's defense, which was odd. The less he involved himself, the better. All he wanted was to see them settled somewhere so he could return to his isolated existence.

"Just double my usual order." He took Kate's elbow. "We'll return for it later." He guided her out of the store. When they stood on the boardwalk, he said, "I'm sorry. But there might be work elsewhere. Let's try the hotel."

Kate nodded, but he could read the discouragement in her eyes, the worry that clouded them.

She had no better results at the hotel. Mr. Kindler had no job available. He was barely making ends meet as it was. If not for the stage passengers twice a week, he would have to close up and move to a bigger town. His wife could handle the housekeeping easily.

Oscar and Kate met Martin Amaker coming out of the bank. He looked as if he had aged five years, his shoulders stooping and the lines in his face deeper.

"Let's go get some coffee at the restaurant," Oscar suggested, stepping between Kate and the wind that whipped around the corner of the building, trying to shelter her from the brunt of the chilly breeze.

Martin shook his head. "No, no, we must not detain you here in town, and we should not spend money on things we can do without right now."

"My treat," Oscar insisted. "Kate needs to get off her feet, and it's getting cold out here." The air was heavy with the smell of snow. Kate's cheeks were red, and she huddled inside her long, drab coat.

Oscar led them across the street to the café, a cheerful little building with blue-and-white-checked curtains at the windows. He held the door for Kate and Martin. The aromas of beef stew and hot bread filled the room.

George Frankel tipped back in his chair, his eyes watery, scrubbing at his nose with a handkerchief. "Hey, Oscar. Come join us?"

Kerchoo! He dabbed his red nose again.

His two companions—his eldest son, George, Jr., who had the heavy-lidded, red-nosed look of a head cold, and Bill Zank, from down at the feed store— scooted their chairs to make room, but Oscar shook his head. "Thank you, but we can't stay long."

He directed Kate to a table in the corner, a bit far from the stove, but away from the Frankel sickness. He helped her with her coat, laying it over the back of a chair, and held her seat for her. When Susan, the waitress, came by, he ordered coffee and, looking at how thin Martin was, beef stew for everyone.

"What did the banker say, Grossvater?" Kate asked. She laced her fingers, resting her hands on the tablecloth.

Martin shook his head. "He cannot loan us any

more money. He said without Johann to work the farm, it wasn't a good risk. We have no savings left, and won't have any income until we can sell the cheeses. And there is more." He did not look up, drawing circles on the tabletop with his finger. "Johann did not tell me this, but he mortgaged the herd to buy that bull. The note is due on the first of the year. We cannot pay both the mortgages with the little we will make from selling our cheeses in Mantorville and here. I don't know what we are going to do. Our only assets are the cows, and they are mortgaged like the farm." His old lips trembled. "I sent the telegram to my brother from the bank manager's office."

Kate sat still for a moment, absorbing this new blow.

What had Johann been thinking to incur so much debt? Oscar shook his head. The decision to buy that bull had proven to be fatal for Johann, and might put an end to his family's ability to keep their land.

Kate leaned forward and covered Martin's hand with hers. "We'll think of something. I'll keep looking for a job. If I cannot find one here in Berne, perhaps I can find one in Mantorville or Kasson, or even Rochester. And perhaps you can find work. Maybe at the lumber mill in Mantorville? You know how to work with wood, and you know leather work. Perhaps there is a saddler or shoemaker that needs help."

Oscar frowned. Kate was in no condition to be driving to Mantorville to work, and any farther away than that and she would have to move to wherever she found a job. He didn't like that idea at all.

The bell over the door jangled, and Pastor and Mrs. Tipford came in, cheeks red from cold, eyes bright.

"Ah, just the people we wanted to see. Mrs. Hale said you were in town." The pastor's voice filled the room. Mrs. Tipford came to Kate and squeezed her shoulder.

"What have you decided? Have you found work?"

"Not yet. Not here in town." Kate pushed out the chair beside her. "We were just talking about some other possibilities."

"The bank cannot help us." Martin laced his fingers around his coffee cup on the tabletop. "I have wired my brother."

Pastor Tipford dropped into a chair, and Oscar braced himself, half expecting the seat to turn to kindling under the impact.

"Times are hard. We've asked around, but there just aren't any jobs or any places that can house all three of you at the moment," the pastor said.

"If it was summer, Inge said we could do what she did as a girl in the Alps. We could live in the haymow, or even in a tent." Martin sat back, his gnarled hands dropping to his lap. "We will continue to look for employment and a place to stay that won't be an imposition on our neighbors while we wait for word from my brother. It should not be more than a day or two if he replies by telegram or a week if he replies by letter."

Mrs. Tipford sent Oscar a loaded look, and his collar grew tight.

"There's no rush. You can stay at my place until you hear back from your relatives." Again Oscar found himself offering hospitality, surprising himself. He wanted them out of his house as soon as possible, didn't he?

The pastor's wife beamed.

Helping this family didn't mean Oscar was ready to rejoin the world. Mrs. Tipford had been after him on her last visit to put away his mourning and perhaps even be on the lookout for a new wife, someone to mother Liesl and be a companion for him...but he had thrust that suggestion away. He loved Gaelle and always would. He had neither the need nor the desire to replace her. Mrs. Tipford was going to have to get used to disappointment if she thought she could pull him back into society and make him forget his beloved wife.

Kate looked at him from under her lashes, clearly puzzled. Oscar looked away, rationalizing the offer he had just made.

It would only be for a week, two at the most, if the brother replied by letter. A day or so if Martin's brother replied by telegram.

Either way, in a week, things would return to normal.

You shouldn't feel so relieved. Nothing has been settled. And yet, Kate did feel relief, a reprieve, if even for only a few days. She'd asked at the café if they needed help in the kitchen, but like most businesses in town, they were getting by but not looking to hire.

The news of the loan against their herd sat like a brick in her chest. *Oh, Johann.*

They returned with Oscar to the mercantile to pick up his order. Grossvater dug into his pocket for the money Pastor Tipford had given him, collected from friends and neighbors.

"Let me pay some. We are costing you money, I know." His hands fumbled with the coins and folded bills.

"Thank you, but no. Put that away." Oscar lifted the first box and headed to the wagon. "Keep that for later. You'll need it."

"But we must pay our way." Grossvater held out the money.

Mrs. Hale was looking on, and Kate's cheeks grew warm. "Perhaps we can talk about this later." She leaned in to pick up another box of groceries.

"Leave that. I'll come back for it." Oscar's tone was sharp, and Kate stopped.

"It's not heavy."

"You shouldn't be lifting things." He shouldered his way out the door.

Grossvater smiled and patted her shoulder. "He is a good man." He picked up the smaller of the two remaining crates and carried it outside. Kate followed.

Oscar was a good man, a bit prickly, but not unkind.

The ride back to Oscar's farm was silent. She huddled in her coat, and when they passed the Amaker farm, she didn't look. Seeing the blackened square where her home had been would be too hard after the day's disappointments. She needed to find a job, to do something to help Martin and Inge and prepare for her baby, but it seemed everywhere she turned was yet another closed door.

God, where are You in all of this? You seem so far away.

Oscar's house came into view, and she had to tamp down a surprising surge of resentment. He had everything here. A nice house, a sweet little girl, land, barns, safety, security. He was a strong man, someone the bank would loan money to without worry.

That's ridiculous. You should be grateful. He's being kind, even though you are an imposition. Pull yourself together.

And Kate remembered that he didn't have everything. He didn't have his wife. He must've loved her very much to have shut himself away from everyone as he had.

He helped her down from the wagon, something she was becoming used to, and set her on the porch steps. She looked up into his face, trying to gauge how he really felt about them staying at his home longer than he had expected. Was he just being polite, enduring them for propriety's sake? Offering because Mrs. Tipford had all but forced him into it again?

His brown eyes gave nothing away, but his hands remained on her arms, as if to steady her. "Go inside and get warm. I'll bring the supplies in."

The door swung open before she reached it, and a little tornado rushed out. "Daddy!" Liesl threw her arms around her father's legs. "I missed you."

Oscar swung her up into his arms, and she patted his cheeks. "You're cold. Come see what we made, me and Grossmutter. That means 'grandmother,' and Miss Kate said I could call her that."

"You shouldn't be out here without a coat. It's too chilly. And you should call her Mrs. Amaker." He set her down and nudged her toward the door. "I'll be there soon. I need to unload the groceries and get the team put away."

Rolf rounded the house, coming up the path from

the barn, his black tail with its white tip plumed high, his tongue lolling. He bounded up to the porch, nudging his head under Kate's hand, begging for a few pats. She stroked his silky, broad head, running her finger along the white stripe between his eyes. He leaned into her.

"You're just a mush, aren't you?"

He didn't disagree.

Oscar and Grossvater carried the supplies into the house, and when he stepped across the threshold, Oscar stopped, breathing in deeply.

Grossmutter and Liesl had been busy. The house smelled of yeasty bread and warm fruit. Grossmutter turned from the oven, her towel-wrapped hands holding a pie tin. "I made *Apfeltorte*, and the *Kind* helped me make bread." She set the hot apple pie—made in the Swiss tradition with no crust—on a trivet. Behind her, on a table near the stove, three bread pans filled with rising dough waited to go into the hot oven.

Liesl climbed into a chair and knelt, leaning on her arms to sniff the pie.

"Take care, sweetling. That's very hot." Kate shrugged out of her coat and hung it on a peg by the door. "Doesn't it smell good? Grossmutter makes the best pie I've ever eaten. Do you like this kind of pie?" She brushed wisps of hair off Liesl's face.

"I don't know. I never had any. Daddy doesn't make pie."

Poor little mite. Her father had isolated himself and, in doing so, had isolated her. Kate bent and kissed the little girl's head. "You're in for a treat, then."

Oscar set the last box on the table. "As long as we

have the team hitched up, Martin and I are going over to your farm to do the milking and chores. We'll be back in a bit. Is it all right if I leave Liesl here with you?"

"Of course." Kate shook her head, surprised that he would even ask.

"You'll be back soon, Daddy? Because I get to help make supper, and I want you to like it." Liesl scampered off her chair and tugged on Oscar's hand.

"I'll be back soon," he promised. "You'll be a good girl?"

"The best."

He looked at Kate. "I don't want to impose. She's my responsibility, and I'll take her if you need to lie down and rest."

"I'm fine. I enjoy her company."

He nodded and went back out.

Liesl chattered away, helping Kate and Grossmutter unpack the provisions, showing them where things went. "There's potatoes in the cellar. That's where we got the apples for the pie. Daddy has apple trees down by the creek. He says Mama planted them when they were baby trees... What's a baby tree called?"

"A sapling?" Kate put a sack of coffee beans into the cupboard.

"Yes, that's it. They were saplings. And this is the first year we got apples, and I got to help. Daddy lifted me up to pick some, and he let me put them into the bin in the cellar, but he said I had to be real careful, because apples can get bruises. Daddy said one bad apple would make the whole bin get rotten."

While Kate and Grossmutter made supper—

chicken and dumplings—Liesl treated them to more of "Daddy says."

When the men returned, they gathered around the table. Kate sat beside Oscar and across from Liesl. The little girl bowed her head and held her hand out to her father. Oscar took it and held his other hand out to Kate.

Slowly, she placed her hand in his large one, and his fingers curled around hers, warm and strong. It had been months since she had held hands with a man. She placed her other fingers into Grossmutter's, and bowed her head, trying to concentrate on the blessing rather than on the comfort she drew from Oscar's touch.

Chapter Five

Oscar couldn't remember when he'd had a better meal. Inge Amaker was a wonderful cook. He ran his hands down his stomach, leaning back from the table. When he'd come into the house with the groceries, he'd stopped cold, inhaling the smell of hot pie and rising bread.

It had been a very long time since he'd returned home to a warm, inviting house, a hot meal and someone waiting for him. Liesl had been well looked after in his absence, and he was reminded of all she was missing by not having a woman in her life to teach her and mother her and show her all the things a young lady should know.

And yet, part of him resented the intrusion on their peace, on the special bond that he had with her. She was calling the elder Amakers Grossmutter and Grossvater, as if they were family, and she had certainly taken a shine to Kate. What would happen in a week or so when the Amakers found a more permanent solution to their problems and left? Would Liesl be devastated? She hadn't known what she was missing before they came. Would she be satisfied with just her father for company after experiencing something different?

"I can't read any stories yet, Daddy. I have to help with the dishes." His little girl hopped off her chair and began gathering the cutlery, bustling importantly. "Grossmutter does the dishes after *every* meal." She relayed this information as if she couldn't believe it.

He smiled and gave her his spoon and fork before rising. He had a few chores to see to himself before he could disappear into his workshop. Three trips to the woodpile saw both wood boxes filled, the one for the stove and the one for the fireplace. The wind had shifted during the day from southwest to northwest, and with it had come both colder temperatures and a few fitful flakes of snow. Oscar inhaled, catching the scent of a storm on the breeze, and added a few more logs to his armload. He walked down to the barn to make sure everything was secure for the night, and dropped a length of wood into the outside stock tank, just in case it froze overnight. The log would bob up, relieving the pressure, and the expanding ice wouldn't break the tank.

When he returned to the house, Kate was drying the last dish, and Liesl was showing Grossmutter her row of books in the glass-fronted bookcase. She looked up when he closed the door. "Daddy, Grossmutter likes stories, too." She smiled, holding the old woman's hand. "And she likes Christmas. She said she would tell me stories about Christmas when she was a little girl in Swizzerland." He smiled at her mispronunciation as did Inge. "Swizzerland is a long, long, long, long way from here, and they have mountains, like in the picture." She pointed to the painting over the fireplace, a wedding gift from one of Gaelle's relatives. Lake Lucerne, with a white boat in the foreground and towering, snow-capped mountains in the background.

Oscar nodded, though his muscles tensed. He didn't want to hear about Christmas. The holiday brought him no joy. He wished he'd never mentioned it to Liesl in the first place. "Do you want to stay out here, or do you want to go work with me?" It had never been an option for her before.

"I want to stay with Grossmutter and hear about Christmas…" She put the end of her braid under her nose like a little moustache. "But I want you to stay and hear, too."

Those big brown eyes beseeched him. "I can't. I have orders waiting." It pinched a bit that she didn't automatically choose to be with him. But he couldn't stay out here and entertain guests. He had work to do.

He carried a lamp into the workshop, an addition he'd built onto the back of the house. It smelled of wood and linseed oil, and he ran his hand over the smooth workbench, taking satisfaction in the neatly arranged tools and clean surfaces. The rest of the house might show a bit of neglect and dust, but in here, neatness reigned.

Oscar picked up a tablet and plucked a pencil from a can, checking to see that the point was sharp. He lit the wall sconces, glad of the reflectors behind the lamps to scatter light to every corner of the room, and began sketching a wedding chest. Commissions for orders had come in during the fall, and this one needed to be finished soon as it was a wedding present for the daughter of one of the sawmill owners down in Mantorville.

Black walnut, cedar lined, with white oak inlay on the top, the chest would be an instant heirloom if he made it well. He concentrated on getting the proportions correct. The inlay design the customer had requested would be tricky. Floral scrolls, two birds with a ribbon in their beaks, a heart.

A slight tap on the door had him raising his head. Kate stood there with two steaming cups in her hands. She nudged the door open farther with her foot.

"Liesl said you usually have coffee after supper."

She set his cup on the workbench and looked around the room. On the far wall, he'd built racks to hold his stock, various species of lumber, various thicknesses and lengths. Some were easy to distinguish, like black walnut or poplar or pine; others took closer inspection. Red oak, white oak, hickory, birch, maple. He even had some cherry shipped in from Pennsylvania. He was saving that for something really special.

"I noticed the beautiful furniture out there." She gestured to the front room. "Did you make it?"

He nodded. "Some of it. My grandfather was a cabinetmaker and wood carver in the Old Country, and he taught my father, who taught me. I farm in the summer and make furniture in the winter." Oscar picked up his coffee and blew across the top. It felt odd to have anyone in here besides Liesl. On winter evenings his daughter played on the floor with blocks of wood and curled planer shavings, talking and singing to herself, pretending the blocks were all sorts of fanciful things, but having Kate here was something different. It felt…intrusive? No, not exactly, but unsettling.

She studied the drawing on the bench. "This is beautiful. But where do you start?"

"I start by asking lots of questions." He smiled. "I try to get the customer to be as specific as they can with what they want—what wood, what size, what deadline. And I try to educate them on what is possible and what isn't. I can do many things with wood, but I can't stop it from expanding and contracting, or splitting, or being too hard or too soft for what they want done." He picked up a piece of pine he'd used to anchor a sheet of paper. "Like this. Pine is light, with a very open grain. When you carve it, you have to be careful, because it can chip out easily. And I don't recommend it for a tabletop, because it's so soft. You'll get lots of dings and dents if you don't treat it carefully."

He strolled to the racks, touching the different woods. "Birch doesn't take stain very well. It's hard to get an even coat. And hickory is very difficult to carve because it's so hard, but it makes a great toy box." He stopped, realizing he'd been going on for quite a bit. Wood might be his favorite topic, but it wasn't likely to be interesting to anyone else.

She tucked her bottom lip behind her teeth for a moment, her eyes showing her surprise at his enthusiasm. Those blue eyes, heavily fringed with dark lashes that, when turned full on him, made his heart beat a bit faster. Her hand went to her belly, pressing slightly.

Oscar remembered the wonder of feeling an unborn baby kicking and tumbling, the surge of joy and amazement at the sign of health and growth. He fought down the memory. He needed to remind himself that the Amakers' stay was temporary and that he wanted it that way, not to dwell on things of the past that made his chest ache.

"I wanted to let you know that we would be gone most of the day tomorrow." She picked her coffee cup up off the workbench. "I need to start another batch of cheese, and it will take all day." Lightly fingering her collar, she looked at the drawing of the wedding chest, a sad light coming into her eyes. Had she owned a wedding chest, now destroyed by the fire? What had she kept in it?

Liesl came pelting into the room, ramming into his knees, hugging him hard and lifting her face to stare up at him. "Guess what Grossmutter told me, Daddy?"

He swung her up onto his arm, grateful for the interruption. "What, Poppet?"

"Grossmutter told me about Advent calendars. She said most everyone in Swizzerland has one, to teach little girls and boys about Christmas and waiting for things." Liesl toyed with a button on his shirt and then raised her hands to press on his cheeks, making sure he was listening. "Some have little doors that you open to show you how many days till Christmas, and some have little pockets with treats in them that you get every day. But Grossmutter and Miss Kate had the bestest kind."

"What kind is that?"

"An 'Ativity calendar."

He glanced at Kate, who was blinking, her fingertips against her lips, eyes suspiciously bright. "You know what, Poppet, maybe you can tell me while you get ready for bed, all right?" He bounced her on his arm before setting her down. "Run out and say good night to the Amakers and I'll meet you in your room for your story and prayers."

"Can Miss Kate come, too?"

"I think Miss Kate is tired. Maybe she can help out tomorrow getting you to bed." And she wouldn't want to listen to a little girl prattle on about a treasure she had lost.

"Oh, I don't mind." Kate smiled brightly, though Oscar could tell it was forced. "I've never helped put a little girl to bed before. Maybe you could teach me all about it, Liesl. Soon I'll have my own little one to put to bed, and I could use some practice." She held out her hand to Liesl, who took it gravely.

"I'll show you how."

Oscar carried the lamp, and Liesl, true to form, talked the whole way up the stairs, into her nightgown and under the covers.

"Daddy tells me a story right before bed, but sometimes he lets me tell one, and I want to tell him about the 'Ativity calendar."

Kate sat on the side of the bed, hands in her lap. Oscar leaned against the doorframe. "Only if Miss Kate says it's all right." She was clearly still raw, her loss fresh.

"She'll like my story. Grossmutter said it was the thing Miss Kate loved best." In Liesl's innocence, she clapped her hands. "The 'Ativity calendar came all the way from Swizzerland, and it had lots of pieces, a new one for every day, and every morning, someone got to put another one out on the sideboard in the dining room. Is that right?"

Kate nodded. "Twenty-five pieces, all of them different." Her voice was husky, but her face kind. "Beginning on December first, one piece each day was added, and we knew we were one day closer to Christmas."

Liesl nodded, bouncing up to her knees. "And on the last day, Christmas Day, the Baby Jesus is born, and He goes in the manger."

"Yes, and that's how I knew, when I was a little girl, that it was finally Christmas."

"Where did the pieces come from?" Oscar asked.

"My grandfather carved them. Sheep and donkeys and camels and shepherds and Mary and Joseph and the stable…each one beautiful. He brought the set with him from Switzerland when he was still a young man, and my father brought it to Minnesota, and I brought it to my husband's home when I got married."

And she'd lost it in the fire.

"And now it's gone." Liesl shook her little head. "Grossmutter looked so sad when she told me that. It makes me sad. I wish I had little donkeys and sheep." Then she leaned over and took Kate's hand. "But—" she shot a look at her father "—I still want a baby for Christmas. That's my one thing that I am going to wish for."

Clearly she hadn't forgotten or changed her mind, and she wanted to make sure there was no confusion on the matter.

Oscar turned toward the hall and rolled his eyes.

He'd have to talk about toys and books and maybe even a kitten, anything to distract her from the baby wish.

Early the next morning, Kate helped Grossmutter clean up the breakfast dishes and then shrugged into her coat to go help with the morning chores at their farm. She really needed to get some new clothes. Her one dress was limp, and her coat still smelled of smoke.

She stepped outside. Her breath plumed in white puffs, and hoarfrost covered every blade of grass and tree branch in lacy, icy fur. The sun topping the trees would soon melt the delicate artwork, but while it lasted, it was beautiful.

Oscar drew the wagon up to the porch and leaped down to help her. "You don't have to come, you know. Martin and I can do the chores."

Kate shook her head. "I have to make a batch of cheese today. I will be staying over there until the afternoon when Grossvater will come get me. It's you who doesn't need to come. I will have all day to do the chores and tend the cheeses." They were already treading on his good graces by extending their stay at his home by several days. He didn't need to be away from his farm helping them when they could take care of things themselves.

"I'm coming." Oscar steadied her as she climbed into the wagon. "You work too hard."

"There is much to be done, and I am the one to do it." She settled into the seat beside him, pressing her hand against her lower back. The baby had been restless last night, and she hadn't gotten much sleep. And it wasn't just the baby keeping her awake. Grossvater had told her not to worry, that God would take care of them, and in the daylight, she could hold fast to that truth, but when night came, and she was alone in her room, fears seemed to grow like mushrooms. It was as if, when she laid down in the dark, her fears perched heavily on her chest, making it hard to breathe.

They rolled into the Amaker farmyard, and the hoarfrost on the blackened ruins of the house covered some of the travesty. Kate averted her face, bracing herself against the thrust of grief that welled up.

"Kate, you go to the *Käsehaus*," Grossvater said as he headed toward the barn. "We will bring the milk to you."

When she entered the low-ceilinged cheese house, Kate took a deep breath, inhaling the milky, earthy, salty smells she had come to love. When she was a girl, she had helped her grandmother and mother make cheese, but always on a small scale, only for family use. When she had married Johann and come to the Amaker farm, Grossmutter had taught her how to make large quantities of cheese to sell. She enjoyed cheese making most days, but now, with so much depending upon the sale of the cheeses she'd made, the task was no longer as pleasurable.

She knelt before the brick firebox and raked out the old ashes before laying a new fire. Opening the dampers to get it going quickly, she moved to the large, brass kettle that could hold sixty gallons of milk when full.

In high summer she could make a new batch of cheese nearly every day, but now, in the fall, she was down to one batch a week, and this would be the last for the year. When the cows were grazing in the lush fields, their rich milk took on wonderful flavor, but now that the grass was brown and they were eating mostly hay, the cheeses wouldn't taste quite as good. Normally, the end-of-season cheeses would be for family use, but this year, they would most likely be sold at a reduced cost to earn something to help tide the Amakers over.

Or to pay the mortgage on the cattle. Or the farm. Or go toward a new house. Or replenishing their wardrobes, food for the winter months, household goods...the list seemed endless.

Kate scrubbed the kettle with a mixture of vinegar and a touch of carbolic to make sure it was really clean, and slanted the damper on the fire to direct heat to the kettle to dry and warm it up.

Grossvater and Oscar appeared in the doorway with the loaded milk cart.

Grossvater also carried a pail. "I skimmed the cream off." He set the bucket on the workbench and draped a square of cheesecloth over it. "I will take the cream to Oscar's for Inge to make butter." He looked into the wood box. "I will bring wood. Oscar..." He straightened with a wince. "Kate is going to need someone to help her with the lifting. I am not much good for that these days, but I can take care of the chores at your farm if you would stay and help her?"

"Oh, Grossvater, we don't want to impose upon Mr. Rabb. I can take care of things here. I will work in smaller batches if I have to." Kate worried her bottom lip.

"That's a good idea, Martin." Oscar put his hands into his coat pockets. "I'll stay and help her."

"We will bring you some lunch, Inge and the little

one and I." Grossvater drew his handkerchief out and blew his nose, coughing a bit. Kate cast him a worried glance. Last winter he had caught a cough before Christmas and it had lasted for months.

"Don't worry about getting wood. I'll do it." Oscar followed him outside, returning with a huge armload of firewood, doing in one trip what would've taken Kate three or four. The wagon clattered out of the yard, and Kate removed her coat, hanging it on a peg by the door. The fire had already heated the small room, and it would only get warmer as she worked.

"You really didn't have to stay. You must have your own things to do." Her lips felt stiff, and she twisted her fingers together. It chafed to be the one on the receiving end of charity when she was used to being the giver, helping others.

"Work is slow now that the harvest is over. What should I do first?" Oscar asked. "I don't know anything about cheese making." He seemed sincere. And he could be a tremendous help to her.

"Would you pour the milk into the kettle? I need to see how much there is so I can mix the things I need to add." She took down her apron, slipping the loop over her head. A smile came as she tied it behind her back. When she wasn't nearly eight months pregnant, she could wrap the apron strings all the way around and tie them in front.

Oscar lifted the milk cans easily, tipping their contents into the massive kettle. "Looks like about forty gallons."

"Do you have your pocket watch?" Kate asked. "I need to keep track of the time."

He slipped a silver watch from his pants' pocket

and handed it to her. She flicked the cover open, and her eyes were drawn to the photograph tucked into the lid. A lovely woman with dark eyes looked back at her. This must be his wife. She'd been beautiful, and Kate could see more than a hint of resemblance to Liesl. She noted the time on a chart she kept on a clipboard on her workbench, and set the watch on the paper.

Kate poked a few small pieces of wood into the fire. "We need to warm the milk to about ninety degrees." She adjusted the damper handle, lining it up with the mark on the brick to allow the right amount of heat to divert to the kettle base. Forty gallons of milk would yield sixteen two-pound cheeses.

"What else can I do?" Oscar took off his coat, too.

"While the milk is heating, I need to go downstairs and brush and turn the cheeses that are curing." Kate dug a match out of the box on the wall and lit the lantern, carrying it by its handle and descending into the cellar under the building. Oscar followed.

She put the lantern on the table in the center of the room as Oscar let out a whistle. Wooden racks stuck out at right angles to the wall all around the room, shelf after shelf of cheeses, from small one-pound rounds to immense forty-pound wheels.

Thankfully, the largest wheels didn't need to be brushed or turned. "Those were made more than a year ago and will be ready to sell soon. The smaller ones here—" she indicated four racks on the right side of the cellar "—are newer, made this summer. They all need to be turned over. And this row needs a fresh brushing of brine." She moved to the brine barrel in the corner and dipped out a small pail. "If you could start flipping each cheese over, I'll follow with the salt brine."

They worked as a team, and Oscar took the brush out of her hand to tend to the cheeses on both the highest and lowest shelves himself. "How many cheeses are in here?"

She shrugged. "Two hundred? Maybe more. All in the Emmentaler style. Grossmutter comes from a village near Emmental. The cheese has a nutty, rich flavor, a good rind and many small holes." Kate poked one of the cheeses that had been curing for a couple of weeks. The top and sides were domed a bit, and it rocked slightly. "The bulging sides mean the air holes have occurred. That's a good sign. A flat-sided Emmentaler cheese is no good."

"You go first." Oscar indicated the stairs, and for good measure, he carried the lantern and held her elbow, guiding her up ahead of him. He really was worried about her and this baby. Johann had died before she'd even known she was expecting, so she hadn't been cosseted or fussed over.

She could get used to this, as long as he didn't overdo.

Picking up her clipboard, she reached up into her bun to take out the pencil she'd stuck there. Keeping careful records made for good cheeses. She measured and mixed the cultures she would need to add once the milk had simmered long enough. "Would you check the temperature? It shouldn't be over one hundred degrees, and closer to ninety is better. We don't want to cook the milk, just warm it through." A thermometer was clipped to the side of the kettle, but she found her hand to be a better judge. "Like bathwater warm, not tea-brewing warm."

He quickly touched the outside of the kettle, and then returned his hand to the metal, nodding. "Warm but not hot. What are you making there?"

She lifted the brown stone jug that held her rennet mixture. "Rennet separates the curds from the whey, the milk solids from the liquids. It's made using the lining of a calf's stomach. And I need to add the culture that will produce the air holes in the cheese, too. Sort of like the way yeast makes bread rise." Kate made careful notations on her clipboard. "I have to keep track of what I put in when, how long the batch cooks, how long I've stirred it. Otherwise, I might forget something important and ruin a whole batch." And money was too dear to do that.

When the milk had simmered long enough, she handed Oscar a long, metal spoon. "I'll pour this in, and you stir. Make sure you reach all the way to the bottom of the kettle." Grateful for his help, she slowly sprinkled the culture powder over the surface of the warm milk.

When the culture had been stirred in long enough to bloom, she poured her rennet solution in. "This one really needs to be mixed well or the curds won't form correctly."

Oscar mixed faithfully while she checked the temperature with her little finger. Warm but not hot. Perfect.

"I'm hoping that the sale of the cheeses this year will be enough to pay off the loan Johann took out from the bank on the herd. If it isn't, I don't know what we'll do." And they still had to pay the mortgage on the farm itself, though with what, she didn't know. She checked the time and lifted the flat, tin cover for the kettle. "We'll let that rest for a quarter of an hour or so."

He put the paddle-like spoon into the washtub on the workbench. "So everything is mortgaged, land and livestock?"

She nodded. "Johann got the loans to build the new house and to buy a blooded bull to improve the herd. The bull was a fine-looking animal, but he was very mean. If Johann had known how mean, he never would've brought him here. Johann was an experienced herdsman, but the bull got loose one day from his pen and attacked Johann, cornered him between the fence and the barn wall. Grossvater had to shoot the bull to get to Johann, but by then it was too late." Now, months later, the shock and first grief had worn off, but the persistent ache remained. The "what if" questions that never seemed to fade.

What if Johann had never bought that bull in the first place?

What if he had been able to fend off the attack?

What if…

She rested her hand on the baby. "He didn't even know he was going to be a father."

"That's too bad. It's life-changing news."

"How did you take the news?"

He frowned, and she wondered if she had overstepped.

Finally, he shrugged. "When Gaelle told me she was going to have a baby, I had to sit down. My knees got wobbly and my head started to spin." A rare smile twitched his lips. "She never let me forget that, either.

She said she didn't know which one of us had the more difficult time when Liesl was born."

It was the first time he had mentioned his wife by name. Gaelle. Pretty name.

"What was your wife like?" Kate admitted to being curious, but more, she felt as if he needed to talk about it.

He leaned on the workbench and crossed his arms. "Like Liesl. Always moving, always chattering, always interested in everything." It was almost as if he was speaking to himself, and his eyes had a faraway look.

"I haven't been around children much," Kate admitted. "Liesl's like a little sponge, following Grossmutter or me around. She wants to try everything." Kate smiled. "She seems very enamored of the idea of Christmas. She and Grossmutter are twins at heart, there. Christmas is Grossmutter's favorite time of year."

Oscar's eyes sharpened, and his lips tightened. "Mrs. Hale tucked a flyer into one of the grocery boxes one Saturday a few weeks ago, about some sales she would be having at Christmas and some of the community events. Liesl asked what it was, and I made the mistake of telling her. Now she can hardly talk of anything else. If it was up to me, I would let the day go by without any notice."

Kate blinked at the bleakness in his tone. Not celebrate the Savior's birth? Why? But his expression forbade her asking any questions. It appeared the time of confidences was over. "Let's check the milk."

Oscar removed the flat lid for her, and she stood on tiptoe to reach into the center of the kettle. "We're looking for a clean break." She slipped her little finger straight down into the coagulated milk and slowly bent it, pulling up. The mixture split in a straight line as her finger broke the surface. "Perfect."

Oscar poked the semi-gelatinous mass, eyebrows raised. "That was fast. Only twenty minutes?"

"Now comes the hard part." Kate smiled. She took one of the cheese cutters off the wall, a wooden frame with wires strung horizontally across it, about a quarter inch separating each strand. Lowering it into the mixture with one side in the center of the kettle, the other against the outer edge, she rotated the cutter in a circle, cutting the curds into half-inch layers. Then she took the other cutter, this one with wires strung vertically, and repeated the procedure, making cubes of the loose curd.

"Could you bring me some water to wash these?" Kate asked, setting the cutters on the drain board. "We'll let the curds rest for a few minutes while we wash up, which will help with separating the whey."

Kate was surprised how easy Oscar was to work with. He had never made cheese before, but he learned quickly, and he only needed to be told something once. When the curds had rested long enough, she gave him the large spoon once more. "We can take turns, but the curds need to be stirred for about forty minutes." She checked the time and made a note on her clipboard.

"You usually do this by yourself?" He bent to his task, scooping deep into the kettle, lifting the curds in long strokes.

She nodded. "Grossmutter helps sometimes, when

the cows are giving lots of milk, but most of the time, I work alone."

He stirred, digging deeply into the mass from bottom to top, his muscles moving under his plaid shirt. He was broader and taller than Johann had been, she noted. His movements were more deliberate, as if he thought about things before acting, unlike Johann's quicksilver ways.

Was it wrong to observe such things? To notice that Oscar was strong and steady, capable and helpful?

They took turns stirring, but he wouldn't let her go as long as he did. After forty minutes, she added more wood to the fire and opened the damper further. "Now we raise the temperature of the curds another thirty degrees or so and go on stirring for another half hour."

"More stirring?" He rolled his shoulders. "I'm in pretty good shape, but I'll be feeling this tomorrow."

The curds, which had started out as half-inch cubes, were now the size of small peas, and much of the thin, yellowish whey had been released. "After this next round, it will be done cooking and you won't have to stir it anymore."

When it was her turn to stir, she forced herself to say what she had been trying to get out all morning. "I wanted to thank you for taking us in. I know we're an imposition, and I hope it isn't for too long, but we are grateful. I don't know what we would do if you hadn't opened your home. And you've taken us to town and helped with our chores, and now with the cheese. I don't know how we can repay you."

He shook his head. "There was no one else, not if you wanted to stay together."

And if there had been anyone else, he would not have volunteered?

"And besides, it's only for a week or two, at the most."

He must be looking forward to the time when they would be out of his house. Until then, they would be as helpful as they could without intruding more than they had to.

Oscar swirled the long spoon in the mixture. "When Liesl woke me up this morning, she was still talking about your Advent Nativity set. I'm sorry about that. She doesn't realize how painful it must be now that you've lost it to the fire."

"It's all right. She's too young to understand. Anyway, it doesn't hurt to talk about it as much as it hurts to keep it all inside." Kate removed wooden cheese hoops from the shelves and began lining them with clean cheesecloth. "I learned that right after Johann died. I missed him so much it was hard to even talk about him, but if I didn't, it was like he never existed at all. It's the remembering, recalling the memories and good times, that hurts and heals."

Oscar frowned, staring into the kettle as he stirred.

"And I didn't want to make others feel as if they couldn't speak of him for fear of hurting me. Grossmutter and Grossvater needed to be able to talk about their grandson—the man they had raised from infancy—without worrying about me bursting into tears all the time." She paused, wondering if he might need to hear of her experience as much as she needed to voice it. "I have learned enough about myself these past few months to know that talking about things makes me feel better. I need to let my emotions breathe instead of stuffing them down. Even if they are emotions I don't want to have, like grief, loss, frustration, fear. The problem is finding someone to talk to about them. I don't want to burden Grossmutter and Grossvater with more than they should carry. So I talk to myself."

She chuckled. "Working alone in the cheese house this summer gave me lots of time to work things out, to pray, to remember. When things got overwhelming, I tried to remember the good times and focus on those. So when Liesl asked about the Nativity set, the pain of loss came up, but it's overlaid with good memories of family and Christmas."

He stirred, looking into the kettle and not at her. "I guess that's where we're different. Talking about Gaelle is…" He shook his head. "At first there was no one to talk to her about, Liesl being so little at the time, and then later…" He shrugged.

Her heart went out to him, newly widowed with a toddler and a farm.

"Was there no one to help you?"

"Gaelle's parents wanted me to let them raise Liesl, but I couldn't do that. They had been none too happy when their daughter married a farmer like me. Didn't even come to the wedding. No way would I let them raise my child. They don't have much contact with Liesl now."

So he hadn't shirked his responsibility and shipped Liesl off, even though it would've been easier on him. He was a man who did what was right, even if it was hard.

Like opening his house to strangers even though he didn't want to.

The sound of a wagon approaching broke the moment, and she glanced out the window. Grossvater, Grossmutter and Liesl. It was too early for lunch. Why were they here? A tickle of unease feathered across her skin.

Liesl peeked around the corner, spotted her father and bounded into the room. "Daddy, guess what? We made butter, and Grossmutter said I am a good helper. Did you know if you shake cream it makes butter? That's what we did. Grossmutter put some in a jar for me, and I shook it and rolled it and it took forever, but then there was butter. And a man came to the door, and he had a telegram for Grossvater, and then we came here."

Oscar lifted her into his arms, brushing a kiss on her head.

Kate checked the curds. They could wait for a bit.

Grossvater followed Grossmutter inside the cheese house, his face sober, no light in his eyes. He pressed his hand to his chest, coughing. Kate hurried over to him, guiding him to the bench along the wall. Grossmutter handed him a dipper of water. When the cough had passed and he had emptied the dipper, he leaned back, a red flush to his cheeks.

"George Frankel brought this out from town since he was headed this way." Grossvater removed the yellow paper from his pocket. "My brother says we should come live with him…"

Kate's heart fell. The most she had hoped for was a loan to tide them over, perhaps enough to build a small house. A loan they would repay, of course, no matter how long it took. But to have to leave the farm…

Grossvater continued. "But he will not have room

for us or a job for me until after the new year. He says to come in January."

Kate took the paper, quickly reading the block letters. A reprieve of sorts, but it didn't solve the immediate problem. What could they do in the meantime? It was seven weeks until Christmas, eight until the new year. In that time, her baby would come. Where would she be when that happened?

"My brother will send more information in a letter, but I know he will say we should sell the farm and livestock and come back to Ohio."

Kate shook her head. She wouldn't. She couldn't. The farm was their home, her baby's inheritance from the father he would never know. There had to be another way. She handed the yellow page back to Grossvater.

Grossmutter went to the kettle and peered in. "This is ready. We should remove the curds." She took off her coat and rolled up her sleeves. Her lined face was grim, but true to her nature, she would work first and worry later.

Kate handed her a strainer and took one herself, dipping into the kettle. They couldn't afford to waste time or their limited resources, but while her hands did the familiar tasks, her mind raced, circled, knotted and spun.

Grossvater put the telegram into his pocket and with slow movements began setting the lined cheese molds onto the slanted, grooved drain board. He had to stop to cough into his handkerchief, his face reddening and eyes watering.

Oscar took over for him moving the molds. "Why don't you sit for a while? I can do this."

"What are you doing?" Liesl asked. "Can I help?" She nudged Kate's elbow.

"We're packing each of the molds, then folding the cheesecloth over and putting a lid on top." Kate scooped a handful of curds into a wooden mold and showed the little girl how to cover it. "You can put lids on all of these." The lid fit inside the mold perfectly. "When we get them all full, we'll press them to squeeze all the liquid out."

They worked quickly, and soon, sixteen cheeses were ready to press. "Liesl, can you bring me a brick?" Kate pointed to the stack in the corner. "Careful, and don't drop it on your toe."

Liesl hefted one of the blocks with an "Oomph." She wrapped her arms around it and staggered over.

Grossmutter made sure the tub on the floor at the end of the draining table was in place to catch the whey.

"What do you do with that?" Liesl pointed to the thin, yellow liquid dripping into the tub.

"We mix it with bran and feed it to the calves, *Schätzchen*." Grossmutter dipped a metal bucket into the kettle, pouring the whey into one of the cans the milk had been stored in. "And Mr. Frankel comes to get some for his pigs when we have a lot."

"You have a lot now." Liesl nodded to emphasize her pronouncement. "What does *Schätzchen* mean again?"

"It means 'sweetheart.'" Grossmutter filled the can to the top and pressed the lid on tight.

"*Schätzchen*. I like it." Liesl beamed.

Grossvater stood, bracing against the wall for a moment to steady himself. "Why don't you and I go feed the calves? They are a bit old for bran and whey now, but they will still like it." He took a bucketful from Grossmutter. "It will be a treat for them."

Kate marked the time on her clipboard for when they had started pressing the cheese, her mind not really focusing on the numbers.

Grossmutter sighed, wiping the now empty kettle with a vinegar-soaked cloth. "What are we going to do? Martin does not wish to work for his brother, or to lose the farm. If it was not winter coming, I would say we should move in here, to the *Käsehaus*. We could sleep on straw pallets on the floor, like I did when we went to the high pastures as a girl. But with the baby coming and now Martin has a cough…"

Oscar leaned on the workbench, arms crossed. "You can't stay here. There isn't even glass in the windows."

Kate brushed her hair back from her temples with both hands, squeezing, wanting to force the desperation out of her head. They couldn't winter in the cheese house.

"We'll have to go to town. Mrs. Tipford has found places for us to stay," Kate said.

"But not together." Grossmutter shook her head. "We would have to be separated. And the baby will come, and we will not be there."

Kate's throat grew thick at the despair in Grossmutter's voice. She wasn't ungrateful for the people who had offered to house them in town, but it made her anxious to think about staying somewhere without her family, of having her baby in a stranger's house.

She looked at Oscar, but he said nothing.

Though disappointment weighed on her shoulders, she couldn't be angry with him. After all, he wasn't obligated to solve the Amakers' problems.

Chapter Six

Oscar went outside the cheese house, his boots hitting the dirt hard. *God, I've done my part. I let them stay overnight, and I extended the stay until they heard from back east. They have other places to go. Pastor and Mrs. Tipford have it set up. They would be better off in town, wouldn't they?*

Because he couldn't have them at his house any longer. Methodically he laid out his reasons, making his argument plain.

Liesl would grow too attached to them. When they left after Christmas, she would be heartbroken.

Having them in the house brought back too many memories. Memories of the good times with Gaelle when they had been a complete family, and there had been love and laughter. It hurt too much having them there, reminding him, digging up the old feelings he worked very hard to keep buried.

And then there was Kate. His biggest concern was that if Kate stayed in his house for another two months, she would be here when her baby arrived.

He couldn't let that happen. What if something

went wrong, like it had for Gaelle? He couldn't be responsible for another expectant mother. Berne didn't even have a doctor. If something went awry, they would have to send down to Mantorville for a physician.

The accusation had rung in his ears when Gaelle's parents had descended on the farm for the funeral. It was his fault for taking their daughter away from the civilized city where she'd been brought up. Away from adequate medical care. By the time the midwife had sent for a doctor, and he traveled through the snow to the farm, it had been too late.

Oscar didn't want to ever live through something like that again, not even just providing a place for his neighbors to stay temporarily. No. They had to go. And sooner rather than later.

Liesl came bounding up the path, Rolf on her heels, barking happily. Her cheeks and nose were pink, and her mittens dangled from the string threaded through the sleeves of her plaid coat. "Daddy, Grossvater says tomorrow is Sunday, and they are going to church. Can we go to church? He says there is singing, and talking about Jesus."

She collided with his legs, looking up, expectant eagerness making her eyes sparkle. A fist closed around his windpipe. He hadn't been to church for almost two years, since Gaelle died. At first, he'd wrestled with God, blaming the Almighty for taking his wife and child. And he hadn't wanted to face the community, the people who wanted to help, to ask questions, to see how he was feeling. How did they think he was feeling? So he just hadn't gone. And after a while, it had become easier and easier to stay home.

Pastor and Mrs. Tipford hadn't been satisfied to let him go, though. They visited regularly, always encouraged him to come back, and he had known he would need to, someday. Gaelle would want Liesl brought up in the church.

But he wasn't ready. He taught Liesl about God at home.

"Please, Daddy?" She used her forearm to brush wisps of hair off her face. "I've always wanted to go."

And by "always," she meant for the last few minutes, since she'd never voiced a desire to go to church before. Oscar touched her cheek.

"We'd love it if you would come."

He turned to see Kate, standing in the cold sunshine, one hand on her middle, the other braced against her back. Her blue eyes caught the light, standing out like forget-me-nots under shade trees.

"See, Daddy, Kate wants us to come, too."

And the next morning, against his better judgment, Oscar found himself following the Amakers into church, Liesl perched on his arm. Her eyes were wide as she tried to see everything at once.

"What's that?" Her loud whisper caught the attention of those around them, and several people looked to where she pointed. The eastern sunshine poured through the stained-glass windows, making blocks of color on the pews.

"What's that?" Liesl pointed to a woman's broadbrimmed hat trimmed with ribbons and flowers. Oscar gently lowered her finger.

"What's that?" His daughter stared at the organ in the corner.

"Shh." He put his lips against her ear. "You must be quiet now. We'll talk later."

Oscar wondered if she would burst with all she wanted to say, all the questions she wanted to ask. She'd never had to be quiet before. The Amakers entered a pew on the left-hand side about halfway back, Martin, followed by Inge, and then Kate.

He would've preferred to sit in the back, and when he was almost ready to slide into the last pew, Kate turned around, her eyes meeting his, her brows raised slightly. Sighing, he took Liesl up to sit with them.

The smiles on both Kate's and Liesl's faces were his reward. His daughter sat on the pew beside Kate, her feet swinging slightly, eagerly looking at the people, the windows, the wall sconces, the pulpit, the high ceiling and pendant lamps.

When Pastor Tipford looked over his congregation, he stopped on Oscar, his smile broadening. Oscar's collar grew tighter.

Mr. Hale rose with his hymnbook, and Mrs. Hale began playing on the organ. She might be nosy and pushy for a shopkeeper, but she could certainly play the organ. Music filled the room. The congregation rose, and Liesl stood on the pew between Oscar and Kate. As they held the corners of the hymnal, she reached up and grasped it, too. Kate smiled softly, catching Oscar's eye.

He looked away. This was wrong. It should be Gaelle here with him, singing the hymns in her soft soprano, Liesl between them, and he should be holding their second daughter, who would be almost two now, on his arm. He shouldn't be feeling so…connected to this woman who stood beside him now.

After the song, Pastor Tipford returned to the pulpit and opened his Bible. "I'd like to continue our series in the book of Philippians. Our text today is from chapter four, verse seven." His voice filled the room. "'And the peace of God, which passeth all understanding, shall keep your hearts and minds through Christ Jesus.'" Looking up, his gaze moved from one face to the next.

Peace. When was the last time Oscar had felt peace?

Liesl fidgeted, and Kate reached into a bag she had brought from his home and pulled out a couple of Liesl's books. He hadn't even thought about how to keep his daughter occupied in church. The four-year-old beamed up at Kate and chose the book about the princess, her favorite.

Kate put her arm around the little girl and drew her up close to her side, tracing little circles on her arm in a repetitive motion that soon had Liesl's eyelids drooping. Oscar reached out for the book before it hit the floor. Kate eased Liesl down until her head rested on Kate's limited lap. She stroked the child's hair gently, and her eyes had a soft light in them that stirred something in Oscar.

How much his daughter had missed through not having a mother. Oscar did his best, but there was a gentleness, a softness, that only a woman could provide.

He forced himself to look away, to try to concentrate on the preacher's sermon, but he kept glancing back at Kate and his daughter.

The service couldn't be over soon enough for him. He needed to get outside. No doubt his distraction was because he wasn't accustomed to being around so many people all at once. But when they were dismissed, he found himself hemmed in. He'd taken the still-sleeping Liesl into his arms, and her head rested on his shoulder. Kate helped him work her hands into the sleeves of her plaid coat before donning her own.

"Oscar Rabb, so nice to see you here today." Mrs. Tipford reached through the crowd to grab his elbow before he could escape. "Now, don't go sneaking off. You look like you want to dash out that door, but there are so many people who have missed you and want to say hello." Neighbors and townsfolk swarmed around, talking, laughing, asking about each other's week.

The Amakers were surrounded, too. There was Mrs. Baker, the one who had said she had a room for Kate. And the Freidmans, from north of town, who had offered to take in Martin and Inge. The folks who would take the Amakers off his hands until they could make arrangements to travel back east.

For the first time, Oscar realized how empty his house would feel with them gone. He shook his head. What a silly thought. They'd only been there a few days. He'd go back to his old ways just as quickly when they'd left.

"We must start a clothing drive," Mrs. Tipford said. "I should've thought about it before now. Martin and Inge won't be hard to clothe, but Kate is another matter. Perhaps Mrs. Frankel would have some clothing that would work for Kate in her current condition."

Oscar studied Kate, who had stepped out into the aisle. She wore the same dress she had worn each of the last few days. Of course she had. Because she'd lost all her other clothes in the fire. And what had Oscar done about it?

Nothing.

Guilt nudged him. He knew what he should do, but…no. He couldn't. God wouldn't ask him to do that, would He?

"George said he delivered a telegram to Martin yesterday. Good news, I hope?" Mrs. Tipford waved to someone across the room.

Oscar adjusted Liesl in his arms. "You'll have to speak with them about that." Mrs. Tipford was a good woman, but she liked to know what was going on with the people of her husband's church, as if she had some proprietary claim. It wasn't that she was nosy like Mrs. Hale, looking for tidbits of news to share with her customers, but Mrs. Tipford did like to ferret out people's needs and plans whenever she could. But Oscar wouldn't be her source this time. If she wanted to find out what the Amakers' situation was, she'd have to ask them.

"It's so good to see you here today, Oscar." Pastor Tipford's voice thundered and heads turned. No way Oscar could just slip out quietly now. In one, loud blast, everyone knew he was here. Mrs. Tipford nudged her husband and pointed to Liesl. The pastor grimaced and lowered his voice to a whisper that still traveled several feet. "Sorry, didn't realize she was asleep. Oscar, I was going to head out to your place for a visit this afternoon. To check on the Amakers and see what they'd learned. Perhaps you can all stay a bit after other folks have left, and we can sort a few things out."

Oscar nodded and edged through the knots of people until he stood with his back to the wall, waiting for the place to clear out.

When it was just the Amakers and Tipfords left, the pastor directed them to sit in the front pews while he scooted the organ stool over and took a seat facing them. Oscar remained standing, swaying slightly to rock Liesl.

"Now, Martin, I understand you've heard from your brother. What did he say, and how can we help?" Pastor Tipford asked.

Martin unfolded the telegram and handed it to the pastor.

"So, they have a place for you, but not until after the new year." Returning the telegram to Martin, the preacher put his big hands on his knees. "That's very generous of your brother."

Oscar watched Kate, who had her head bowed and her fingertips against her lips. Tiny wisps of brown hair teased the nape of her neck under her upswept hair, making her look vulnerable and fragile.

He knew she was strong. He'd watched her work hard all day yesterday making the cheeses, and he knew that if he hadn't been there to help her, she would've done it all alone.

She had survived the loss of her husband and her home, and though he had heard her crying once in the privacy of her room, he hadn't seen her break down or despair.

She cared for her husband's grandparents as if they were her own, tending them, respecting them, putting their needs ahead of hers.

She was definitely strong.

But who took care of her? Who listened when she

needed to talk? Who shouldered her burdens and lightened her load?

"So." Mrs. Tipford drew his attention back to the conversation. "What do you want to do? The Bakers and Freidmans are still willing to have you." She cast an inquiring look Oscar's way. "But if things are working out for you to stay where you are, that's fine, too, isn't it?"

Oscar remained motionless, but inside, he was shaking his head. Yesterday he had outlined some very good reasons why the Amakers should find somewhere else to stay. He needed to think about what was best in the long run for himself and Liesl, didn't he?

Martin and Inge looked up at him, no expression on their faces beyond weary acceptance of whatever he decided. Pastor and Mrs. Tipford had their heads together, no doubt discussing logistics and plans of action for when he refused.

Then Kate looked up. Her eyes weren't exactly pleading with him, but there was a hope there that shook him.

"It's working out all right for now. They might as well stay at my place. After all, it's only for a few weeks." He heard himself say the words, make the offer that he had promised himself he wouldn't. But when she looked at him like that, what else could he do?

He could keep to himself over the next few weeks, that's what. Though he worried about Liesl's growing attachment to the Amakers, he would have a word with Kate about it. She would understand and take pains to keep things aloof.

* * *

A tiny corona of warmth glowed around Kate's heart as she entered Oscar's house and pulled off her gloves. Being in church had felt like rain on parched soil. Her burdens and responsibilities were the same, and yet, they were lighter, too, through having her spirit fed through worship and fellowship.

Rich aromas greeted her. Grossmutter had put a chicken into the oven to roast before leaving for church, and now, she shed her coat and kerchief and checked on the bird.

"How can I help?" Kate asked.

"Kate." Oscar took her coat and hung it up. "I'd like a word with you, if you don't mind."

He'd been quiet on the way to his farm, but then again, he was usually quiet. She'd been afraid to hope that he would let them stay on at his place for a little while longer, and when he had offered, it had been all she could do not to jump up and hug him.

Not that she was jumping much these days. She pressed her hands to her lower back as she followed him through the sitting room and into his workshop. Accustomed all her life to being slim and agile, carrying this baby was difficult to get used to. And it was only going to get worse. If only she wasn't so short. Her center of gravity had altered, making her slow, and clumsy.

Oscar leaned against the workbench. Behind him, the walnut wedding chest was taking shape. Last night when she'd brought him his cup of coffee, he had been using a hand plane to smooth the joints where he had glued boards together, running his hand over the wood, and switching from the plane to a piece of sandpaper as he worked. When he'd finished, she couldn't feel a single joint it was so smooth.

Now he crossed his arms, his face sober.

She hurried to speak. "I can't thank you enough for extending hospitality to us again. We're very grateful. I know we could stay separately with other families, but it means so much to me not to be parted from Martin and Inge. And with the baby coming..." She laughed. "It was beginning to feel a bit like a trip to Bethlehem. 'No room at the inn.'" She pressed her lips together. "Anyway, I am grateful."

He nodded, but his face went from sober to grim. "I wanted to talk to you about that, and a couple other things. Have you seen a doctor about the baby?"

She shook her head. "No, but you don't have to worry. I am young and healthy, and the baby is quite active." As if to illustrate her point, the baby kicked her ribs, and she placed her hand on the spot. His eyes followed the movement. "There wasn't much money before, and even less now. We can't pay for unnecessary doctor's visits. Grossmutter will be with me when the time comes. That's all I need."

"I would prefer if you at least got checked out by the doctor, just to make sure things are all right. I'll drive you to Mantorville myself, tomorrow." He nodded, as if his plan was quite reasonable.

"But I told you, I'm fine, and there's no money for a doctor right now." Though she could pay him with a cheese, she supposed, if he was willing to barter. And if Oscar would take her to Mantorville, she could possibly make arrangements with the stores there to buy her cheeses. Some of the early-summer ones could be sold now, as well as the largest wheels from last year. She drummed her fingers on the table, thinking.

"It would set my mind to rest," Oscar said.

He had asked for nothing from them in return for his hospitality. Surely she could do this one thing, though she felt it unnecessary.

"All right."

He lowered his arms and turned away, bracing his weight on his palms on the workbench. His suspenders crossed on his back, black against the white of his Sunday shirt. The shirt was in need of a good ironing, as if it had lain folded in a drawer for a very long time.

"Did Mrs. Tipford talk to you about some clothes?" he asked.

Kate glanced down at her dress. Though she laid it out every night, and sponged it, the garment needed a good washing. And she would dearly love a change from the skin out. Still, she should be thankful for what she had.

"She didn't say anything to me, but if we're going to Mantorville tomorrow, perhaps we can stop at the farm and pick up some cheeses to take with us. I can sell them at the store and perhaps have enough for a few clothes or, at the very least, a few lengths of fabric to make some."

He didn't say anything for a moment, and then, "My wife left some things. They might be a bit long and need hemmed up, but they should work for you." He didn't turn around.

Wear his dead wife's clothes? As grateful as she would be for something else to wear, how would she feel using a dead woman's things? How would that make him feel?

"Are you sure?"

"No sense letting them go to waste when someone could use them." His voice sounded forced, harsh. "Mrs. Tipford said she'd be by with some things for Martin and Inge, but finding clothing for you might be a bit tougher. But my wife was in the same condition…" His shoulders hunched and his head lowered.

She wanted to go to him, to put her hand on his back, to say she appreciated his sacrifice, his generosity, but something held her back.

He seemed to get hold of himself, and when he turned around, there was no vulnerability in his eyes or his voice.

"There's one other thing we need to talk about."

"Yes?"

"It's Liesl. Before you came, she hadn't met many strangers. For quite a while, it was just her and me. It appears she's taking quite a shine to you. All three of you. But I don't want her getting too attached. I didn't say anything right away, because I thought you'd only be here a day or two, or at most a week. But things are different now. You're going to be here a couple of months, and when you leave, it's going to go hard on her if you've gotten close."

Kate's brows rose. "What is it you want us to do?" She couldn't rebuff the child. Was she supposed to ignore her? Not answer her thousand and one questions? Not braid her hair or read her stories or…

Oscar scrubbed his hands through his hair. "I don't know. Maybe just remind her from time to time that you'll be leaving soon. That way, maybe she'll be more ready for it when it happens. And another thing, she's still holding on to the idea that I can get her a baby for Christmas. Maybe, if we don't talk about your baby when she's around, we can try to get her thinking about something else as a Christmas gift?" He shrugged. "Anyway, I just don't want her to be disappointed or hurt when things don't work out the way she hopes. When she gets her heart set on something, it can be hard to budge her."

Kate could understand his concern, but she didn't know how to prevent herself from caring about Liesl, or to stop the little girl from caring about her. And the bond between Grossmutter and Liesl was a beautiful thing.

"It will be difficult on everyone when we go." Well, perhaps not difficult for Oscar. He seemed to be doing a fine job holding himself aloof. "And I don't think you can stop Grossmutter from talking about Christmas. It's her favorite time of the year." And for Grossmutter, the celebration started weeks ahead of time with the planning and preparing. "She's been through so much this year, I don't want to dampen any joy she might get out of the Christmas season. But I'll speak with her."

He nodded. "I'll show you where the clothes are."

Upstairs, in the room she had been using, he knelt before a dome-topped trunk under the window and drew a key out of his pocket. "Mrs. Tipford packed these things away for me right after the funeral."

Small feet clattered on the stairs, and Liesl bounded into the room. "Grossmutter says dinner is ready."

"Liesl, you should call her Mrs. Amaker. She isn't your grandmother." Oscar rested his hands on the closed trunk lid.

The little girl wrinkled her nose and tilted her

head, clearly puzzled. Kate's heart went out to Liesl. Oscar was asking the impossible—for the Amakers not to care about his daughter, and for Liesl not to care about them. Still, Liesl was his daughter, and the Amakers would need to respect his wishes.

Oscar unlocked and opened the trunk, the scent of lavender rolling out. He stepped back, putting his hands in his pockets. "You're welcome to whatever might work for you."

"Thank you." Kate moved aside a layer of tissue paper. Mrs. Tipford had wrapped everything with care. A cheesecloth sachet of lavender buds lay atop the clothes. She blinked. Lavender was one of her favorite scents, and she'd kept a crystal bottle of lavender water on her dressing table, a gift from Johann.

"What's that?" Liesl asked.

Kate lifted it and smelled it, inhaling the herbaceous, floral scent, and then she held it under Liesl's nose. "It's called a sachet, and ladies use it in their dressers and armoires to keep their clothes smelling nice. I had some sachets like this once." Before her house burned down. "I love the scent of lavender."

Liesl breathed in deeply and then sneezed, giggling. "Daddy, can I have some in my dresser, like a grown-up lady?"

Kate looked at Oscar, holding the lacy bundle and tilting her head toward Liesl. At his nod, she handed the sachet to the child. "You may have this one."

"Thank you." She hugged Kate's side and scampered out, no doubt to put the scented packet in her room.

Oscar followed her, pausing at the door, but continuing on, his boots thumping on the stairs.

Kate lifted the first garment from the trunk, grateful to be alone. The maternity clothes were on top, which made sense. A blue dress with black trim, and a brown dress with small, red flowers scattered over it. She held the brown one up to her, testing the length of the sleeves and the hem. Gaelle Rabb must've been several inches taller than Kate.

Beneath those two garments in the trunk lay a lovely red shawl. Red was Kate's favorite color, and she had used it whenever she could in trims and accents in her own clothes.

Under the shawl, Kate found a heavy, burgundy cloak. She held it up, feeling the weight. Something to wear other than Johann's coat.

A tap sounded on the doorframe. It was Oscar, holding a lidded, square basket. "Thought you could use this." His eyes went to the cloak and flicked away. "Sewing kit."

"Oscar." It was the first time she had called him by name, and he went still, his hand gripping the doorframe. Kate swallowed, and took a deep breath. "Are you sure about this?" She wondered how she would feel if it was a neighbor going through her husband's things, preparing to wear his clothes.

He nodded. "The clothes aren't doing anyone any good packed away. I should've given them to Mrs. Tipford a long time ago, so she could hand them out to folks in need. I guess now I'm glad I didn't."

Again Kate had that feeling, the feeling that she wanted to go to him, to touch his shoulder or squeeze his hand, to let him know that she understood his loss, the need to move forward but the reluctance to do so, to comfort him.

And perhaps to be comforted, too.

Chapter Seven

Kate rode beside Oscar in the farm wagon, heading south to Mantorville, the midmorning sun bright and almost no wind. The overnight frost had long since melted away, promising a lovely fall day, warm for this time of year. She'd left her coat behind, opting for the red shawl instead.

Oscar pulled his hat down, shading his eyes. "I'm of half a mind to bring Martin's cows over to my byre to save on time going between the farms. I've got the room, especially since I moved the young bullocks out to the pasture with the shed." He shook up the reins. "And I was of half a mind to bring Martin with us today and have the doctor check out his cough. I could hear him all over the barn when we were milking this morning. I asked, but he refused to come, said he would be fine."

"I wish you had been able to persuade him. He was ill last winter with the same cough, and it lasted for months. Grossmutter is worried about him, too. I feel guilty going to see the doctor when I'm healthy, and he's in need and staying home." Kate shifted on the

hard wagon seat. Finding a comfortable position…
any comfortable position…was proving more difficult these days.

"You *both* need to see the doc." He glanced behind
him into the wagon box. Thirty-two cheeses rested
on a bed of straw, each carefully sewn into a cheesecloth bag. "I'm glad you're done making new cheese
for the winter. Now that you've shown me which ones
need brushed and turned in the cheese house, you can
leave that chore to me."

"You don't have to do that. It's my job. You have
enough to do with your own chores and your woodworking and all." He'd insisted she stay home this
morning and finish the hemming she and Grossmutter had started the afternoon before to alter Gaelle's
dresses to fit her. Kate wore the brown and red dress,
which matched the red shawl perfectly. When Oscar
had first seen her in the new-to-her clothes, he'd
looked thoughtful, but said nothing. She didn't know
if she was disappointed or relieved at his reaction, but
it felt nice to have fresh clothes to wear.

Oscar raised one booted foot to rest on the kick-
board, and propped his forearm on his knee. "If you
have to go over there every day to turn them yourself, then I have to go with you. I don't want you on
those rickety cellar stairs with no one else there. And
if I'm going to go, I might as well turn and brush
them myself."

Kate felt guilty causing him so much more work.
He hadn't asked for any of this. How could they repay
his kindness? In her life, she had often been on the
giving end of charity, but never before had she needed
so much assistance.

Mantorville was a bustling, busy town, several times the size of little Berne. Built on the north bank of the Zumbro River, the town rose up from the river to the plains. Coming in from the north as they were, the town spread out and down as they reached the outskirts. On the left, the large, limestone county courthouse rose, its pillared front entrance and domed central tower a testament to law and order in Dodge County.

Oscar pulled up at the intersection of Main Street and Fifth. A square brick building stood on the corner, and hanging over the door, Dr. Horlock's shingle swung in the breeze.

Across the street, the three-story stone Hubbell House hotel and restaurant sat solidly, white trimwork gleaming. Johann had taken Kate to the restaurant once as a special treat.

Oscar helped Kate from the wagon and held the door open, revealing a set of stairs. "Doc's office is on the second floor. I've never met him, though George Frankel says he's a good doctor. Horlock took over Doc Easterly's practice when he retired last year."

An enormous Boston fern sat in front of the windows, and a set of horsehair-silk furniture that had gone out of style years ago was grouped around a small, low table. On an inside door, a small sign hung from a nail. The Doctor Is With a Patient. Please Take a Seat.

Kate eased herself down into a chair, felt herself sliding on the slick upholstery and pressed her toes into the rug. The furniture reminded her of her grandmother's parlor, and being scolded for sliding off onto the floor on purpose when she was a little girl.

Oscar clasped his hands behind his back and paced the small space. His scowl made Kate feel even worse about taking up his time like this, especially when it seemed so unnecessary.

"You don't have to wait for me. You said you needed some supplies from the hardware store and the sawmill. I could meet you somewhere when I'm finished here. Maybe at the mercantile?"

"I'll wait." He stopped pacing to study a painting on the wall and then moved to read the book titles on the case in the corner.

The door opened, and Dr. Horlock came out, wiping his hands on a towel. A burly farmer followed, ducking his head to come through the doorway. "Have your wife put a poultice on the wound for a couple of days. Boils can be nasty things, and the heat will help draw out the infection now that I've lanced it." He spied Kate and Oscar and smiled. "Ah, hello. I didn't realize anyone had come in." He nodded to the farmer. "If you aren't better in a week, stop in again."

The man nodded, put on his hat and clomped down the stairs, not looking at anyone.

"A man of few words." Dr. Horlock grinned. He was about thirty, Kate guessed, but looked older. He had thinning blond hair and wore wire-framed spectacles. Slender, and not much taller than Kate, he finished drying his hands and folded the towel neatly. "Now, which one of you is the patient?" He raised his eyebrows, pretending not to notice Kate's expanded middle.

Kate scooted to the edge of the chair and began to push herself upright. Before she got far, Oscar was there with a hand under her elbow to help.

Dr. Horlock nodded. "Come right in." He waited for her to go in ahead of him and then looked over his shoulder. "Do you want to come in with your wife?"

Oscar was already shaking his head. "She's not my wife."

The doctor's brows rose, and heat filled Kate's face.

"She's my neighbor. Mrs. Amaker."

"I see." He nodded, though he was still clearly puzzled. "Well, then. You can wait out there. We shouldn't be long."

The examination room had a desk and chair in one corner, a padded leather table and glass-fronted shelves full of bottles, jars and instruments. Atop the desk stood a black bag, open, and filled with the tools of his trade.

"Now, Mrs. Amaker, what can I do for you?"

Kate stood beside the exam table and spread her hands. "I don't know. I am fit as a fiddle, and I feel fine, but I promised Mr. Rabb that I would see a doctor." She smoothed the ends of the red shawl. "My relatives and I are staying at his house, and he's concerned about me and the baby."

Dr. Horlock pushed the office chair around so she could sit, and leaned against the desk, crossing his arms. He looked relaxed, friendly, and his air of competence calmed Kate. She'd never been to see a doctor before, and didn't know what to expect, but his kindness put her at ease, and she found herself telling him about the fire and her husband's death and Oscar's kindness.

"You say he's a widower and has a little girl?"

"Yes, his wife died in childbirth a couple years ago."

The doctor removed his glasses and polished them on his handkerchief, holding them up to the sunlight. "I can understand his concern for you, then. Shall we do what we can to allay his fears?"

Kate had expected to feel horribly embarrassed, but Dr. Horlock was quick and discreet, listening to the baby's heartbeat, asking her some questions and feeling the rambunctious movements going on inside her. "You're correct, Mrs. Amaker, you are fit as a fiddle. That is one active baby in there. Due in six or seven weeks, I'd guess?"

She nodded. "Around Christmas."

"That will be a nice way to start the new year. Now, who will be with you when you deliver? Do you have a midwife?"

"My husband's grandmother. And one neighbor across the road, Mrs. Frankel, she has twelve children, and she said I could send for her when my time came, too."

"That's fine. And if you need me or you have any concerns, you only have to send for me." He went to the pitcher and bowl on a small stand and washed his hands again, giving her some basic instructions about getting rest and putting her feet up for a while each day.

Kate picked up her shawl. "Doctor, there was one other thing. My grandfather—" it was easier to refer to Martin as her grandfather rather than explain the relationship "—is ailing, but he won't come to see you. He's got a terrible cough, the same as he had last year. Is there anything we can do for him?"

By the time she left, she felt as if she'd made a friend. She clutched a packet of powders and a bottle of cough syrup for Martin along with instructions for their preparation and use. Dr. Horlock opened the door, and she thanked him.

"Oh, I nearly forgot. I don't have the money to pay you, but I brought something I hope you'll take in trade." She looked to Oscar, who was staring at the medicines in her hand, his brows bunching. "I make cheeses, and I have several nice ones with me down in the wagon."

The physician nodded. "Ah, lovely. You wouldn't guess it, but my wife actually put together a list of things to bring home from the grocery, and would you believe, cheese was on it?" To prove his words, he pulled a paper from his pocket. True enough, cheese was listed third. Relief made Kate smile.

"Shall we bring one up for you?"

"I'll get my bag and go down with you. I have a few calls to make." He plucked his suit coat off the rack and buttoned it up. "I can drop the cheese off at my house on the way."

When Oscar and Kate stood alone on the walk, Oscar asked, "What is the medicine for? Is the doctor worried about the baby?"

Kate shook her head, touched by the concern in his voice. "No, we are fine, Baby and I. The medicine is for Martin, for his cough. I might not be able to get him to the doctor, but I can still get him the medicine he needs. And Dr. Horlock was very nice. Do you think one cheese was enough?" She tucked the medicines under the straw in the wagon bed.

"He said it was. And now that I know how much

work goes into making one, I'm sure you overpaid." Oscar took her elbow, guiding her around the corner toward the general store.

The Mantorville Mercantile was three times the size of Hale's in Berne, and not nearly as inviting and cheery. Shelves packed with canned goods and patent medicines, cases stuffed with collars and buttons and suspenders, tables piled high with shirts and pants. A barrel of salt pork in brine sat near the front door, and a keg of vinegar balanced atop it.

Kate had never dealt with the owner. Martin and Johann had done the cheese-selling in the past. Johann had always thought the proprietor to be cross-grained and difficult to negotiate with. A tremor went through Kate, but Martin and Inge were counting on her to strike a favorable bargain, so she must be brave.

"Mr. Watterson runs things." Oscar kept his voice low. There were several patrons in the store, and the man behind the counter was tying up a paper-wrapped bundle for one of them. None of the customers were ladies.

Kate watched him struggle with the length of string. It was short, almost too short to accomplish his wishes. But he finally got the knot tied, with only about an inch of extra twine sticking up from the ends. Parsimonious.

When the customer left, Kate stepped forward, her hands trembling slightly. "Mr. Watterson?"

He gave her a sharp-eyed stare, his thin lips a flat line in his face, no warmth or helpfulness in his expression.

"Hello. I'm Kate Amaker. I believe you have

purchased cheeses from my late husband, Johann Amaker?"

"I have purchased a few."

Kate felt as if a cold wind had rippled over her. She forced a bright smile. "Well, I've brought some into town today to sell. All two-pound cheeses, but I do have larger wheels...if you prefer to have them in the store for selling wedges and slices."

"I am not accustomed to dealing with female vendors. Send your husband in to do business if you want to sell products to me." Mr. Watterson's glance flicked from her middle to Oscar, who stood a few steps behind her. "Is there something I can get for you, sir?"

Oscar shook his head. "The lady was here first."

The shopkeeper looked as if he had just sampled straight whey.

"Mr. Watterson, I cannot send my husband. He's dead." Kate kept her voice flat and businesslike, though it was difficult.

The storekeeper looked at her from down his narrow, long nose. "Very well. How much?"

Kate named her price per pound.

No reaction from Mr. Watterson.

"Sir?"

"I'm sorry. I was waiting for the rest of the joke. You are joking, are you not? That price is ridiculous." He busied himself with straightening his ledger book and pencil.

"That is the price you paid last year." Kate had seen the receipt. This store had received thirty pounds of cheese, paid in cash, eleven months ago.

"That was last year. Times are tougher now. The harvest was lean, and people are buying less. I can neither afford to keep as much inventory, nor pay as much for local products." He spoke patronizingly, as if she, a mere woman, was too simple to understand.

Her heart sank, but she refused to show it. "Very well. I shall have to take my product elsewhere." She tightened the strings on her reticule, and turned away.

"Wait, I didn't say I wouldn't buy some, but not at that price." He placed his hands flat on the counter-top. "I'll pay half."

Half wouldn't even cover the cost of making the cheese in the first place. She might as well roll the wheels of Emmentaler into the ditch. Every doorway to the Amakers staying in Minnesota seemed to slam shut in her face. But she couldn't meet Mr. Watterson's ridiculous offer.

"No. That's not enough."

Shrugging, Mr. Watterson turned his back and began taking canned goods out of a box and setting them on the counter. "Suit yourself. You know my price."

"And you know mine. Good day." The lump in her throat made speech difficult, but she managed to at least be polite.

She headed toward the door, expecting Oscar to follow, but when he didn't she looked back over her shoulder. He stood at the counter, hands braced flat, leaning in. His voice was low, and she couldn't make out what he was saying, but clearly it wasn't what Mr. Watterson wanted to hear. He leaned away, his face mottling in red blotches.

Then Oscar was at her elbow, opening the door, ushering her outside.

"I think we should have some lunch, don't you?"

His tone was so mild she blinked. "At the Hubbell House? They serve a good meal there." When she paused her step, he shrugged. "My treat."

The restaurant was pleasantly busy, but not crowded, and they were shown to a seat in the main dining room. The waiter handed Oscar a printed card. "We've still got pot roast and pork chops, but the next stage is just arriving, so you might want to hurry."

Oscar raised his brows at Kate. "Either is fine," she answered his unspoken question.

He ordered chops for them both, and the waiter hurried away.

"I'm sorry about that business at Watterson's."

Kate unfolded her napkin, smothering a weak smile at the lack of room on her lap to put it and wondering if she should just spread it over her belly. "It's not your fault. There are men like Mr. Watterson who don't think women should be doing business, or think that they're too simple to understand. Or they hope they can take advantage of them, drive a hard bargain, and the woman will just fold her tent and go away."

"I'm glad you didn't cave. Half price." He leaned back and toyed with the cutlery. "That's robbery."

"The problem is, Watterson took a lot of inventory from us last year. If I don't sell to him this year, what can I do with the rest? Mrs. Hale will take some, but not much, and the other two stores here in Mantorville only take about ten pounds each. With there being a creamery in Rochester, the stores there don't need to buy from me." As she worked down her list of possible sales, the worry mounted. She'd invested time and money in the production of the cheeses, and if she couldn't sell them, the Amakers would have nothing to show from a year's work.

The stagecoach arrived, clattering to a stop outside the window. Through the rippled glass, Kate watched the passengers descend. The driver jumped down, coiling his whip and reaching back up for the mail bag. Hostlers hurried to unhitch the horses and lead them away, bringing fresh animals from the stables behind the hotel.

A large man edged between the tables, his long coat catching on chairs. Mr. Siddons. Kate tensed. Everyone in Dodge County knew who Mr. Siddons was.

"Mrs. Amaker?" He smiled, but his pale eyes glittered without warmth. Reptilian and cold. "I thought that was you." He nodded to Oscar. "Rabb."

Oscar shook his hand, half rising.

"Mrs. Amaker, I was sorry to hear about your house fire. A total loss, I believe?" He gripped his lapels. "I understand you might be selling out and heading back east? If that's the case, I would like to be the first to offer cash for the farm and livestock."

And just where did you hear that bit of news? Mr. Siddons was the wealthiest man in the county, and at every opportunity, he gobbled up more and more farmland. He had an immense dairy between Kasson and Mantorville, and Kate's heart hurt at the thought of Johann and Martin's beloved Brown Swiss cows being absorbed into the immense Siddons holdings. They would cease to be individuals with names and personalities and become numbers, worthy of being kept only if their milk production numbers merited it.

"We have not yet decided if we'll go east or stay here, but I will convey your interest to Martin and

Inge." Kate didn't like the way Mr. Siddons rocked on his toes, looking down at her alongside his bulbous nose, as if calculating her net worth and productivity. The Amakers might have to sell out, but she'd rather give the farm to George Frankel rather than see it in the hands of Mr. Abel Siddons.

The waiter brought their food, and Mr. Siddons spied someone else he wanted to speak to and took his leave.

Oscar bowed his head, said a short grace for their food and took up his fork. "I was thinking, I need to make a trip to Saint Paul to deliver some furniture to a store. I could take the cheeses along with me and sell them there. You're more likely to get a better price, too."

He spoke as if the Siddons interruption hadn't happened. It took Kate a moment to switch her thoughts and concentrate on what he was saying. "You'd do that?" A spark of hope lit in her chest. If he could sell the cheeses for enough, maybe they could find a way to keep the farm.

Nodding, he spread a roll with butter. "It won't take me much out of my way, and the sooner you have the cheese money, the sooner you can make your plans with Martin's brother."

Kate's appetite fled at this reminder that he was eager to get them out of his house and his life.

Oscar loaded the rest of the lumber into the wagon box—including the special dimensions he'd ordered at the last minute—careful not to bump the cheeses still resting in the straw. Kate had sold ten of them to the remaining stores in town. Those, with the one she'd given to Dr. Horlock, meant she was returning home with twenty-one unsold.

She sat on the wagon seat now, wrapped in the red shawl, hands in her lap. He was glad he'd taken the time to give her some lunch at the Hubbell House, but she'd only picked at her food. The offer from Siddons must've killed her appetite. Either that or the unpleasant encounter at the mercantile.

His jaw tightened, remembering Watterson's uncivil treatment of Kate. Yanking on the ropes securing the lumber, Oscar wished he was yanking on the lapels of Watterson's coat. The bounder, trying to take advantage of Kate because she was a woman in desperate straits. He had known Watterson was a cold miser, but he hadn't known the extent of his antipathy toward women.

At the second store, he hadn't missed how Kate had run her hand over a bolt of soft, white flannel, a wistful look in her eyes. It had hit him like a blow to the chest. She had probably spent months making things for her coming baby, only to have them all burned to ashes in the house fire. To his knowledge, she didn't have so much as a diaper pin left.

Which made the cheese money all that much more important.

And he didn't have anything in a bureau or trunk at his house to give to her. When Gaelle and the baby had died, he'd packed up all the baby things and sent them over to George Frankel's house. The Frankels could always use baby clothes and such, and Oscar had known he would never need such things again. He'd kept Gaelle's clothes, but he'd gotten the baby things out of the house quickly.

He climbed up into the wagon and gathered the reins, chirruping to the horses. Kate grabbed the seat and her belly as the wagon lurched, headed up from the riverbank sawmill to the top of the hill and the level prairie.

She looked tired, her shoulders drooping a bit. When they got home, he'd insist she sit for a while. Gaelle, near the end of her pregnancies, had suffered from swollen ankles and a tired back. Oscar peeked toward Kate's feet, but her long skirt covered her shoes.

That skirt. Gaelle's. It had been her favorite maternity dress. Not because she was fond of the color, but because she said it was comfortable and easy to put on.

Seeing Kate in it when he drove up to the house this morning to pick her up had brought back so many memories. Surprisingly, though thoughts of Gaelle still brought a pang, they hadn't hurt like he'd been expecting. Which troubled him. It was supposed to hurt, wasn't it? He was supposed to be battling his resentment and grief, wasn't he?

"Oscar," she said, turning to him. "Before we get to your home, there's something I need to ask you."

He slowed the horses to a walk and gave her his attention, caught by the gravity of her tone.

"You asked me not to speak about Christmas to Liesl, and to ask Grossmutter to do the same." She twisted her hands in the red, yarn fringe of the shawl. "I'd like to ask you to reconsider that request." When she put her hand on his arm, she looked up at him with those blue eyes, filled with concern. "I don't think you can understand how important Christmas is to

Inge. She looks forward to this season all year. The town has several events, and she helps Mrs. Tipford and the other ladies plan them all. The Star Singing, the Advent tour, the church program and gift giving. She bakes once-a-year treats and decorates and anticipates."

Oscar listened. Gaelle had been like that, too. It was one of the reasons Oscar had abandoned all the trappings of the Christmas season after her death. It reminded him too much of all the good times.

Kate bit her lower lip and then continued. "This might very well be the last Christmas we have in Minnesota." Her voice faltered a bit. "I know I should be grateful that Martin's brother is willing to take us in, but none of us wants to go, to leave this place we've worked so hard to build, the place we have our roots. From what Martin has said, his brother isn't a pleasant man, and the work Martin will do in the tannery isn't pleasant, either. I'd like to do everything I can to make this Christmas special for Martin and Inge. It isn't easy for anyone to uproot their lives and start over somewhere else, but it's especially hard when you're elderly. I understand your concerns about Liesl, but I'm concerned about my family, too. Surely giving them a good Christmas won't hurt Liesl too much."

He rubbed his hand down his face, feeling like an ogre. Or that fellow in the Dickens story, Scrooge? He'd used Liesl as an excuse, yes, but in reality, he hadn't wanted to think about Christmas because it was too painful for himself.

Perhaps he could let them have their fun and just stay out of it. Yes, that's what he would do. They could celebrate however they wanted, and he'd hold himself out of the jollity.

Slapping the lines, he urged the horses on. "It's fine. Do what you like. Give yourselves whatever you can as far as a nice Christmas is concerned." He almost said he wouldn't mind, but that wouldn't have been true.

Kate's shoulders relaxed, and she smiled, worry lines smoothing on her brow. "And I thought, if you like, I might be able to make something for Liesl. She showed me the princess dress in her storybook, and if you wanted, I could sew one for her as a Christmas gift. That might get her mind off a baby for Christmas." She smiled softly. "I love to sew, and it would be no trouble."

That baby for Christmas notion. Oscar sighed. Every night that request headed Liesl's prayer list. "It would be a load off my mind if you could get her fastened onto some other Christmas gift, that's for sure. Maybe you two can go to town and look at fabric? And not just for a Christmas present. If you'd be willing, I could pay you to make up a new set of dresses for Liesl for the next couple of years or so. She grows so fast, and I feel like I'm always looking for a seamstress to make new clothes for her."

"I'd like that. And you wouldn't have to pay me. It would be a way we could give back to you for your hospitality."

Kate's smile was a fine reward in itself. And he had a few thoughts on how to compensate her for her time if she wouldn't accept money.

They pulled into the yard, and Oscar stopped the horses in front of the house. There was hardly room, what with all the buggies and traps parked out front. He recognized the flashy chestnut of the Tipford's, so the pastor and/or his wife were here, but who were all these other folks?

He leaped down and reached up for Kate. "Looks like a party. Do you know what's going on?"

She shook her head. "I'll go see." She reached into the straw where she'd put the medicines she'd gotten for Martin, and Oscar led the team around the back of the house to his workshop door to unload the lumber. Rolf gamboled around, bushy tail wagging, tongue lolling.

Martin met him inside the workshop door, rheumy-eyed, dabbing his nose with a handkerchief. "You might want to stay out here." He coughed. "Hen party going on in the house."

Oscar slid a couple of boards toward himself and grasped them under his arm. "What's it all about?"

"I don't know. I got out of the way first thing, me and the dog. Mrs. Tipford showed up with a basket of clothes for Inge and me that have come from the church people who wanted to help." Martin plucked at the new, blue wool shirt he wore. "It's nice, yes? Then the other ladies came, and the kettle was heated and I left. It is the wise thing for a man to do when the women get together." He shrugged, good-natured about it. "I went down to the barn and swept out the feed and tack rooms, and I fixed the broken hinge on that end stall door."

Something Oscar had been meaning to get to for weeks. He'd noticed over the past few days how handy Martin was to have around, fixing little things, tidying up, always doing something. "Thanks." He slid the boards into the rack and went back for more. Martin met him in the doorway, a four-by-four under each arm.

"Where do you want these?" Martin turned his head, coughing in a tight bark, wincing at the small explosions.

"Walnut goes in the middle rack, soft maple in the upper, but I can get it. Why don't you take a rest?" The old man looked like a stiff wind would topple him.

Martin shook his head. "It is good to stay busy. I am not fast, but I am steady." He eased past Oscar and into the workroom.

In no time they had the wagon empty of wood. Oscar rolled a cheese toward himself. "Let's put these down in my cellar. Save a trip back to your place."

As they stacked the rounds on an empty shelf, Oscar told Martin what had happened at Watterson's. Martin's shoulders sagged.

"I should have gone to town myself. Kate has no experience with men like him." Regret lined his face. "Last year Johann sold all the cheeses. He had a way of dealing with men like Watterson, getting us a good price for our product." He rubbed his hands down his face. "I miss my grandson very much."

Oscar nodded, feeling a kinship with the old man. If Johann was here, so much would be different for all the Amakers...and for himself.

"I had a few words with Watterson before I left." Not that it would do much good. Still, someone had needed to stand up for Kate. "You don't want to do business with him if you can help it. Anyway, I told Kate I would take some of your extra cheese to Saint Paul with me at the end of the month and sell them there. I have to deliver some furniture pieces to a store there, and I am sure the grocers in the city would buy some of your inventory."

Martin raised his head, a hopeful light in his eyes. "We might get a good price if you're already going up there. It was always too far to justify the expense of a trip, but if you're going, anyway..." His step had a bit more purpose as he went up the cellar stairs.

Oscar followed him up, pondering the notion that what a person really needed to keep going was hope more than anything. Hope that things would be better down the road, hope that someone cared, that there was a way forward.

After unhitching and turning out the horses, Martin picked up a broom, brushing aside Oscar's protests. "I will sweep out the wagon. Then I will come to the house."

Oscar nodded and headed to the pump to wash up. He respected that Martin wanted to work, needed to be doing something, but Oscar would need to find light jobs, preferably indoors, until the old man was feeling better. He opened the kitchen door and stepped inside. The pocket doors into the parlor were wide open.

His sitting room was crammed with females. Skirts and bonnets and chatter and scent. The smallest of the lot spied him and shot off the footstool, crashing into his knees. He swung her up, and she squeezed his neck. "Daddy, look. We're having a tea party." Liesl squirmed with glee. "Grossmutter... I mean... Mrs. Amaker let me wear my bestest dress, and I got to drink cammic tea, and eat cookies, and I've been really good. I got to help hand out the teaspoons." Her brown eyes sparkled, and her smile was contagious. He had no idea what cammic tea was, but she looked like she was having fun. He hadn't known what a social creature his little girl was.

Kate turned from the stove, carrying a tray, and Oscar lowered Liesl to the ground and took it from her. Here she was supposed to be resting, putting her feet up, and she was carrying heavy trays and waiting on people.

"Thank you. I just brewed another pot. Would you like some tea, or would you prefer coffee?"

He leaned close to whisper in her ear. "I would prefer that you sit down and let someone wait on you. You have to be tired from your trip to town. I can make my own coffee."

Her lashes flicked upward, their looks colliding, and he read the surprise in her eyes. It made him feel good to catch her off guard with a little care. She spent so much time looking after everyone else, it was high time someone put her first. He set the tray on the table in front of the fireplace, and Mrs. Tipford nodded.

"Hello, Oscar. Thank you for letting us use your parlor for our meeting." She gave him a bright smile, most likely well aware that he'd had no say in their being in his house. "I'll pour. Now, Inge, you have the lists of food for after the Star Singing? We'll combine the Star Singing with the Christmas Eve service, and we'll have the treats at the church afterward. That seems to work best. And, Gussie, you'll have the usual school program?"

Gussie Slocum, the schoolteacher, nodded, taking notes on a tablet.

Oscar realized he'd stumbled smack into the Berne

Christmas Committee's plotting session. Oh, no. He refused to get sucked into this. They could plot and plan to their hearts' content, as long as they left him out of it. He quietly took his leave, heading into the kitchen and sliding the pocket doors nearly shut behind himself. Martin had it correct. When women gathered, it was wise for men to scamper.

Liesl followed him, squirming through the narrow space between the doors. "Daddy, Grossmutter... I mean, Mrs. Amaker...says I can be in the Sunday school Christmas program, and that all the children get to be in the Star Singing, and that when December finally comes, we will go visiting every night. And she will teach me to make Christmas treats." She climbed onto one of the kitchen chairs, kneeling and propping her elbows on the table, her chin in her hands. "And we can make decorations, and learn new songs, and we will read about Baby Jesus." She drummed her toes on the seat.

Oscar listened, but didn't pay much attention, used to her prattling. He slid the coffeepot to the front of the stove and reached into the cupboard for the coffee beans. But the little sack wasn't there. Rows of canned fruit and vegetables stood neatly on the shelves.

"The church ladies brought those, some from each of them. Mrs. Tipford said it was to help you feed the Amakers. Grossmutter..." She looked at him out of the corner of her eye, and he knew she was "mistaking" the name on purpose, but he let it slide. "She took everything out of the cupboard and put it all back in different places. The coffee is in here." Liesl scooted off the chair and went to the corner hutch. She tugged open the top bin. "See, it's close to the grinder, too."

She pointed to the coffee grinder on the wall. "It's more…'fishent, Grossmutter says."

Which he took to mean "efficient." Her vocabulary was certainly expanding with the presence of guests in his home. He quickly ground some beans, wincing at the noise, and got the coffee brewing.

Martin came through from the workshop, wiping his hands on a towel, his cheeks red from the cold. A hot cup of coffee would do the old man some good. Oscar glanced at the clock. It was nearly time to head over to the Amaker farm to tend the chores, and he wanted to have a word with Martin beforehand.

Liesl beamed and patted the chair next to her. "You can sit here. Daddy, guess what we did today? Before the ladies came, me and Grossvat—Mr. Amaker fixed that bridle you said was broken. I got to hand him the tools, and he poked a new hole in the strap…" She went on for several minutes, detailing the repair with surprising accuracy, while Oscar nodded his thanks to Martin. Yet another chore he'd meant to get to that was now done.

The ladies' meeting broke up. The pocket doors opened, and several of them streamed through. In their bright dresses, chattering away, they reminded him of a flock of birds. They put on bonnets, tugged on gloves, gathered belongings, talking all the while.

As he dug a pair of thick-walled enamel cups from the cupboard—thankfully, the dishes were in the same place they'd always been—he noted that Kate had remained seated in his big armchair, and someone had pushed the footstool in front of her. She was talking to one of the older ladies, holding her cup of tea on her rounded belly, clearly enjoying the company.

What was it about women that seemed to get them so happy and full of energy just by being together? Being around too many people for too long made him edgy and tired, but Gaelle had thrived on company. He poured the coffee, handing a steaming cup to Martin and taking up his own.

"Oscar." Mrs. Tipford bustled over, tying her bonnet strings. "Thank you again for opening your home. Liesl may have told you, but if not, I wanted to let you know that the church ladies all raided their larders and sent along some canned goods and supplies to help the Amakers. And I brought some donated clothing for Inge and Martin." She put her hand on his arm. "Kate tells me that you are responsible for her clothing. That's so considerate of you."

Oscar jerked his chin, letting her know he heard her.

"Anyway," she said brightly. "We've got things well in hand now for all the festivities. Hard to believe it's only a few weeks until Christmas."

He set down his cup and headed outside to help the ladies into their wagons and buggies. They all thanked him, telling him how glad they were to see him at church that week, how they missed his wife at their gatherings. He nodded, reminded over and over why he had avoided town and church and people for so long. He felt smothered, and when the last visitor pulled out of the drive, he sighed with relief.

Returning to the house, he let Rolf inside. The dog went first to Liesl, nosing her, licking her face, checking on her, then to his water dish, lapping happily before trotting into the living room and nudging Kate's hand. She had clearly become a favorite of Rolf's.

Inge began picking up teacups and spoons, piling things onto the tray. Liesl hopped off her chair and joined her, bustling about, mimicking the older woman in a way that made Oscar smile but also ache a bit. Another reminder of how much she'd missed by not having Gaelle in her life.

Kate, he was thankful to see, remained in the chair, her head tucked into the wing, eyes closed. Rolf flopped onto the rug beside her.

He turned to Martin. "I was thinking, to make things easier on both of us, it might be a good idea to bring your cattle over here to my place. I've room in my byre if the weather is bad. Otherwise, they can stay in the pastures here, and it would save all the trips next door. Most of your cattle are coming into their dry season, so they wouldn't be much work, and since I only have the one milk cow, and she's a Jersey, they'll be easy enough to tell apart. I can haul feed from your place by the wagonload before the snow flies."

Martin frowned into his cup, but before he could speak, he tucked his mouth into the crook of his elbow and coughed. The spasm lasted for a while, and when he was done, his face was red, and he held his chest. "It *is* a lot of trouble for you to make so many trips to help with the chores."

"It's not that. I don't mind, but it would put my mind to rest if you were able to stay indoors until your cough is better, and it *would* save me a heap of time if all the livestock was in the same place."

The old man nodded. "And perhaps we could discourage Kate from needing to help with the chores."

Oscar sensed he had an ally. "Exactly. I already

told her I would see to her cheeses, though I'll be glad when this last batch is done being turned and such and can just sit there on the shelf and ripen. I don't want her on those open cellar stairs by herself." He helped Liesl, who was struggling to pull a chair up to the washtub, lifting her to stand on the seat.

Inge set a plate of oatmeal cookies on the table. She had an apprehensive bend to her eyebrows, and a tentative look in her brown eyes.

"Herr Rabb..." Her voice was meek as she refilled his coffee cup.

"Please, call me Oscar."

"Oscar, there is something I would like to ask." She fingered the knot of the kerchief she often wore over her snowy hair.

Kate stirred, blinked a few times and yawned, stretching. She spied them through the pocket doors, and pushed herself up. He frowned. Her nap hadn't been long enough.

She came into the kitchen, bracing her hands against her lower back. "I'm sorry. I must've dozed off."

"Daddy," Liesl said, plopping teaspoons into the wash water. "Grossmutter says we can have an Advent window here in our house, if you say it's all right. The big one in the parlor. On day sixteen." Liesl hopped on her toes, her braids bouncing on her shoulders. "And then people from town will come, and we will have good food and music and singing."

He paused, a cookie halfway to his mouth.

"I don't think Grossmutter meant to tell your daddy so suddenly, sweetling." Kate cupped Liesl's head. "Oscar, the ladies were organizing the Advent tour.

The Amakers have always taken one of the days, and Mrs. Tipford thought, since we were staying here, you wouldn't mind if we took our turn using your front window."

Oscar was familiar with the Advent tour. When Gaelle was alive, their house had been one of the stops. But that had ended two Christmases ago, and he had no desire to resume the tradition. If they wanted to plan the town events and go to every single one, he wouldn't stop them, but he refused to be included.

Liesl hopped off her chair and came to lean into Kate's side, looking up. "Tell me again what happens to the window?"

Kate sat herself at the table, and put her arm around the child. "Every day, beginning December first, people decorate their front window for Christmas. Pine boughs, paper chains, strings of beads, paper stars, whatever they think will look pretty." Her eyes had a faraway look, remembering. "Each evening, visitors go to the next house on the list, singing and eating good food and sharing the Christmas season. One after another, houses are visited, until it is Christmas Eve night."

"What happens then?" Liesl's eyes were round, and her lips parted in anticipation.

"On that night, we all gather in the center of town, and the children of the town carry lovely stars they have made, and they sing songs about the Baby Jesus coming to earth to be our Savior. They walk through the town, sharing the Good News. Then we meet at the church for the Christmas Eve service, and afterward there will be hot chocolate and Christmas goodies."

"And we all go home to wait for Christmas Day!" Liesl clapped, bouncing and grinning. "And there are presents and good food and the Christmas story."

"Yes, and family and being thankful for all God's blessings, especially sending us Jesus to be our Savior." She smoothed Liesl's hair and gave her a squeeze.

Oscar swallowed the last of his coffee, forcing down bitter thoughts. Christmas wasn't a time of thankfulness and family for him. It was a huge reminder of his loss. And now his house was going to be on the Advent tour? He should put his foot down, insist that they keep his place off the list. It was one thing to let Inge make some Christmas food, and for Kate to help him with a gift for Liesl, but to have half the town visit? To be expected to visit them? Because he couldn't have them come to his place and not reciprocate.

No, he wouldn't do it.

Kate rubbed her stomach. Was the baby moving around in there? She leaned over and dropped a kiss on Liesl's head, a gesture so natural it stunned him.

He was reminded that she had been nothing but gracious to his rambunctious daughter, answering her thousand questions every hour, teaching her through example, always kind. At a time when no one would blame her at all if she was concerned with nothing but her own future, she was trying to make things better for her family, and his.

She cast him a glance, and with a guilty start, she dropped her arm from around Liesl.

He'd told her to keep her distance and not let his daughter get too attached.

With the way Liesl was looking up at Kate right now, it was probably too late.

Chapter Eight

"What about this one?" Kate held up a length of pale blue fabric scattered with yellow flowers.

Liesl pursed her lips, tapping them with one finger, so serious Kate wanted to laugh. "No. That's not it."

"Well, sweetling, we're just about out of choices. And time. You need to make up your mind." Kate moved aside the blue calico while Mrs. Hale waited behind the counter to cut the fabric once they reached a decision. Oscar and Grossvater would be returning for them soon, and Grossmutter already had her foodstuffs purchased and ready to go.

Still, Liesl dithered, touching one fabric after another, doubt in her eyes. She'd chosen several already, but those were for everyday dresses. This one was supposed to be for her new Christmas dress.

At last, her hand dropped, and her chin lowered. Before Kate knew what was happening, a fat, glistening tear rolled down Liesl's cheek and splashed on the floor.

"What is it, sweetling?" Kate wished she could kneel easily so she could look the child in the eye.

Spying a ladder-back chair by the door, she took Liesl's hand, drawing her along. When Kate was seated, she wrapped the girl in her arms, kissing her head. "Sometimes there are so many choices we get overwhelmed, don't we? It's all right."

Liesl burrowed her head into Kate's shoulder, hiccupping sobs forcing themselves out of her throat.

"Are there just too many choices?" Kate asked.

"No-o-o-o."

Patting her back, rocking her slightly, she rested her cheek on Liesl's hair. "What is it, then?"

The bell over the door jangled, and a gust of cold air came in with Oscar. Kate took the ends of her cloak and wrapped them around Liesl, who continued to cry.

"What's wrong?" Oscar dropped to one knee, his big hand covering his daughter's back. "Is she hurt?"

Kate shook her head. Liesl tugged away from her and launched herself into Oscar's arms, sobbing into his neck. He held her close, rising to his feet, and Kate stood, too, feeling a failure. How had a shopping expedition for a Christmas dress turned into a crying child?

Oscar hugged her close and whispered in her ear, swaying slightly. "Shh, just tell me what's wrong."

"I...don't...want...a...Christmas...dress." The sobs nearly strangled the words, but she got them out.

"Why not, Poppet? I thought you wanted a pink dress with blue flowers."

"You said I could only make one wish for Christmas." She straightened in his arms, her face tear-streaked. "If I can only have one wish, I want a baby, not a dress."

Oscar's eyes met Kate's over Liesl's head, wide and a bit panicked. So Liesl hadn't been deterred by thoughts of a pretty dress. She still wanted a baby.

Kate dug in her reticule and drew out her handkerchief. She stepped close, dabbing at Liesl's wet cheeks, aware that Mrs. Hale was hearing every word and that Oscar had no idea what to say.

"Sweetling, you don't know what you're asking. Babies aren't something you can just ask for as a Christmas present. A book or a toy or a new dress, yes, but not a baby."

Liesl frowned, drawing back. "But I have been praying, every night. Daddy, you said Jesus hears and answers our prayers."

Kate turned away, smothering her smile, not wanting Liesl to think she was laughing at her. Ah, the faith of a child.

Oscar puffed out his cheeks. "Poppet, that's true. Jesus does hear and answer our prayers, but sometimes, the answer is no." He leaned his forehead down to touch hers. "And that's what I am telling you. No. You cannot have a real baby for Christmas. I know you don't understand." He put his hand gently on her lips to stifle the protests coming. "But someday you will. For now, you need to trust me. Is there something else you would like for Christmas instead?"

Her brown eyes swam with tears, and her chin quivered, making Kate's heart break. "No, Daddy." She buried her face in his shoulder again.

"All right." He cradled her head, a frustrated tilt to his mouth.

Grossvater stepped into the store, bundled to the

eyes in a coat and scarf. He tugged down the muffler. "Are we ready?"

Buttoning her coat, Inge nodded. Kate raised her brows to Oscar. "We got a few yardages cut, enough to start on the wardrobe you asked for."

He nodded. "You go ahead. Liesl and I will be along in a moment."

Mr. Hale accompanied them, carrying the groceries, and Kate took the paper-wrapped bundle of fabric and notions from Mrs. Hale with a tight smile. Outside, the cold wind took her breath away. It had snowed overnight, a few inches, and now the snow lay in hard-packed ridges and drifts, while some areas were blown clear of snow altogether by the brisk wind.

"Today I can believe that Christmas is only six weeks away." Inge tugged on her mittens.

"All set." Mr. Hale put the box of groceries into the wagon bed. "See you folks on Sunday if the weather holds."

Kate clambered up over the front wheel, and when she got into the wagon, she felt a pang along her side. Gasping, she pressed her hand to her abdomen.

"You are all right, Kate?" Martin asked, helping his wife get settled on the board seat in the back.

She winced, rubbing her side. "Yes, just a twinge." Forcing a smile, she eased down onto the wagon seat and turned. "Nothing to worry about."

Inge nodded. "The baby has not so much room now."

Not much at all. Another six weeks seemed a long time, and yet it was rushing by, too.

Oscar and Liesl emerged from the store, and Liesl had a happier look on her face. Oscar carried a large, paper-wrapped bundle, and Liesl had a smaller one clutched in her hands. After placing their things in the back of the wagon, Oscar swung Liesl aboard. She hurried to sit between Martin and Inge on the board seat.

"What have you got there, little one?" Martin asked.

"It's a surprise." She held the little package primly in her lap.

"Ah," he said, his eyes twinkling. "Surprises can be fun."

Kate turned to face forward. Surprises could be fun, though not always.

"It is a good thing," Martin continued, "that God is never surprised, though. He always knows everything. What we are thinking, what we are feeling, what has happened in our lives and what is going to happen. We do not need to fret or worry, because God is never surprised."

"But He can surprise *us* from time to time." Oscar slapped the lines and chirruped to the team.

Kate nodded. This entire last year had been one surprise after another, and not many of them what she would consider good. But, she reminded herself, God was good, and He wasn't surprised, and she would trust, because He had never failed her.

When they arrived back at Oscar's home, Kate couldn't help but wonder at the sense of comfort walking into the farmhouse gave her. She felt more at ease here than she'd thought possible after that first, awkward night and morning when Oscar had made it clear he was uneasy having them there.

What about now? Would he be relieved to have

them gone? To have his house back? No more trips to town for errands that were not his, no more extra chores, no more people cluttering up his life?

Kate untied her cloak slowly, realizing that whether he would miss them or not, she would definitely miss him and Liesl. Oscar might be a man of few words, but his actions spoke volumes. He had denied them nothing they needed and given them much that they did not.

Liesl marched into the room, the bobble on top of her hat wobbling as she ran to the parlor and put her "surprise" packet onto the ottoman. She shrugged out of her little plaid coat, dropping it on the floor.

"Miss Liesl." Kate looked at the coat.

"Oh, I forgot." She brought the garment to Kate to hang by the door.

They stepped out of the way as Martin and Oscar brought in the packages and boxes. Grossmutter was already at the stove, stirring up the fire. She dipped water into the kettle.

"Some hot tea will warm us up."

"Can I have cammic tea again?" Liesl climbed onto a chair and began removing foodstuffs from the carton.

"Of course, *Schätzchen*." Grossmutter brushed her hand over Liesl's hair. Kate loved the bond growing between those two. Having the high-spirited little girl around had helped take Grossmutter's mind off their troubles.

Oscar carried in the package of dress goods. "Where would you like this?"

Kate took it. "I'll put it in the parlor for now." She'd wait until the kitchen was clear to spread out fabric and begin cutting out dresses, pinafores and nightgowns for Liesl. It still bothered her that the child had been so upset about a Christmas dress. What else might they give to her that would make her happy?

Martin sat at the table, his shoulders hunched. His cough was a bit better, though he still looked tired. The medicine Dr. Horlock had sent helped, but what he really needed was a long rest without worries.

Oscar returned from putting up the team, and he carried one more package. Shrugging out of his black coat, he dropped it onto a hook and set the paper-wrapped bundle on the end of the table.

"Can we do it now, Daddy?" Liesl asked.

Oscar smiled at the little girl as she hopped on her toes. Kate marveled at how quickly her moods could change.

"Let me get warmed up first, Poppet. The surprise will keep for a few more minutes." He pulled up a chair and sat, taking the cup Grossmutter handed him.

"Look, Daddy. I have cammic tea."

"Just what is 'cammic' tea, anyway?" He looked into her mug.

Kate smiled. "I believe she means cambric tea. It's tea and milk." Mostly milk, in fact. "I remember when my mother first gave me cambric tea. When the church ladies came over for a quilting bee. I felt quite grown up drinking tea with the ladies."

"Where is your family now?" Oscar asked.

She rubbed her belly as the baby thumped her side. "My parents passed away when I was fourteen. I lived with my mother's aunt until I married, and she's gone now, too. Martin and Inge are my family now."

He looked thoughtfully at her, and she felt her

cheeks heating for some odd reason. She wanted to smooth her hair and fuss with her collar, find something to do with her hands. So strange.

Martin set his cup down. "I had a letter from my brother." He reached into his sheepskin-lined vest and pulled out an envelope.

Inge's lips trembled, and the lines on Martin's face grew deeper. He handed the envelope to Kate. "Would you read it, please?"

Oscar lifted Liesl into his lap. "Do you want some privacy? We can go into the other room."

"It is all right. I have read the letter, and you will need to know what it says."

Kate took the envelope, drawing the pages out with a sense of foreboding. She smoothed the papers out on the table. The letter had been written with a bold, clear hand, easily legible.

"Martin,
"I hope you got my telegram. You did not send an answer, so I am following with this letter.

"Too bad about your house, but maybe it is for the best. Father never wanted you to leave Cincinnati in the first place to take up farming. After we broke our backs farming in Switzerland, he wanted better for us in America. I know you always hated the tannery, but it looks like you need it in the end. Though you are old enough now, you should be thinking of retiring. I am not sure what good you will be in the factory, but I will find something."

Kate looked up, hurt and angry for Martin. His brother, many years his junior, sounded so unfeeling, unkind. As if it were a foregone conclusion that Martin would fail as a farmer and have to return to the family business.

Martin looked into his tea mug, and Inge rested her hand on his forearm.

Kate continued reading.

"I will not have a place for you to stay until after the new year. The factory janitor is retiring, and I suppose you can have his position. The job comes with a two-room apartment at the back of the factory as part of the wages. I know you said you had your grandson's wife with you. Is she needing a job, too? I'm not running a charity here, Martin. She will have to live with you in the rooms I can provide, or she'll have to find a place of her own. It's one thing to help out my old brother, but my great-nephew's relict? That's asking a bit much.

"Can you manage the train fare to get here? If not, I suppose I can advance you the money against your wages. Still, you have the farm to sell and the livestock. That should bring in enough to get you here, even if you have to split it with the widow."

He signed the letter "Victor."

Kate let the pages fall to the table. This was the man upon whose mercy they were to throw themselves? Someone who only reluctantly would give his aging brother a janitor's job and a pair of rooms in a tannery? Someone who had no sympathy, no thought for how hard it would be to leave their home?

Someone who clearly didn't want her as part of the arrangement?

This was the situation into which she was supposed to bring her baby?

Oscar's mouth was set in a line, and his eyes looked hard. "He sounds like a real gem. Is there nowhere else you can go? Or better yet, no way you can find to stay here?"

Martin patted Inge's hand and shook his head. "Not without becoming a further burden on our friends. Do not judge Victor too harshly. He is a busy man, and it has always been his way to put business before people. At least I will have a job, and we will have a place to live." His faded brown eyes closed for a moment. "Victor was always afraid that my father would go back on his word and leave half of the tannery to me, though when I left home to become a farmer, Father said I would have to do it alone, that if I was turning my back on the family business, I would receive nothing from it. And though he stayed true to his word, Victor has never forgiven me for leaving."

Kate leaned forward and put her hand over his and Inge's. "You were born to be a farmer. Just as Johann was. We have a few weeks yet before we have to go. Perhaps the Lord will make a way for us to stay."

Though what that could be, she didn't know. She'd thought of little else for the past three weeks now and come up with nothing.

Oscar slid his chair back and whispered in Liesl's ear. "I think it's time for our surprise, Poppet. Why don't you go get yours?"

Anything to dispel some of the gloom in the room. That letter. Victor Amaker sounded like a skinflint. Oscar had been by one of the tanneries in the Twin Cities, and the smell was horrendous. He couldn't imagine anyone living in the factory. Working there would be bad enough. With Kate and a baby and Martin and Inge crammed into a two-room apartment inside the factory...?

Liesl ran back from the parlor clutching her parcel, brown eyes bright. "Now, Daddy?"

"Now. And don't forget what you're supposed to say."

She went to Kate, eyes downcast for a moment. Squaring her shoulders, she looked up. "Miss Kate, I'm sorry for acting out in the store. Thank you for helping me choose fabric for new clothes and making them for me." She put the soft bundle into Kate's hands.

Kate didn't open the package right away. Instead, she leaned forward and cupped Liesl's face in her hands. "Sweetling, I will love sewing for you. You didn't have to get me a gift." Her glance flicked to Oscar's face. "But I am so glad you did. I love presents, don't you?"

Liesl nodded, beaming, everything right in her world again.

"Will you help me open it?" Kate loosened the string and held the gift out for Liesl's help. The little girl pulled off the wrappings, revealing a pair of white, knitted baby booties.

"Aren't they precious?" Liesl asked. Oscar smiled. Those were the words Mrs. Hale had used in the store when he'd lifted Liesl up to look into the glass case of baby things, bonnets, booties, little gowns. His daughter had picked out the white booties right away.

"They are that and more." Kate hugged Liesl.

"I picked them out all by myself." She shot her daddy a guilty look and squirmed. "Well, Daddy helped."

Kate laughed. "You both did a lovely job." Her grateful glance spread warmth through Oscar's chest. She held the little bits of footgear on the palm of her hand. "My baby's first shoes. The only thing I have for him or her so far."

Oscar cleared his throat, and pushed the other package across the table toward her. "This is from Liesl and me, too. To say thank you for sewing some clothes for her." His voice felt rough, like he was coming down with a cold or something.

With wondrous soft eyes, she pulled the twine on the bundle, peeling back the paper to reveal several lengths of flannel. Thick, fluffy white for diapers, thinner, patterned yardage for blankets and gowns... at least that's what Mrs. Hale had said it was for. What Oscar knew about baby clothes would fill a thimble and leave room leftover, but he trusted Mrs. Hale.

"Oh, my."

Then the waterworks started. She clutched the fabric to her chest, tucked her chin down and just started sobbing. Oscar got to his feet, unsure what to do. Didn't she like the stuff? Had he gotten it wrong?

Liesl shot him a panicked glance, but no more panicked than he felt.

"We can take it back, I'm sure." Oscar shifted his weight.

Inge chuckled and got up, tugging a hanky from her sleeve and pressing it into Kate's hand. "Do not mind her. She loves the fabric. Sometimes mamas who are expecting weep when they are happy."

Kate dabbed her eyes and gave Oscar an apologetic, watery smile. "Thank you so much. I was so worried about how to outfit the baby when it came. You didn't have to do such a nice thing, but I'm so glad you did."

Her blue eyes still swam with tears, but sunshine was breaking through. Oscar rubbed the back of his neck. He would never understand women, but as long as she was happy, he was happy.

Which gave him pause. He wasn't really concerned about Kate Amaker's happiness, was he?

Rolf rose from his place by the fire and gave a bark, staring at the door. Oscar eased the curtain aside to look out the window. A black buggy was pulling into the yard drawn by a pair of high-stepping grays.

Mr. Siddons.

Oscar met him on the front porch, wary. Mr. Siddons wasn't alone. He had a driver. The small man got out of the buggy and held the horses, and Mr. Siddons descended, looking over the house and barn and grounds like the tax man come collecting.

Rolf, at Oscar's side, lowered his head, growling deep in his chest, his back rigid. Oscar snapped his fingers, and Rolf quieted, but he didn't relax. Odd. The dog was usually quite friendly.

"Mr. Siddons."

"Afternoon, Rabb. I was out this way and thought I would call in." Siddons wore a navy, woolen topcoat and fine leather gloves. He held out his hand and shook Oscar's firmly. "Thought I might come in and talk to Martin Amaker if he's here."

"He's here." Oscar, in just his shirtsleeves, felt the cold bite his skin. Or maybe it was just the cold, calculating look in Abel Siddons's eyes.

He ushered his guest inside, turning back to see if the driver was coming.

"Don't worry about him. He'll wait with the horses." Siddons waved his hand as if swatting a gnat and stepped into the house. Again his eyes took in everything, from the cupboards to the coat rack to the coffee grinder on the wall.

"Are you sure about your driver? It's mighty chilly out there."

"He's paid to stay with the horses." Siddons again made that brushing-off gesture. "Ah, Amaker, just the man I wanted to see."

Martin rose slowly, his back bent with age, but his manners courtly and impeccable. "Mr. Siddons." He gave a small bow. "What can I do for you?"

Without waiting to be asked, Siddons took a chair and looked at Inge, who stood by the stove with her hands folded. "You wouldn't happen to have some coffee, would you? It was brisk riding in the buggy today."

Liesl had gone to stand by Kate, staring at the stranger who had barged in and taken over the room. Inge looked to Oscar, a question in her eyes. He nodded, and she went to fill the coffeepot.

"I'll get right down to it." Siddons hadn't even un-buttoned his coat. "I've heard you're going to be selling up, Amaker, and I want first crack at your land. I'll offer you a fair cash price. The same offer I made to…" He frowned and looked at Kate. "To this young woman when I saw her in Mantorville last week. I'm sure she told you."

Martin's surprised look said that Kate hadn't passed on that information, but he quickly composed himself.

"I thank you for the offer, and I will keep it in mind. We are not certain what our plans will be, but the land will not be for sale before the new year." Martin turned his teacup on the table.

"Hmm, I'd like to get things settled before then, maybe even get started on a house for a tenant to move into soon. I have a mind to plow the pastures and put in an early crop of peas, then a crop of carrots. And I'd tear down that big barn. No need for it without livestock on the place. The wood could build a new equipment shed with some left over for a house."

Kate gasped, her hand going to her lips. "Tear down the barn?"

"It's a waste of space and wood. I have to say, you're squandering the land's potential keeping it as cow pastures for so few head. And Brown Swiss? They might be good milkers for cheese production, but I prefer Holsteins any day. If you'd have put the land into crop production instead of cows, you probably would've had a tidy little nest egg built up and could afford to build a new house now."

Inge set the coffeepot on the stove with a bit of

force. Kate's arm tightened around Liesl, and her jaw came up a fraction. Oscar frowned.

"Mr. Siddons," Oscar said. "The Amakers are good farmers, and they have the best herd of dairy cattle in the county. They make excellent cheeses, and they take care of their land."

"Well, they used to, didn't they? But word around the county is that you'll have to sell up to pay the rest of your loan. Big risk mortgaging a property. And then to mortgage your herd just to buy one single head of livestock. You'd have been better off either renting a bull from one of your neighbors or just buying some scrub bull. Doesn't matter what kind of calf you get, as long as you keep the cows in milk production."

The smell of coffee brewing filled the kitchen, but Inge made no move to pour a cup for Mr. Siddons.

Mr. Siddons turned to Oscar. "You could do better by your place, too. All that land along the river, I'd let some firewood cutters in there to clear-cut those trees. You get the money from the firewood and bring more acres into farming production. I tell you, so many farmers around here are stuck in the old ways. Bigger farms, more crops, modern methods. That's what we need. We're growing a nation, and we need to move along with the times."

Oscar spread his hands on the table and levered himself up. "Mr. Siddons, you've made your offer and your views plain. Now, I hope you'll excuse us. It's coming up on chore time, and we have a lot to do." He walked to the door and opened it.

Siddons sat for a moment, looking from one face to another, then levered himself upright. "Fine, fine." He donned his gloves, pressing the gaps between his fingers to fit them on snugly. "You'll keep me in mind, though. I'll match anyone's price."

"Good day, Mr. Siddons." Martin scooted his chair back.

As the buggy drove away, Liesl tugged on Oscar's pant leg. He lifted her up on his arm.

"Daddy, I don't like that man. He's scary."

Kate stood at his elbow, watching the departing buggy. She hugged herself, rubbing her upper arms, eyes troubled. She had so much to worry about, and now this.

Oscar found himself wanting to put his arm around her, to shield her from the life-blows she'd been taking.

Which brought him up short. What was he doing thinking about a woman that way? His heart belonged to Gaelle, and it always would. He had no business having tender feelings for anyone else. What was wrong with him?

"I've got chores to do and then I need to get into the workroom. Orders are backing up with all the time I've been spending on other things." He let Liesl slide to the ground, but in spite of cautioning himself, his thoughts were still on Kate and his reaction to her.

The death of her husband, the house fire, the awful letter from Martin's brother, the casual way Siddons had come in and scythed through their achievements and dreams. Those were hard things, but they weren't really his concern. He'd done more than he'd intended already—housing her, feeding her, even clothing her. That was neighborly, and that was also where he drew the line. He'd share his material possessions up to a point, but he would not share his heart. That belonged entirely to his dead wife.

He needed to be by himself to get his head on straight. Too much time spent with the widow Amaker was making him forget himself.

Chapter Nine

Kate handed Liesl the red pencil, and the little girl marked a red *X* through November 30 on the calendar hanging on the kitchen wall. It was hard to believe that almost a month had gone by since their house had burned, since they'd moved in with the Rabbs.

"It's almost time, isn't it?" Liesl hopped off the chair, her braids flopping. "To tear off 'Vember so it can be December?"

"Almost." Kate leaned back so she could take a deep breath. The baby was taking up so much room now, it felt as if she couldn't get her lungs quite full of air most of the time.

"And tomorrow Daddy and Grossvater will be back?"

"Tomorrow or the next day." Kate looked out the window at the fat, falling flakes. It had been snowing since before sunup, and already several inches blanketed the landscape. Oscar had been gone for six days, delivering the furniture orders he'd completed to Saint Paul.

And Martin had gone with him, driving another

wagon full of several hundred pounds of cheese. Most of her summer's efforts. With so much inventory still to sell, the men had thought it best for Martin to drive his own wagon, accompanying Oscar all the way to the big city. He'd packed the cheeses in straw and burlap to keep them from freezing or being jostled too much.

Oscar had refused to allow Kate to help him carry the cheeses up the stairs to load the wagon, so she'd remained in the cellar directing him as to what should go and what wasn't ready yet.

"You might as well take everything you can, to make the trip worthwhile. No sense leaving any of it behind," he'd said.

His words had pressed deep on her heart. In the end, the cellar had been almost empty.

She'd stood in the center of all the shelves, close to tears. This would be the last time. Next summer, she would be in Cincinnati and, most likely, Mr. Siddons would own the farm. Would he raze the cheese house the same way he planned to tear down the barn? If she came back in five years, would she even recognize the place they had worked so hard to build?

She wished she could talk to someone about it, but there wasn't anyone. Not wanting to burden Inge and Martin with her disquieted thoughts, she had kept them to herself. And Oscar…it felt as if he had taken a step away from the Amakers ever since Victor Amaker's letter had arrived. He worked hard outside, preparing things for winter. Every day he hauled at least one load of hay from the Amaker barn, stacking it in his barnyard to feed the small herd of Brown Swiss he'd brought over to his farm to make choring easier.

Every night, he retreated to his wood shop to work on furniture pieces. And he and Martin had been gone for a week now.

Kate felt as if she hardly saw him anymore.

"Are we going to sew, Miss Kate?" Liesl tugged on her sleeve.

Pulled from her thoughts, Kate smiled at the little girl. Liesl was an excellent tonic against the megrims. "We sure are. Come stand on the table, sweetling. Once I get this hem pinned up and sewn, we'll be just about done with your new dresses." The table was strewn with fabric, pins and scissors on one end, and bowls and flour and spoons on the other. Grossmutter was making *Zopf*, the special bread she loved. It was usually reserved for Sundays, but with Martin expected home soon, she was making it as a treat for him. While she kneaded the dough, she muttered under her breath.

Kate smiled. Grossmutter always recited Scripture and prayed while she worked bread dough. It was a good time to talk to the Lord, she always said.

Liesl let Kate remove her shoes and dress and climb up on the table. Arms out, she held still while Kate dropped the new dress over her head and buttoned it up the back. It hung in folds on her little frame. Kate had made this one extra big, allowing room for Liesl to grow into it.

Not that Kate would be there to see it. The thought made her heart hurt. As much as Oscar had feared that Liesl would grow too attached to the Amakers before they moved out, Kate knew it would hurt her just as much to leave the little girl who had grown so dear.

Estimating how tall Liesl might be in a year or two

wasn't easy. But Kate would put an extra-deep hem in, so that it could be let out when needed. Maybe Mrs. Tipford or Mrs. Frankel would make the alterations in a couple of years.

"You look like a little brown robin," she said. The chocolate-colored wool brought out the deep brown of Liesl's eyes, and the red trim at the cuffs and collar were bright splashes of color.

"Daddy says I look like a princess."

"That's true, but you know that it's what you do that makes you pretty, not your face or your clothes?" Kate spoke around the pins clamped between her teeth.

"Daddy says that, too."

"Your daddy is a smart man."

And kind, and gentle, and strong, and steady.

Kate had been thinking about him way too much, especially the last several days, since he'd left for the Twin Cities.

Placing the final pin in the hem, Kate walked around the table, checking for evenness. "That should do it. Hold still while I get it off you. I don't want you to get any pinpricks." She eased the dress over Liesl's head, holding the hem wide. "There. I'll work on that tonight."

Liesl sat on the table and scooted to the edge, hopping off in her bare feet and scampering over to get back into her clothes. "Now will you make baby gowns?" She had been an avid observer of Kate's progress with the flannel.

"Maybe later. Let's get the sewing cleaned up and help Grossmutter with the baking, all right?"

The wind buffeted the house, sending a swirl of

snowflakes against the windowpane. But the kitchen was toasty, the house snug.

When the bread was rising in the warming pan near the oven, Kate drew Liesl to her side at the flour-dusted table. "Would you like to play a little game with me?"

Liesl's smile was Kate's answer. The little girl loved games.

"Watch." Kate drew in the flour a capital *A* with her finger. "This is *A*. *A* for apple. Can you make one?"

Liesl drew a lopsided *A*.

"Beautiful. Now try this one." Kate drew a *B*. "*B* makes a 'buh' sound. What word starts with a buh sound?"

"Buh...baby!" Liesl beamed.

"That's right. *B* is for baby." Kate hugged her. Liesl had stubbornly clung to the notion that she would receive a baby for Christmas, though she didn't speak of it as often now.

They continued to make letters in the dusting of flour, wiping it smooth over and over. The kitchen smelled of yeasty bread and the stew simmering on the back of the stove. The wind blew hard, and Grossmutter lit the lamp against the falling darkness.

Everything was cozy, but Kate found herself uneasy. Rolf, too, seemed unsettled, pacing from room to room, head up, sniffing the air.

"I'd best bundle up and finish the barn chores before it gets too bad outside." Kate brushed her hands together to rid them of flour, and stood. Even Johann's big coat didn't quite meet over her middle anymore, but she buttoned it as far as she could. The burgundy cloak was too nice to wear for doing barn work. "Chores will take me a while, so don't worry. And I'll bring Rolf with me."

Grossmutter handed her a pair of mittens from the box by the door. They must be Oscar's, because they almost fell off Kate's hands, but they would help keep her warm. "We will have hot stew and bread when you come in, and I will keep water on for tea."

The cold sliced through Kate's coat and made her shiver as she walked down to the barn. Icy hard snowflakes stung her cheeks, and she pulled her scarf higher to cover her nose. The lantern guttered and sputtered. Rolf stayed by her side, head low as they leaned into the north wind. She thought of Martin and Oscar, traveling home in this weather. Surely the storm would delay them. Hopefully, they were somewhere warm and dry, waiting it out.

Stepping into the barn was like someone slamming a door. Quiet, warmth, the smell of bovines, hay, dust and grain. Kate took a few deep breaths and hung the lantern on a peg high on a post.

She'd brought the cattle in this morning in anticipation of the storm. Oscar's little Jersey and all ten of the Brown Swiss. They stood in a row down the byre, tails out, some lying down, all quiet. Only two of the cows were still giving milk, less than a gallon each, so milking wouldn't take long. The heifer calves shared a pen down at the far end.

Kate opened the back door of the barn, and the cattle filed out to the water trough. A thin sheet of ice covered the surface, and she broke it with the hatchet tied there. While the cattle milled outside, drinking their fill, she returned to the barn to clean up and spread fresh straw. She filled the mangers, always easier when the byre was empty.

When she let the cows back inside, they each went to their place and began tearing at the hay in the racks. She milked quickly and, because they still had plenty of milk in the house, poured the two buckets into the metal trough in the calf pen, saving out a small pan for the barn cats.

With only the chickens to feed, Kate went into the granary. The coop was attached to the barn, so she didn't need to go outside. A dozen reddish-brown hens and one cranky rooster clucked and pecked in the straw. She tossed down a couple of ears of dry corn and a turnip for them to squabble over and filled the feed pans with cracked corn. They still had plenty of water.

One last check that everything was secure for the night, and she was ready to brave the cold again. Rolf met her at the door, but as she latched it behind her, his head came up and he gave a bark, disappearing into the swirl of snowflakes.

"Rolf, come!" she shouted, but her words were sucked away. The dog had bounded away into the dark and swirling flakes. Kate trudged up the path, careful where she stepped, watchful of not slipping in the snow that was piling up, ankle-deep already. She held the lantern high to light the way, and every few steps, she stopped and called for the dog.

He barked from somewhere up ahead, and emerged from the darkness, only to turn and run away again. Kate was almost to the front porch, eager to get inside, when she heard a rattling sound. She listened hard, tugging the scarf off her ears.

It was a wagon, hoofbeats, snow-muffled, but unmistakable. Who would be out on a night like this?

Whoever it was, they turned into the farm lane. The sounds grew nearer. Kate raised the lantern, and through the blowing snow, she saw the heads and shoulders of a pair of horses. Then their bodies, and finally the wagon they pulled. A figure sat high on the seat, hunched and bundled, snow on his shoulders and hat. Rolf leaped and ran, circling the wagon, barking. The horses paid him no mind, heads lowered into the wind.

Behind the wagon, another team emerged from the darkness, and Kate's heart leaped. Schwarz and Grau, Martin's farm horses.

The first driver pulled up in front of the house and raised his head.

Oscar.

Her heart bumped hard against her ribs. He was home. They were home.

"What are you doing out here?" He tugged down the muffler over his face and beard. "Get inside before you freeze. We'll be in soon." He slapped the lines and headed toward the barn.

His voice was gently chiding, and she hurried to obey.

"Liesl, Inge, they're home." She burst into the kitchen. "Oscar and Martin. They're just putting away the horses, and then they'll be here." She couldn't keep the excitement out of her voice, the joy at having the menfolk safely home.

Inge looked at her with speculation in her eyes, and Kate felt heat rush to her cheeks.

"I was afraid they might be caught out somewhere

in the storm," she hurried to explain. "I didn't want Martin's cough to return, and I was hoping they were somewhere safe. Liesl, why don't you set the table? I'll start the fire in the parlor fireplace."

Kate took off her coat and gloves and scarf, trying to cover her confusion. It really was only relief that they were safe, wasn't it? But if that was it, why was her heart thrumming so fast and her skin tingling?

Liesl happily plunked cutlery onto the table. Inge checked the bread in the oven, and Kate opened the parlor doors wide. She swept the ashes out of the fireplace and laid a new fire, hoping to take the chill out of the room so they could all retire there after supper. She angled Oscar's chair just right and straightened the afghan covering before she caught herself.

She really *was* only glad they were soon to be out of the storm. That's all there was to it.

Oscar was mighty glad to be out of the storm. His hands hurt, his feet were numb and his lungs felt as if someone had scoured them out with broken glass. The barn was warm and quiet, smelling of grass and grain and cattle.

In spite of his best efforts, he hadn't made it home in time to prevent Kate from doing the evening chores. He had hoped to spare her that. It had been one of the worst parts about leaving and taking Martin with him, knowing Kate would have to see to the barn chores all by herself.

But as he curried the tired horses, he looked around the barn. He couldn't fault her. She'd done a very good job. Everything was right and tight. By lantern light, he and Martin finished with the horses, and he dumped a generous portion of grain into each feedbox and made sure the water buckets were full. "Have a good rest, boys. You've earned it."

And so had he and Martin. He followed the older man up to the house, peace settling over him as the light from the windows shone out on the snow even though his muscles ached from the long, tense ride. It had been a quite a spell since he'd felt a peaceful homecoming.

A gust of warm air hit him as he stepped into the kitchen, and the smell of supper and hot bread wrapped around him. He hadn't even stomped the snow off his boots before Liesl had launched herself into his arms. He held her away.

"Whoa there, tornado. Let me get out of my snow duds first or you'll get chilled."

"I missed you, Daddy. I counted every day, see?" She pointed to the wall calendar, red *X*'s marching like soldiers across the lines. "And we sewed and baked, and I learned some of my letters."

This week was the longest he'd been separated from Liesl since she was born, and he'd felt every minute of their time apart, but oddly, he hadn't worried about her, knowing she'd be well cared for in his absence.

The minute he was free of his coat, he scooped her up and kissed her cheek. She patted his beard. "Your face is cold!"

"All of me is cold. You'd think it was January out there instead of November. And after such a mild fall." He went to the stove and sniffed, Liesl perched on his forearm. "What's that cooking? Is that possum fritters and bullfrog soup?" He waggled his eyebrows at Liesl.

She giggled. "No, Daddy. It's stew. And bread. We made Zoffy bread today."

"Zoffy?"

"Mmm-hmm. Grossmutter says it's special Sunday bread, but we should have it now because you would be coming home soon. But we thought you wouldn't come home till tomorrow or the next tomorrow."

"We decided we didn't want to stay away so long. That supper smells good, and I'm so hungry I could eat a whole possum, fur and all." He smiled at Inge. "Hello, Mrs. Amaker. I've been thinking about your cooking the whole week. We sure didn't have anything as good out on the road."

Martin came and put his arm around his wife, bending to whisper something in her ear that put a sparkle in her eyes. She leaned into him for a moment, resting her white head on his shoulder before straightening up and moving toward the stove.

"Come, sit. We will eat, and you will tell us about your journey." Inge put a loaf of braided bread on a cutting board on the table. "The *Zopf* is still very hot, but we will have it now, anyway."

Kate stood off to the side, watching. She had a wistful look on her face, and it hit Oscar that he had Liesl, and Martin had Inge to greet, but Kate had no one special coming home to her.

"Hello, Kate." He put Liesl into her chair and scooted it in for her. Rolf twined around his legs, snuffling and wiggling. "Everything looks fine down in the barn. I'm sorry you had to do the chores tonight. We were hoping to get back in time, but the storm held us up." He pushed aside Rolf's wet nose and pulled out a chair for her.

She sat, lowering herself carefully, hand braced against her belly. "Was it a successful trip?"

Martin dug into his pocket and handed her a slip of paper. "This is another reason we were late. We stopped in town."

She took the paper, scanning it quickly, then bit her lip, tears springing into her eyes. "Is this real?"

He nodded. "We sold all the cheeses, and there was enough to pay the mortgage on the herd with some left over. We can make this year's payment on the farm mortgage, or we can save it for if we move to Cincinnati."

Oscar hated to think of them leaving the area, but he was glad they would have at least a little nest egg when they went.

"If and when we sell the herd, at least they will be freehold." Martin sighed. "We could sell most of them and pay the entire mortgage on the farm off, but without the herd, there would be no more cheeses, and no money still to build a house. I have wrestled with the problem every way I can think of, but I cannot see a way we can stay on the farm. Even if the house had not burned down, without Johann it was going to be hard."

Oscar and Martin had discussed it at length on the trip. Martin worried about "his girls" as he called them. And Oscar got a glimpse of how much Martin did not want to have to take them to his brother's place in Cincinnati.

Kate folded the paper again and slid it across to Martin. "At least the herd isn't mortgaged any longer.

I'm glad of that. It felt wrong the whole time. Mortgaging land is one thing, but this felt like getting a loan on friends." She turned to Oscar, and the force of the blue in her eyes jabbed him in the chest. "Was your trip successful, as well?"

"It was. The buyers were pleased with the commissioned pieces, and I sold the two extra bureaus I took along." And they'd sold well, too. He'd never made so much money on his furniture before.

"Were you able to complete your shopping?" She inclined her head slightly toward Liesl, who was busy with her supper.

"I found a few things." Including a length of pink fabric with blue flowers. He'd ask Kate to sew up a Christmas dress for Liesl to wear to the Star Singing, since she now had her heart set on participating. And he'd found a little something for each of the Amakers.

Christmas shopping had never been so difficult. When he'd been married, Gaelle had made it easy for him, giving him a list of three or four things, saying she'd be happy with anything. And she was, being a generally happy person. Anything he made or bought for her had brought smiles and kisses.

"While you were gone, Mrs. Tipford came by to finalize the plans for the Advent window tour, and she brought Liesl a little present." Kate spread butter on a slice of bread and put it on Liesl's plate.

"Oh, yes, Daddy. Look what she brought." Liesl slid off her chair and ran into the parlor, returning with a worn bundle of papers. "It's a whole catalog." She flopped the tattered book onto the table.

"Mrs. Tipford said she found it in a cupboard in the church basement," Kate explained. "She thought

Liesl might like looking at the pictures. I think we've been over every page at least three times, haven't we, sweetling?"

"I like the toys and the dishes best." Liesl climbed into her chair once more. "And the hats and shoes. Daddy, did you know you could buy a hat with a bird on it?"

"Ah, so, is a bird hat what you want for Christmas now?" he teased.

She shook her head, eyeing him soberly. "No, Daddy. Not a hat with a bird."

So she hadn't abandoned the idea of a baby for Christmas. He only hoped the idea he'd come up with on the drive home from Saint Paul would please her. He'd have to consult Kate and enlist her help later.

After supper, he rose and stretched. "That chair in the parlor is mighty tempting, but I had better get into the wood shop. I have a few more Christmas orders to complete for folks around here, and they won't finish themselves."

Liesl pushed her chair up to the bench. "After I help Grossmutter with the dishes, can I come play in the workroom?"

"Sure, Poppet. I'd like that." It was how they spent most winter evenings before they'd taken in houseguests, him working on a piece of furniture and Liesl playing under the table with the shavings and wood scraps. He'd missed her chattery company.

He pushed open the door to the shop, inhaling the familiar scents of cut wood and linseed oil. This was the one place that usually brought him comfort... which had been hard to come by the past few weeks. Lighting the fire in the small woodstove helped take the chill from the room, and he went to the rack to select some of the special stock he'd purchased at the sawmill in Mantorville. The plans for a hall tree lay on his workbench, and once that was finished, a what-not needed to be stained and varnished. And there was the project that has been forming in the back of his mind for a while, but that would have to wait until other work was done.

"Daddy." Liesl skipped into the room. "Do you have some little pieces for me? I want to build something."

It was a common request, and Oscar slid a box out from under the bench with his boot toe. "I've been saving these for you."

She pounced on the box, dumping the contents onto the floor with a clatter. Ends of boards, a bit of crown molding, a chipped spindle he'd had to abandon when a knot blew out as he was turning it on the lathe. To him they were orts, but to Liesl, they were treasures and fuel for her lively imagination.

Kate tapped on the door, bringing in a tray with coffee cups and a glass of milk. "Martin and Inge have gone upstairs to bed already. I think the trip tired out Martin more than he wanted anyone to know."

Oscar took the tray and set it on the workbench. He had also missed the nightly routine of drinking coffee with Kate in his workroom. "He was a man on a mission. I could hardly keep up with him as we went from store to store. He's proud of you, told every shopkeeper we talked to about how good you were at cheese making. Said your Swiss-style cheese was the best to be found outside the Alps."

She smiled fondly. "He's such a sweet man." Her

face sobered. "I can't imagine him being a janitor in a factory in the middle of a big city. It will crush the life out of him."

Oscar picked up a wood plane and drew it over the edge of a drawer, flicking the long curl of poplar under the table for Liesl. He felt so helpless in the face of the Amakers' troubles. All they wanted was to stay on their farm, but it seemed as if everything conspired against them, and it all started with poor choices...

"If it weren't for the loans on the cattle and land, you wouldn't be in this fix. Every cent you have is going to service the loans, and there's nothing to build another house with. If you didn't have the initial loan, the bank would advance you enough to build, but a second mortgage is out of the question. What was your husband thinking? He put your whole way of life in jeopardy, and for what?"

He regretted the question the minute she sucked in a sharp breath. She set her coffee cup on the tray, her lips tight. "Johann was forward thinking. A visionary. He had big dreams and plans, and he wasn't afraid to take risks. He mortgaged the farm to build a house big enough for his grandparents, his wife and his future children. And he mortgaged his herd to buy better bloodlines, because he dreamed of enlarging our cheese-making business and breeding better cattle." She blinked, her hand going to her unborn child. "Everything he did was to make a better future for us. There was no way he could anticipate that his life would be cut off too soon."

"Kate, I'm sorry—"

She held up her hand to stay his apology. "I loved my husband's enthusiasm, his big dreams and ideas, his fearlessness. He wanted more for his children than he had, and he wasn't afraid to work hard, to take some risks and to trust that God would honor his efforts. I don't expect you to understand, someone who hides away from life, afraid he will be hurt again if he lets anyone get too close." Her blue eyes snapped fire, something he hadn't seen from her before. "Don't worry. We'll soon be out of your house and your life, and you can go back to hiding and playing everything safe."

"Daddy?"

Kate jumped as if she'd forgotten the child was in the room, and she bit her lower lip.

Liesl edged out from under the table, planer curls tucked behind her ears, and startled questions in her eyes. She looked from him to Kate and back again, seeking reassurance.

He reached for her, cuddling her close, feeling horrible that he'd hurt Kate's feelings and scared his daughter in the bargain. Why hadn't he kept his thoughts to himself? He'd spoken out of frustration for the plight of the Amakers, wanting to find someone to blame for their hardships, but he'd managed to trample Kate's feelings in the process.

She studied her gripped hands for a moment and then raised her chin. "I'll say good night." Her voice was muted, as if she struggled to force the words out. "See you in the morning, Liesl."

And she was gone. Her footsteps sounded on the stairs, and his heart jerked to Christmas, two years ago, but he shoved the memory aside. That was in the past. Kate wasn't Gaelle. History wouldn't repeat itself.

"Daddy? Are you mad at Miss Kate?"

"No, Poppet. I'm not mad at Miss Kate." He was mad at himself. Brushing a kiss across her hair, he hugged her tight.

"Is Miss Kate mad at you?"

Probably. And she had every right to be. He'd blamed a dead man, her husband, someone who couldn't defend himself. Someone she undoubtedly had loved as much as he loved his dead wife. He should've kept his thoughts to himself. Still, perhaps it was for the best, putting some distance between them. He'd felt much too comfortable in her presence, to the point that on the trip he had found himself missing her.

"It's nothing for you to worry about. Sometimes we say things we don't mean to and hurt someone's feelings. It will be better in the morning." He hoped. "Let's get you ready for bed."

"With a bedtime story? I missed the bedtime stories when you were gone."

"Sure, Poppet. We'll have a bedtime story." And then he would return to his workshop and start the project he'd been thinking about for almost a month, only now he wondered how it would be received.

Chapter Ten

Kate opened her bedroom door and nearly collided with Oscar, the one person she didn't want to see this morning. Her outburst the previous evening had cost her sleep last night and made her cringe now.

"Good morning, Kate." He looked as if he hadn't slept too well, either. Was he going to apologize? Should she make the first overture?

From an outsider's perspective, it might have seemed as if Johann had been foolhardy in his plans, but she knew the truth. If he hadn't died, his dreams would be coming to fruition. Even now, if they could only find a way to keep the farm, some of his efforts were maturing. Ten Brown Swiss cows were in calf with purebred Brown Swiss offspring that would be worth a fair bit when they arrived. Johann would've been more than able to pay off the mortgage on the herd and the farm, and they would've had the cheese money to pay for their expenses for the coming year.

But Oscar couldn't know any of that. And she'd snapped at him like a cornered shrew last night. She would definitely need to apologize.

Before she could, he said, "I don't want you on the stairs by yourself from now on. Wait until I can accompany you. It's too risky. You might fall." He took her elbow and led her to the top of the stairs. "It's narrow, so let me go down first, and keep your hand on my shoulder."

"Really, Oscar, I'm not an invalid. I can walk down a flight of stairs without help." Here she'd been ready to apologize, and he was bossing her around and treating her like a soap bubble about to burst. He didn't have to remind her she was clumsy and fat. She'd awakened this morning with swollen hands and ankles, and had to let out the waistband on the borrowed dress yet again, which made his criticism sting all the more.

"I'm not taking the risk while you're here." He went down two stairs, turned back and picked up her hand and put it on his shoulder.

Heat seeped through his shirt, and the muscles moved under her hand as he turned away. But he didn't release her hand, clamping it with his own to keep her from disobeying him. Slowly, with deliberate steps, he went down the stairs, and she had little choice but to follow. When they reached the bottom, he let go of her hand, but he stayed close, head bent.

"I want you to promise me you won't use the stairs unless I'm with you."

"But, Oscar, that's ridiculous."

"Promise me. I ask very little of you. You can do this one thing for me."

Her breath snagged in her throat as she looked into his eyes, so intense, so close. He was right. He didn't ask much of her.

"Fine. I think you're being ridiculous, but I'll humor you."

"Thank you." His tone was dry, but he stepped back. "Oh, and I don't want you going outside by yourself, either. The temperature warmed up for a while last night, and it rained on top of the snow, then froze again. It's too dangerous."

She could see the wisdom in what he said, and she had no real desire to go outside, but she was out of sorts, from their spat last night, from her lack of sleep and from the grinding burden of the decisions that needed to be made regarding the Amakers' future. She swept past him...at least as sweeping as a woman in her condition could be, and went to the stove to stir up the fire for breakfast.

Liesl called from upstairs. "Daddy, I'm ready for my shoes."

Moments later Oscar brought her down on his arm, dressed and ready for the day, except for her hair. She wore one of the dresses Kate had sewn for her, pretty yellow fabric with some smocking that Inge had done across the front. She looked so sweet and fresh Kate wanted to hug her, but as she came close, the little girl's brow puckered, and she stuck her finger into the corner of her mouth, looking at Kate from under her lashes.

Her wariness made Kate feel terrible. This had to be about her sharp words with Oscar last night. "Good morning, Liesl. Would you like me to fix your hair for you?" She spoke gently, smiling. "You look nice this morning. The fabric you chose is perfect for that dress."

Liesl smoothed her skirt, eyes still troubled.

"Sweetling, I am very sorry for what happened last night. I spoke too sharply, and that wasn't kind." Chagrin prickled her skin, and she avoided Oscar's eyes, focusing on Liesl. "I am sorry for upsetting you. I am not angry with your daddy, and I'm certainly not angry with you."

This time her gaze did flick to Oscar, and some of the tension went out of his shoulders. Had their squabble upset him, too?

Liesl nodded, studying her. She must've been reassured, because she squirmed to get down and brought her hairbrush and the leather ties to Kate.

"Hop up on your chair. Would you like to try something a bit different today?" She took the brush, grateful to have something else to focus on. She drew the brush through the silky brown strands, parting it down the middle.

"Different how?"

"Well, I thought I might fix your hair like I used to wear mine when I was a little girl in school."

"I'm going to go to school someday, Mrs. Tipford says. What happens at school?" Liesl wrinkled her nose. "Is it like Sunday school?"

"Sort of like Sunday school. I'm glad you liked going to Sunday school, singing and learning Bible stories." She'd talked of little else each of the three times she'd gone in the last month. Kate divided Liesl's hair and fashioned a smooth braid behind each ear. "School is a wonderful place. You learn your letters and numbers and how to read and write and cipher. And you learn about history and geography and literature. You'll make lots of friends, children your age." Something that was sorely lacking in Liesl's life at the moment. "And there's recess where you play games and run outside. And there are lots of books, and a globe, and chalkboards."

"That's a few years from now." Oscar filled the coffeepot. "She's too young for all that."

"I'm learning my letters already, Daddy. Miss Kate is teaching me. In the flour."

"In the flour?" His brows came down. "She's teaching you letters already?"

Kate finished tying the second braid and removed two hairpins from her own hair, tightening and moving others to compensate. Then she crossed Liesl's braids over the top of her head and pinned them. "There you go, sweetling. What do you think?"

Liesl felt the braids, her eyes going wide. "Like a grown-up lady," she whispered.

"Well, not exactly, but close. I always wore my hair that way. It kept the little boys from dipping the ends of my braids in the inkwell." She smiled at the memory. That seemed a long time ago.

"What's this about you teaching Liesl her letters? She's too young for that." Oscar folded his arms across his chest. "She's only four."

"Liesl, honey, run upstairs and put your hairbrush away. But be quiet. I think Grossmutter and Grossvater are still sleeping." Kate handed the brush to the little girl and waited for her to climb the stairs. "Oscar, she's not too little to learn her letters and numbers. She's very bright, and you've read so much to her, she's catching on very quickly. Learning now can only help her later. I learned to read before my fifth birthday. Lots of children do."

"What's this about flour? Teaching her with flour?

Or do you mean flower, like the plant?" He drew his hand down his beard, brows bunched.

She shrugged. "My family was not well off, and paper was dear, as were slate pencils. My mother used to dust the table with flour when she kneaded bread, and when she was done, she taught me to trace my letters and numbers in the flour left over. Easy and not expensive. Liesl loves it, and she's doing really well."

He shook his head. "I'm not ready to think about her going to school or learning to read."

"Ready or not, it's going to happen. I'm sorry if I've overstepped. I never dreamed you wouldn't approve." It seemed ever since he'd gotten home from his trip, she'd put one foot wrong after another.

Spinning a chair around, he straddled it, parking his chin on his wrists. "It's not that I don't approve. It just surprised me. Seems like only yesterday she was a bald little mite in a bassinet, and now she's outgrowing her dresses and thinking about how her hair looks and learning to read."

"I think that's a common feeling among fathers. That their little girls grow up too quickly." Kate stoked the fire and opened the breadbox to remove the left-over *Zopf*. It would make excellent egg-battered toast. "My mother used to say that when a father looks at his newborn son, he sees all the things they will do together as men—the hunting, fishing, building and the like. But when he looks at his newborn daughter, he can only see his little girl who should remain a little girl forever."

Liesl clattered down the stairs, and Kate winced at the noise. At the bottom of the steps, Liesl stopped, hunching her shoulders and scrunching her face. "I'm sorry. I forgot."

Kate glanced at the clock. Past seven-thirty. That was a fairly good lie-in for Martin and Inge. It shouldn't matter too much.

Oscar stood, adjusting his suspenders on his broad shoulders. "I should get down to the barn. Then I'm spending the day in the workshop."

"Breakfast will be ready when you come back." Kate paused as she set the skillet on the stovetop. How many times had she said that to Johann as he headed out for morning chores?

Liesl scooted her chair over to the calendar as he shrugged into his coat. "Look, Daddy. It's here."

"What's here, Poppet?" He wrapped his muffler around his neck and dug into his pocket for his gloves.

"It's the Christmas month." She pointed to all the red *X*s on the November calendar and tore off the page. "Miss Kate, does that mean we get to go visiting tonight?"

December 1. The first night of the Advent season, and the first visit to one of the Advent houses. "It is. The parsonage is hosting tonight. Mrs. Tipford asked for the first night so she would have plenty of time between her Advent window evening and planning the Star Singing and Christmas Eve service."

Oscar frowned while Liesl beamed. "And we will sing and have treats and see people." She clapped her hands.

"That's right, sweetling, but for now, how about if you set the table? I hear Martin and Inge stirring upstairs. We'll surprise them with having breakfast all ready when they get down here, all right?"

By midmorning, Kate wanted to take a nap. She was so tired, and her back ached. But there were so many things to do. The house smelled wonderful, though.

"What are these called?" Liesl asked.

"*Zimtsterne*. It means 'cinnamon stars.'" Kate rolled out the dough and gave Liesl the tin cookie cutter that Grossvater had fashioned. "You cut out the stars. While these are baking, Grossmutter will make the icing."

Grossvater shouldered his way through the kitchen door, the screen banging behind him. He carried an armful of wood. "Will you need more?"

Kate checked the kettle and the coffeepot, both full of nearly boiling water, and the reservoir on the back of the stove, full to the brim. "That should do for a while. Could you gather all the laundry from upstairs? Oscar has—" she almost said "forbidden" but that seemed harsh "—requested that I not use the stairs alone. He's worried that I will fall." She waited for someone to scoff, to say he was being overprotective, smothering her like this.

"He's a good man." Grossmutter lifted the washtub off its peg in the little pantry and set it on the end of the table away from the cookies.

Liesl cut the star-shaped cookies out of the dough, her spread fingers echoing their shape. "Daddy is the best daddy in the whole world."

"Is somebody talking about me?" Oscar emerged from the workshop, wiping his hands on a towel. "And what smells so good?"

"I'm making cookies, Daddy."

He came over and dropped a kiss on her crisscrossed braids. "And when they're done, I can eat them all?" He waggled his eyebrows.

"Nope. These are for the party tonight. For Mrs. Tipford. Grossmutter says the recipe has been in her family for a long, long, long, long time. And they will have frosting, and we can put them in a pretty box to take to town." She put the last cutout on the baking sheet. "I'm done."

Kate lifted the handle on the full water bucket in the sink, but Oscar was beside her, taking it from her hand. "Don't lift that. It's too heavy for you. I'll get it."

"Thank you. We're determined to wash every bit of laundry in the house today."

Grossvater came down from upstairs, his arms full of bedlinens. He dumped the sheets and pillowcases on the already-full laundry basket on the floor. "That is everything I could find."

Kate pressed her hands to her lower back. "That will be more than enough to be going on with, I think. We'll be hard-pressed to get it done before we head into town."

Oscar frowned. "Maybe you should stay home tonight and rest. You look worn out now."

She sent him a grimace. "Just what every woman wants to hear. I'm fine, and that laundry isn't going to do itself." She edged past him, noting that he smelled of varnish and sawdust, a masculine mix if there ever was one. "I wouldn't dream of staying home tonight. It's the first day of December."

"We're all going, aren't we, Daddy?" Liesl slid off her chair and came to stand beside him, looking up.

He lifted her in his arms, and she took his face between her little hands, dusting his beard with flour, making Kate smile. "Daddy, it's the most biggest day I ever had."

"Well, I can't disappoint you on the 'most biggest day,' can I? But Miss Kate is going to have to rest before we go, so how about you and I help her with the laundry so she'll have time to maybe get in a nap or at least put her feet up before it's time to go?"

Kate paused. "What about your woodworking?" She knew he had pressing orders to complete.

"I need to wait for some finish to dry. Can't work on anything else because I don't want sawdust to settle on the wet varnish. There's more than enough time to help with laundry." He took her by the elbow and led her into the parlor. "Just sit a spell and relax. You do too much around here as it is."

Kate let herself be seated in the chair he often used at night, sinking into the soft upholstery. "What about the baking?"

"Stop trying to control everything. Let somebody help you once in a while." He winked at her, and a bloom of…fondness?…burst into her chest.

Settling back, she let herself relax, watching his form as he went back into the kitchen. It was nice to be cosseted. She should probably take advantage of it, since in the coming weeks it would most likely be in short supply.

Oscar drew the wagon as close as he could to the manse. Wagons, horses, buggies and the like surrounded the house, and he was forced to pull up several houses down the street. People milled in the clear night air, and light streamed from every window at the parsonage.

He didn't want to be here. He didn't want to celebrate the season. He didn't want to remember...and yet, forgetting felt wrong. He needed to hold on to the memories, the feelings, everything. Forgetting meant betraying everything that went before.

"Lookit, Daddy." Liesl stood behind him, hanging on his shoulder and pointing. "It's the Advent window." Her voice held awe and anticipation.

Sure enough, the large window on the front porch stood open, and Mrs. Tipford leaned out, handing mugs to folks milling on the porch. Greenery framed the opening, and a pair of lamps sat on small tables on the porch to illuminate the area.

Liesl hopped and tugged. "Can we get down? I want to see."

"Patience, Poppet. You'll get your turn." He wrapped the reins around the brake handle and leaped to the ground. "Let me help Miss Kate first."

He reached up for her, and instead of assisting her to climb over the side, he carried her across the packed snow. She threw her arms around his neck, and gave a squeal of surprise. "Oscar!"

"Hold tight. We'll be on the porch in a trice." He went carefully, mindful of what a fall would do.

"You can't carry me. I'm as big as a house."

He raised his eyebrows. "A house?"

She swatted his shoulder. "You know what I mean. I'm perfectly capable of walking. I even promised to hold on to your arm when I was on the snow."

"This is easier." And, if he admitted it, nicer. She was a small woman, her pregnancy notwithstanding, and she wasn't much of a burden. Her head rested briefly against the black wool of his coat, and a rip-ple of awareness went through him. He inhaled the scent of soap and lavender, a feminine combination that made his thinking a bit fuzzy.

"I'm going to be a spectacle, being carried around like an infant. What will folks say?" Her whisper brushed across his cheek.

"That you're being well taken care of? That you have good sense in not risking a fall in your condition? Anyway, it's nobody's business but ours."

She did draw some curious looks, but folks parted to allow him through, and others called greetings.

"Here you are." He deposited her on the front steps. "Wait here. I'll be back."

He noted her flushed cheeks and sparkling eyes as he turned away. He'd definitely surprised her. And himself. He hadn't planned on carrying her. It had just sprung into his mind at the last moment, and he'd done it.

She'd fallen asleep this afternoon almost as soon as he insisted she sit down for a moment, confirming his suspicions that she was tired and needed more rest. And she'd looked so peaceful, her hands resting on the mound of her unborn baby, her head tucked into the corner of the big chair, lashes fanning her cheeks.

Pretty as a picture.

He stopped in the snow on his way back to the wagon, guilt stomping hard through his chest. Digging under his coat, he found his pocket watch and flicked it open, tilting it to catch the moonlight.

Gaelle's picture stared up at him, tucked into the lid of the watch, her eyes warm, looking right at him, her hair coiled high and falling in a cascade over her shoulder. She had given him the picture as an engagement present, cutting it to fit into his pocket watch so he would always have it close to him.

She was the love of his life, the only woman who would ever have his heart, and the only woman who should ever even have his notice. He loved her with everything in his being, and he had promised at her graveside that he would never love another.

And he had no intentions of going back on that promise.

Anyway, what woman would want him, when he would forever love Gaelle? He'd never ask a woman to take second best.

He glanced at the photograph once more before closing it and tucking it into his pocket. It was good to remind himself of his priorities. He'd made a promise to his dead wife, and he should focus his attention only on raising their daughter. His boots scrunched on the snow as he threaded his way back to the wagon.

Liesl all but flew into his arms as the elder Amakers climbed out of the wagon box. "Hurry, Daddy. I see children."

A fist squeezed his heart. It had never occurred to him that she might be lonely for someone other than him to play with. Not until they had company in the house and he saw her blossom. "We'll get there. You won't miss anything."

Mrs. Amaker carried the square box of cookies, tied up with a red ribbon. Her lined old face caught the light from the front windows, and Oscar was startled by the change that came over her. Her smile broadened, and a glow he'd never seen lit her expression. It was as if she'd shed ten years and a ton of burden. He began to see what Kate had meant about Inge Amaker's love of the season and Kate's desire to make this one extra special for her. They all walked up onto the porch.

"Happy Christmas, Mrs. Tipford." Mrs. Amaker handed over the box. "Your home looks very…festive. Just what my heart needed today."

Mrs. Tipford leaned far out over the sill and opened her arms to hug the older woman. "Ah, Inge, it is so good to see you smile. Happy Christmas. I can't wait to see what you brought. You always make the best Christmas treats."

"Happy Christmas, Mrs. Tipford," Liesl recited as she had been practicing at home. Then she grinned and blew the pastor's wife a kiss. Oscar's brows rose. She wasn't just emerging from her shell, she was exploding from it.

His eyes sought Kate, who stood off to the side, chatting with Mrs. Frankel, who held a blanket-wrapped baby. George had a toddler on his arm and his hand on the head of a boy of about four or five. Other Frankel children milled around, eating cookies, laughing and talking.

Per Schmidt and his family arrived, and Mrs. Schmidt carried a fruitcake on a platter. The thing looked like it weighed a good five pounds and was studded with fruit and nuts.

"Oscar, good to see you. We're heading out to the hill behind the house for some nighttime tobogganing." Pastor Tipford had a lantern and a pole. "Lots of folks brought their lanterns, so we should have plenty of light. It's not much of a hill, but it works for the kids. You'll come, right?"

Oscar looked at Liesl, still in his arms, wearing

her plaid wool coat, her face surrounded with a white rabbit-fur trimmed hood. "Can we, Daddy?"

Her eyes pleaded with him, brown and deep and so like Gaelle's it almost hurt. He didn't want to toboggan. He didn't want to pretend to be having a good time, and yet, he couldn't disappoint her. She needed this, even if he wanted no part.

"Sure. I haven't been on a toboggan since I was knee-high to a short horse."

George came off the porch, several children in his wake. "We'll come, too. The ladies said they'd get the hot chocolate heating up."

As Oscar trudged through the snow, he wondered at how much his life could be turned upside down by giving one act of kindness…kindness that he'd been sort of coerced into. Offering a single night's hospitality to a family in need had changed everything. For the last month, he'd done things he'd never anticipated, like making cheese, and giving his wife's clothes to another woman, and attending church regularly, willingly doing laundry, and now a community function with more than a dozen families.

He missed his peaceful, quiet days where he had Liesl all to himself, didn't he?

"Do you want to ride with me?" he asked his daughter.

"Yes. Can we go fast?"

So fearless. He hugged her and strode to the top of the hill to wait their turn. At intervals along the slope, townsmen had hung their lanterns on poles to light the path. There were a few sleds and toboggans to share, and with whoops and hollers, riders swept down the snowy track.

When it was their turn, Oscar put Liesl in front of him, settling her between his legs, and wrapping his arms around her. "Ready?"

"Go, Daddy!" She bounced on her seat.

He pushed off, and down they went, the night air like a cold rushing river against his face. As Pastor Tipford had said, it wasn't a very long or very steep hill, just right for kids, and almost before they started, they were at the bottom, piling off and laughing.

Liesl brushed her hair out of her face with her pale blue mittens, giggling.

"Can we go again, Daddy?"

One of the older Frankel girls came over and bent at the waist to talk to Liesl. "I'll take you if you like. You can ride with Frannie and me." She indicated her sister.

Liesl looked up at him. "Can I, Daddy?"

He looked up the hill, and then at her eager face. She shouldn't come to any grief riding with the older girls. "You may. I'll be here waiting when you come down."

Liesl beamed and the elder of the girls offered her hand.

"I'm Nancy."

"I'm Liesl."

"I think you live across the road from us."

They climbed the hill, Liesl's laughter reaching him, and a piece of his heart cracked a bit. She was getting big, no doubt about it. His baby wasn't a baby anymore. It was good that she was getting out and about, meeting people, but he hated the idea of sharing her.

"You look like you could use this."

He turned. Kate stood there with a mug of hot chocolate.

"What are you doing out here? I thought you were staying on the porch." He frowned.

"Relax. It's a very short way, and Mr. Hale lent me his arm. I wanted to see the fun. It's hard not to join in." She lifted her delicate chin. "I'll have you know, I'm a champion tobogganer, and if I wasn't in my current state, I'd be racing to get to the top of that hill and have a ride."

A laugh surprised him. "I imagine you would be. Good thing you're grounded." He took the mug. Even through his gloves, he felt the warmth of the hot chocolate. Mrs. Hale carried a steaming kettle, several coffee mugs hooked over her fingers, and Mrs. Tipford passed around plates of cookies. It seemed everyone had come to the base of the hill to watch the sledders.

When all the hot chocolate had been drunk and the last ride had been taken, Pastor Tipford gathered everyone together. "Friends, before we depart tonight, I want to thank you all for coming, and I think it appropriate that we pray and thank our Heavenly Father for this Advent season. Won't you join me?"

Everyone formed a circle, joining hands. Kate put her red-mittened hand into Oscar's palm, and Liesl took his other.

As the pastor prayed, disquiet rose in Oscar's chest. It felt too right to be here. Too nice. He wanted to yank his hand away from Kate, scoop up Liesl and run to the safety of their home. He wanted to remember why he had withdrawn from the community two years ago. He didn't want to celebrate a season that only punctuated his sense of loss and regret.

But he stood there in the snow, cheeks tingling with cold, holding a woman's hand. A woman he admired for her courage, her resiliency, for her loyalty. A woman whom he couldn't seem to get out of his thoughts.

He'd been worried about how Liesl would feel when the Amaker family left, but now he realized that he wouldn't be unaffected himself.

Which made him feel all the more guilty.

What would Gaelle say?

Chapter Eleven

"I need you to promise, Daddy." Liesl sat up in bed and took his face between her hands.

"I already said it was all right." He took her hands in his and lowered her to her pillow. "Now, you've had a big night, and it's time for sleep. Nobody will disturb your box under the sideboard." Though why she cared about a cardboard box, he couldn't imagine. But she did, and she was earnest about it. She had talked about it the entire ride home from the Tipfords', surprising Oscar. He'd thought she'd fall asleep in the wagon after all the excitement of the day.

"You'll make sure Miss Kate and Grossmutter and Grossvater know you've promised?" She let him tuck her arms under the blankets.

"I'll make sure they know. Are you going to tell me what this is all about?"

Shaking her head on the pillow, she pressed her lips together.

"All right, Poppet. Keep your secret. Sleep well." He pushed himself up from the side of her bed and reached for the lamp.

"Daddy?"

She was stalling. "What is it, and this better be the last thing for tonight."

"Is it all right to pray to Jesus for what we want for Christmas?"

He paused. "I think it is fine to ask for what you want, but you have to be ready for whatever answer Jesus gives. Sometimes He has to say no, just like I do. It doesn't mean that He doesn't love you. It means He wants the best thing for you, and that might not be the thing you think you want." Oscar sat on the side of the bed again and stroked her hair. "And that doesn't just go for little girls. It goes for grown-ups, too. We don't always get what we want, just because we pray for it."

And didn't he have reason to know it?

"What is it that you're praying for now?" Though he had an idea.

"It's a secret. For me and Jesus."

"Is it about a baby?" He couldn't keep the sternness out of his voice. "We've been over that. You might get a doll for Christmas, but you're not getting a real, live baby."

She blinked, and her eyes looked suspiciously bright for a moment, but she shook her head. "It's something else."

He pinched the bridge of his nose, shutting his eyes. It had been a long day, and if tonight was any indication, it was going to be a long month, especially if everyone in his house insisted on attending every Advent party. Tomorrow it was the Zanks' place, and the night after the Slocums'. Though he should be relieved that Liesl had apparently abandoned the notion of getting a real baby for Christmas, now she had something else on her wish list, and she wasn't sharing.

Still, there were three and a half weeks until Christmas. She'd probably let him know before then what it was.

"All right, Poppet. You say your prayers and get some sleep. There's lots to do tomorrow."

He stood and took the lamp, leaving it on the hall table with the wick turned down low. He left her bedroom door open halfway. When he came to bed, he'd blow out the flame.

When he got to the kitchen, Inge was hard at work, mixing bowl in her arm, stirring something with a wooden spoon. Martin sat at the table with Kate, several papers spread in front of them. Oscar recognized the letter from Martin's brother, Victor.

"What if we sell the yearlings? They aren't purebreds, so we'll only get the beef price for them, but it would be something," Kate said. She drew one of the pages toward her, pencil in hand. "With the rest of the cheese money and the sale of the yearling calves, we could make the mortgage payment."

Martin nodded. "We could, but we would then have no money to build a house to live in. And no money for food and supplies for the next year until we could sell cheese again." He dragged his hands down his face. "The money we have is like a handkerchief. And we keep trying to stretch it into a tablecloth. We can make the mortgage payment, but only if we spend every last cent, including money from selling the yearling calves, when it is not the time to be selling. We will not get top dollar for them. Not until spring when the buyer can turn them out on grass instead of having to feed them through the winter."

Kate leaned back, tossing her pencil onto the pages. "And building the house wouldn't be enough. We would have to furnish it with something. Beds, blankets, food, clothing. If we paid off the mortgage, we wouldn't have enough for even the barest necessities, not for an entire year. And with the baby coming, we'll need even more things. And I can't get a job, not and care for the baby and make cheese all summer."

"I think we have no choice. We will have to take my brother's offer. We can sell the farm, pay off the entire mortgage and have some left over. Perhaps enough that we can take our own rooms somewhere in the city and not have to live in the factory."

"Are there any other options?" Kate asked. "Is there any way we can keep our farm?"

Martin pushed his spectacles up on his forehead and rubbed his eyes.

It seemed there was little else the Amakers could do than sell out. Even if they didn't have the mortgage to pay, replacing the house and possessions would've been hard. As it stood, they'd be at least able to get away with a bit of a nest egg once they sold the farm.

"Will you sell to Siddons?" Oscar didn't fancy him for a neighbor. Not that Mr. Siddons would live on the farm. He'd install tenant farmers, sharecroppers.

"If we had more time, we could have an auction. For the land and the livestock." Martin butted the papers together into a neat stack. "But with things the way they are, we will need to take the best offer we can get. Mr. Siddons has indicated his interest, but I have not settled on my price."

Inge opened the oven door and pulled out a hot pan, while Oscar leaned in the doorway, hands in his pockets. The smell of baked chocolate filled the kitchen, cozy and homey.

Oscar sniffed. "What's that you're making, Mrs. Amaker? It smells wonderful. In fact, my house has smelled like fresh bread and cookies every day since you walked through the door. There's always something tasty in the cupboards now."

Inge set the mixing bowls in the washtub. "It is *Brünsli*. Christmas brownies. For tomorrow's Advent window visit. It is the Zanks' turn, and we must bring a gift."

Oscar had never been to Bill Zank's house. He wasn't even sure where the feed store owner lived. The prospect of another trip to town, another evening of fellowship with friends...he inhaled again the fragrant, chocolaty aroma coming from the oven.

"If we're going out again tomorrow night, I had best get into the workshop and finish up the wedding chest. We can deliver it when we go to town." He started to turn away, then stopped. "Liesl wanted me to remind you that the area under the sideboard is not to be disturbed." He pointed to the walnut cupboard that sat up on legs, leaving perhaps eighteen inches of space underneath. A cardboard box lay on its side, the open top facing the kitchen.

Nothing else. Just the box.

"I don't know what all goes on in that little head of hers, but whatever this is, it's important to her."

Kate pushed herself up from the table. "I've never known such an imaginative child. She can make worlds out of any old thing you give her to play with.

It must be all those bedtime stories you read to her."
She pressed her hand to her lower back and rounded
the table. "Would you mind if I brought my sewing
into the workshop? Martin and Inge are going to turn
in soon, but I would like to get on with hemming diapers. I hate to sit alone at night. If I wouldn't be dis-
turbing you?"

She would, but not in the way she might think.

He brought a chair from the parlor into the workshop and set it near the little stove. She settled in with
a pile of white flannel squares, her thread and thimble.

Cozy. As if she belonged there.

Oscar forced himself to get to work.

The wedding chest had turned out better than he'd
hoped. The inlay work was as smooth as glass…and
so it should be for all the hours he'd spent sanding
and fitting the pieces together. Oscar opened the lid,
inhaling the tangy, woodsy smell of the cedar lining.

"All this needs is the hardware. I already set the
hinges, but not lock." He ran his hand over the satiny walnut.

"It's beautiful. I'm sure the bride will treasure it."
She had a wistful echo in her voice, and he was reminded that if the Amakers had family heirlooms,
they had been lost in the fire.

He found a pencil and his ruler and marked the
exact spot the hole for the lock should be cut. Then he
measured again, his father's voice in his ear. "Measure twice and cut once."

Kate laughed, and he realized he'd said the words
aloud. Not looking up from her sewing, she said, "My
mother said that, too, but she was talking about fabric.
She took in sewing to make a little extra money, and

she knew if she got a pattern piece wrong, it would come out of her profits."

"That's where you learned your dressmaking skills?" He selected a chisel, testing the edge for sharpness. He would need to create a mortise to drop the locking mechanism into, and he needed to be careful not to gouge too big a hole.

"Yes." She drew her thread quickly through the flannel, whipping the edges of the cloth into a tight hem. "Liesl was asking me if she could learn to sew. I put her off until I could check with you. I didn't ask before I taught her some of her letters, and I didn't want to overstep again."

"Isn't she too young to sew? Only four?" He didn't like the idea of her with a needle in her little hands.

"I wasn't much older than that, but I thought we might start with some lacing cards and yarn. They're easy enough to make, just punching holes in cardboard and winding a piece of thread around the end of a length of yarn to make it tight. She can practice all kinds of stitches with the yarn." Kate bit her thread to break it and reached for her spool and another square of flannel. "I thought it could be a Christmas gift from me to her. We don't have much we can give, but we want to give Liesl something."

"You don't have to. She isn't expecting anything from you." He tapped the chisel with his wooden carving mallet, taking small chips of walnut at a time.

"I know. But we'd like to do something. And Grossvater and Grossmutter wanted me to let you know they would be paying for the baking supplies Grossmutter was using to make the Advent treats she's taking to the celebrations."

He put his tools down and looked at her. "There really is no need for that."

She lowered her work to her lap. "Please, Oscar, let them. They know they are costing you more than you would normally spend at the mercantile, especially with all the baking supplies. If they can't contribute, they won't feel right going to the parties."

Test-fitting the lock, he noticed it sticking in one of the corners. With a rounded rasp, he filed off a bit of wood at a time, trying the lock again. He could appreciate the Amakers wanting to contribute, to pull their weight, so to speak, but…he realized, they'd been doing that and more.

"Things sure have changed around here in the last month. I didn't realize all the tasks I wasn't getting done, or that I wasn't getting done well, until you all showed up." He dropped the lock into the mortise where it fit snugly. Now to affix the top plate. "I haven't cooked a meal, washed a dish or swept a floor. Every piece of harness and tack has been soaped and oiled, every loose board and hinge is tight, and my horses have never been groomed so often. I'd say you all were contributing more than your share. Not to mention what you've done with Liesl."

He glanced up and saw she was pressing her hands against her stomach, breathing quickly, eyes closed. His heart leaped into a gallop, and he dropped his screwdriver with a clatter. "What is it? Is it your time?" Panic clawed up his windpipe, making it hard to breathe.

She shook her head, eyes still closed, lips tight. After a moment she eased, taking a deep breath. "No, I just took a bad kick to the ribs. I had no idea a baby could be so strong." She rubbed her right side. "He's been doing that a lot lately, and I'm getting sore. I guess he's protesting the lack of room."

Oscar bent to pick up the screwdriver, but he didn't feel any relief. She was going to have a baby. He'd known it in his head, but he'd put off really thinking about it, especially after she'd gotten the all clear from Dr. Horlock. It had been easy to push the reality aside, think about it sort of obliquely, because there was so much to do in the here and now, so much else to think about, the birth was something that would happen "later."

But later was rushing upon them. The baby would come, and it would come while she was staying in his house.

"Maybe I should send for the doctor in the morning, have him come check you out, just to make sure everything is all right?"

She picked up her sewing again, as if the most terrifying and life-altering thing that could befall a person wasn't going to happen to her within the month. "That would be a waste of his time."

He tightened the screws on the faceplate and felt as if he were tightening the screws on his heart.

Kate looked at the calendar on the kitchen wall, grateful that the sixteenth of December had finally arrived. They wouldn't have to go out tonight. After more than two weeks of evening visits to the community, she was more than ready to stay home.

Not that tonight would be any more restful. This evening, the Amakers and Rabbs would host the Advent celebration.

The house smelled like a bakery. Grossmutter had been hard at work since sunup, making *Chrabeli*, the delicate little claw-shaped cookies that were Kate's favorites. She had plates of *Brünsli*, *Zimtsterne* and *Zopf* covering the table, each under a tea towel. And as the time for visitors drew near, *Kinderpunsch* would simmer on the stove, filling the house with fruity sweetness and tantalizing spices.

Liesl came through from the workshop where Oscar was putting the finishing touches on a rocking chair to be picked up by the Slocums tonight, and tripped across the room, a block of wood in her hands. She knelt by the sideboard and set it in among the others.

It had taken Kate three days to realize what Liesl was playing with the box and scraps. Every day, she added a new block of wood, chatting to herself, arranging the pieces to suit the picture in her mind.

It was Liesl's version of the Advent Nativity she had heard Grossmutter talk so much about. The box was the crèche, the wood blocks the sheep, shepherds, donkeys and camels. Sixteen pieces as of today, nine more to come.

"Which one is that?" Kate asked.

"It's a wise man." The child set the block up on end. She angled it, moved it a couple of inches, then pushed it back. "There. How many wise men were there?"

"Our Nativity had three wise men, though Scripture doesn't really say how many there were. I suppose tradition says there were three because there were three gifts that they brought to Jesus." Kate closed her eyes for a moment, remembering the beautiful carving, the satiny finish of the family pieces. Her favorite wise man had been made of walnut. He wore a crown with tiny carved jewels, and the curls of his beard had looked so real.

"Sweetling, would you like to move your set up on top of the sideboard instead of underneath? We can clear off the top to make room."

"Yes." Liesl hopped up. "And then we need to decorate our window, right? Daddy said he would bring in the branches, and Grossmutter said we could make some paper chains and popcorn strings, too."

Kate began moving items off the sideboard to make room. "How about we put a tablecloth on here, though, to keep from scratching the wood?" She opened the top drawer and removed a pale green cloth. "You can pretend this is the grass."

"Don't we need the white one, to pretend it's snow?" Liesl clutched several "sheep" blocks.

"Depends. Jesus wasn't born in Minnesota. He was born in Israel. It's mostly warm there, and there was grass growing for all the sheep to eat. But it's up to you. We can use white if you want."

The child considered this for a moment, her lips pushing out as she thought. "Green. Then there will be grass for my sheep, too."

"Kate, can you come here for a minute?" Oscar called.

She pushed a chair up to the sideboard for Liesl to stand on to arrange her pieces and hurried into the workshop. "Yes?"

"Tell me what you think." He dusted the shiny back of the rocking chair with a bit of old flannel. "Think Mrs. Slocum will like it?"

"Oh, Oscar, it's beautiful." She touched the satiny wood, setting the chair into motion. "What kind of wood is this?"

"It's quarter-sawn red oak. See these marks?" He pointed to the headpiece. "Those are called sun rays or sunbursts. You only see those in quarter-sawn wood." Turning the chair slightly, he waved his hand. "Give it a try."

Kate lowered herself into the chair, bracing on the arms to ease herself down. The chair embraced her, and she settled in, pushing with her toes to rock gently. "It's perfect." The arms curved at just the right angle, the back fit snugly into the bend of her spine. "Mrs. Slocum is going to love it. She won't want to get up and tend to any chores."

His smile warmed her. Over the past couple of weeks, he'd asked her to come in and inspect every new piece of furniture, as if he couldn't wait to share his creations with her. "I hope so. It took a long time to steam and bend all the wood for this one."

"What do you have left to finish before Christmas?" She rocked, feeling the ache in her back a little less than when she was on her feet.

"Just a jewelry box and a checkerboard." He glanced at the door and lowered his voice. "And I was thinking of making a dollhouse for Liesl. Would you be able to make some little curtains and rugs and things if I did? She's so fascinated playing with those wood blocks, pretending they're a Nativity scene, I thought she might like a dollhouse for Christmas."

Kate laced her fingers under her chin. "Oh, she would love that. And I would love to help you with it."

"I drew up some plans last night." He reached into

his pocket and pulled out a folded paper. "I thought I'd make it sort of like our house now. Well, half of it. With a kitchen and parlor downstairs and two bedrooms upstairs. Simple, you know?"

She opened the paper, her mind already envisioning the little house and the pieces she could make for it. "She'll be thrilled. She's such a little homemaker already. And so imaginative."

He rubbed the back of his neck. "It's going to be pretty hard for her when you all leave. I thought this might fill some of the hours."

Who was going to fill the hours for Kate? She was going to miss the little girl dreadfully. Just then the baby gave a *thump, thump, thump.* Smiling, Kate rubbed the place. *I suppose you will fill up my time, but that doesn't mean I won't miss sweet little Liesl.*

"Since the chair has your stamp of approval, I guess it's time for me to head out and get some pine for that Advent window."

"Can Liesl and I come with you? We'd love to help." She found she wanted to pack in as much time with them both as possible.

He frowned. "I don't want you to fall out there."

"It's not icy. And the snow would be a soft place to land. I promise to hold on to your arm the whole way there." And that wouldn't be any hardship at all. His brawny arms were one of the things that made her feel the safest. As if, should he put his arms around her, she would be impervious to any harm or hurt.

She studied her hands as warmth spread up her cheeks. Here she was, only days away from the birth of her first child, imagining what it would be like to be held safely in the arms of Oscar Rabb. Was this disloyal to Johann? Or unseemly?

Without a doubt, she had loved her husband. When they were married, she'd never thought about another man like this, never wanted to. But Johann was dead. She missed him, and she knew she always would. But she was alive.

"If you promise to take it slow, you can come with me."

She looked up, wondering what Oscar would think if he knew her thoughts. He'd probably be shocked and hustling to find somewhere else, anywhere else, to house the Amakers until they had to leave for Cincinnati.

So she must never let on that she had a…tenderness…for him. Anyway, it was probably just that he was so steady and kind. Not like she was in love with him or anything. Grossmutter had warned her that pregnant women sometimes got emotional, thought silly thoughts. That's all this was, a passing attraction. She and Oscar were friends. Just friends. And friends enjoyed each other's company.

"I'll get my cloak."

He was at her elbow, helping her up, and she wished for a moment that she didn't resemble a grain silo in roundness and proportions. She blew out a breath. "I once saw a picture of a walrus on the beach. That's what I feel like these days."

Shaking his head, he put his hand to the small of her back to guide her to the door. "Why do women always think they look their worst when the opposite is true? If you ask me, there's nothing prettier than a woman being just as God made her to be. You're doing some important work there, housing Junior until he decides to make his appearance. Nothing unsightly about it."

She felt every finger of his touch, and his opinion was like balm on her chafed heart. His words would be mulled over in the coming days, she had a feeling.

Bundled up, she and Liesl waited on the front porch for the sleigh. Last week when the snow had gotten deep, Oscar had taken the wagon box off the wheels and put it on sled runners. And at Inge's request, he'd attached a string of bells to the horses' harness. Now the bells chimed out merrily as he drew up to the house.

Liesl hurried off the porch, and Oscar swung her up high, depositing her gently into the straw piled in the back of the wagon. Rolf barked and leaped aboard, tail wagging like a white-tipped black flag. Kate waited for Oscar to come to her, mindful of his strictures on this little jaunt.

"Is it too cold for you girls?" He put his arm around her waist and took her hand in his other one.

"No. We're tough Minnesota women, aren't we, Liesl?" Kate bragged. "We don't get cold."

Oscar's brows rose. "Really?"

Liesl giggled and fended off a lick from Rolf. Soon they were on their way to a grove of pines along Milliken Creek where it ran through the pasture on the Amaker farm.

"In the summer, when it gets really hot, the cattle come down here and stand in the water to cool off," Kate remembered. "With all this snow, it's hard to recall the hot days of summer."

"But in the summer, it seems to me I can recall

every snowflake of a blizzard." Oscar slapped the lines. "Probably because we're tough Minnesotans, eh? We like to brag and complain about the ferocity of our winters, no matter the season."

They reached the pine grove, and Oscar led them into the trees, a handsaw over his shoulder and Kate's arm tucked into the crook of his elbow. "How much will you need?"

"Enough to hang in the window and decorate the sill. And maybe some to form a wreath for the front door. Liesl, would you like a wreath on the door?" Kate called ahead to the little girl, who was lifting her feet high and trying to navigate the drifts. Rolf ran and leaped and rolled in the snow, clearly joyous at being out with them.

"Yes! Grossmutter would like that, wouldn't she?" Liesl called back over her shoulder.

Oscar wasted no time. He soon had an armful of fragrant branches. Long-needled white pine and the shorter, stubbier blue spruce. "You wait here while I load this in the wagon. I'll be back for you."

He disappeared through the trees, and Kate bent and picked up a handful of snow. She put her fingers to her lips and motioned for Liesl to do the same. "We'll ambush him when he comes back, right?" she whispered to the little girl.

With a giggle, Liesl packed her own snowball and crouched behind a pine tree, eyes alight.

The moment Oscar came into the small clearing, Liesl jumped out and let fly, her snowball arcing and falling well short. Kate's was more accurate, and her missile exploded against his dark coat front.

"Gotcha!"

He froze, eyes wide, then a grin spread across his face. "So, you want to have a snowball fight, do you?" He leaned down and gathered a handful of snow, not packing it.

Kate laughed, edging backward. "No, I just realized that I don't, really."

"Me, either." Liesl giggled and scrunched her shoulders. Rolf circled, barking and leaping, eager to join in.

"You can't change your mind now." Oscar gently tossed his snow at his daughter, who dodged it easily. "There's a price to be paid."

While he was distracted with Liesl, Kate packed another snowball, this one sailing forth and hitting him in the back. He whirled.

"So, you're a baseball player in disguise, are you?" He scooped up a huge armful of snow and shoveled it her way, sending a cascade of flakes showering over her, gentle but cold.

"Brrr." She brushed the snow off her face, laughing.

"I thought a Minnesota girl like you didn't get cold." He stepped close and took the end of his muffler and wiped at the snow still clinging to her hair and cheeks. His breath plumed in a cloud, and she smelled the scent of sawdust and pine.

This close, she could see greenish flecks in his brown eyes. His mouth curved into a smile, and his beard looked so soft she wanted to touch it to confirm her suspicions. She didn't feel the cold at all. In fact, she was tingling and warm, her blood zipping along quickly.

At that moment, a barking something hit the back

of her legs and she cannoned into Oscar, tumbling to her knees in the snow, hands splayed to catch herself. She landed hard, jarring everything, and quickly rolled onto her side, stunned.

Oscar had staggered back with a shout, then yelled, "Rolf, get out of here." He was on his knees beside her, his face a mask of worry. "Kate, are you all right?"

She took stock of herself, feeling the cold seeping through her cloak. Blinking, she studied the treetops and the bright, pale sky overhead, then took a deep breath, shaking a bit from the surprise of it all. Rolf's big, furry face blotted out everything, his tongue lolling and swiping at her cheek.

"Get back." Oscar pushed the dog away.

"Miss Kate?" Liesl squatted beside her. "Are you hurted?"

"I'm fine, I think. Help me sit up." She tried to brush the hair out of her eyes and only succeeded in dumping snow from her mittens onto her face.

"No, lie there for a minute." Oscar pushed the dog away again. "That was quite a tumble. When you're ready, I'll carry you back to the wagon and get you home."

She was a bit rattled, but nothing like it appeared he was. His hand shook as he rubbed it down his pale face.

"I'm not hurt. I can get up." She propped herself up on her elbows, but she would need help to get any farther, half-buried in the snow as she was and on a slight slope.

"You'll do no such thing. Are you sure you're not injured?" He reached out as if he wanted to touch her belly, but he pulled his hand back. "Liesl, go get into the wagon and stir up the straw nice and fluffy. Push aside the pine branches so there's a place for her. I'm going to bring Miss Kate and lay her there."

"Really, Oscar, I don't need to lie down in the back of the wagon. I'm perfectly capable of walking there and sitting on the seat."

She might as well have left the words unsaid for all he listened. "Does anything hurt?"

"No, though I imagine I might have tender spots tomorrow, but this Minnesota girl is getting cold lying on the snow." And she felt awkward and huge.

"If you're sure, then put your arms around my neck. I'm going to lift you, but if anything hurts, you must tell me right away." He leaned close, eyes tense with worry, hands gentle.

She did as he said, torn between gratitude for his solicitous care and frustration that she needed it. He tucked his hand beneath her knees and under her back and picked her up, steadying himself in the snow, peering into her face for the first sign that she was in pain.

With careful strides, he brought her to the wagon and laid her on the straw in the back as if she was made of spun glass. Liesl had piled up the straw as best she could and stood in the box, mittens clasped tight together, her face pinched and her mouth wavering.

"Sweetling, I'm fine. Don't worry. Come, sit by me and we'll keep each other warm." Kate patted the straw. "Doesn't it smell nice, all these pine branches? Grossmutter is going to be so pleased."

Oscar lost no time getting the horses started, but he didn't rush them, keeping them to a brisk walk so as not to rattle the wagon too much. Embarrassment at her situation flitted across Kate's skin. How ridiculous she must look, taking a tumble into the snow, then being conveyed home like a trussed-up turkey.

When they reached the farmhouse, Oscar carried her up the steps, and Liesl went ahead to open the door.

"Inge? Can you come with us? Kate took a tumble." He didn't stop in the kitchen but marched right up the stairs to her room.

"Really, Oscar, put me down."

"You're going to bed, and you're going to let Inge take a look at you. I'll be back in a bit with the doctor."

He set her on the bed, and she swung her feet over the edge to stand. "That's ridiculous. I don't need a doctor. There's nothing wrong with me. Yes, I had a little fall, but it was into a pile of soft snow. I was more surprised than anything, but sending for the doctor is—"

His hands were firm on her shoulders. "Lie down."

"Grossmutter, tell him." Kate appealed to Inge. "There's too much to do with the Advent celebration here tonight for me to lollygag in bed."

The elderly woman looked at Oscar's uncompromising face, his crossed arms and his strong stance, and shook her head. "*Schätzchen*, perhaps it would be wise to rest for a while."

Liesl clambered up on the bed beside Kate, kneeling on the quilt. "You should do what Daddy and Grossmutter say, Miss Kate."

Feeling she had no choice in the face of so much opposition, Kate relaxed against the pillows. "Fine, I'll rest here, but I don't need a doctor."

"You're having one, and that's that. Inge, please, get her into some nightclothes and under the covers, and check her out. I'll be back with Doc Horlock as soon as I can." He strode out of the room and down the stairs. The kitchen door closed briskly, and the clop of horses' hooves on the snow-packed drive faded.

What had he been thinking, taking a pregnant woman out in the snow and cold, just to cut some pine branches? And why had he let her out of the wagon? And what had come over him to toss snow all over her, getting Rolf excited and precipitating the collision?

Oscar slapped the lines on the team's rumps, urging them into a trot. With the snowy roads it would take him better than an hour to get to Mantorville.

"Lord, please let Horlock be in his office and not out making house calls somewhere."

The sled skidded as he made the turn onto the main road, but he didn't slacken the pace...and he didn't stop praying.

The Amakers were under his roof, under his protection, and it was his job to see that they were well cared for and safe. And what had he done? Let his head be turned by a pretty woman who made him forget all his self-imposed and hard-learned lessons. He'd given in to those lovely eyes asking him to let her go with him to the pine grove.

And now she might have to pay dearly for his mistake.

Chapter Twelve

Kate plucked at the blanket stitch surrounding the Dresden plate pattern on the quilt. It seemed strange to be in her nightgown in the middle of the day, especially when she wasn't ill. Inge bustled about the room, pulling another blanket from the chest and spreading it over Kate's feet.

"You are sure you are fine?"

"Yes. I was more surprised than anything. You're all overreacting." She pressed her head back into the pillows and closed her eyes. She *was* tired, but it was the same old weariness she felt every day.

Inge sat on the side of the bed, taking Kate's limp hand in hers. "Child, do you know how precious you are to us? If something happened to you or the baby, I don't know what we would do." Her grasp, tight but somehow soft, too, pressed into Kate's fingers. Kate opened her eyes, feeling chastened for her churlishness.

"I love you, too, Grossmutter, but nothing is going to happen to me. I wish this baby would just go ahead and show up so everyone could stop worrying about that and focus on what we're going to do in a few weeks."

Martin tapped on the doorframe. He held the towel-wrapped handle of the warming pan. "The kettle is boiling."

Inge went past him into the hall. "I will bring some tea."

"There isn't anything I can do," Kate asked, "to persuade you to let me get up and on with the preparations for the party?"

Shaking his head, Martin slid the bed warming pan under the edge of the quilt. Kate turned half on her side, drawing her knees up as far as she could as he rubbed the warming pan over the sheets. "It is no light matter for you to fall these days. And Oscar was clear in his instructions to keep you in that bed. You gave him quite a fright."

"I'm sorry to cause you all so much worry." She moved her feet down, savoring the warmth from the heated sheets as he withdrew the brass warming pan. The feather mattress was nice, and the pillow so comfortable. She'd just rest for a while. Her eyelids began to droop, and she slipped over the edge into sleep.

"Mrs. Amaker." Something pressed on her shoulder, giving it a small shake.

Kate didn't want to open her eyes. In fact, she wasn't sure she could, her lids were so heavy, her mind so muzzy from slumber. She didn't recognize the voice, anyway. Perhaps she was still dreaming.

"Kate."

She knew *that* voice was Oscar's and it sounded

concerned. In a moment, when she was more awake, she would see what he needed.

"Kate, wake up. Please. Dr. Horlock is here."

Managing to crack open one eyelid, she tried to focus. A yawn welled up and threatened to split her jaw. She barely got her hand up to cover her gaping mouth. "Sorry." She blinked, struggling up out of somnolence.

"Is there something wrong with her? Why isn't she alert?" Oscar paced at the foot of the bed.

Dr. Horlock set his bag on the quilt and smiled. "I think it's because she's sleepy. So would you be if you rarely found a comfortable way to sleep, or if you had a person living inside you who was seemingly trying to kick his way out the moment you finally snatched some rest. At least, that's what my wife claims. She's due in three more months." He motioned for Oscar to go out into the hall and turned back to Kate, who rubbed her eyes and pushed her hair back from her face.

"Now, young lady, Oscar tells me you were plowed over by that shaggy beast of his." He took her wrist in his fingers, finding her pulse and comparing it to his pocket watch. "Can you tell me what happened?"

"It wasn't much of anything, really. The dog bumped me in the back of the legs, and I went down face forward into the snow. I caught myself on my hands and knees, and I sort of fell over onto my side so I wouldn't land on my middle."

The doctor nodded, pursing his lips, keeping his eyes on the watch.

"So you got shaken up a bit."

She nodded, and he glanced up, letting her wrist

drop. "Yes. A bit. I was more surprised than anything."

"I'd like to listen to the baby. Have you felt him move since the fall?"

Kate paused. Had she? She'd become so used to the baby rolling and kicking and tumbling that unless he delivered a hard smack to the underside of her ribs, she didn't take much notice. A frisson of worry flicked across her chest.

"I don't know."

Dr. Horlock drew his stethoscope from his bag and gently turned back the quilt. Placing the small bell end against her abdomen and the tong ends into his ears, he closed his eyes. Slowly he moved the bell from one place to another, listening, his face calm and untroubled.

Finally, when Kate was ready to grab his lapels and beg him to get on with things, he opened his eyes. "I think he's sleeping. But I can hear his heart going nice and strong. I imagine he'll be waking up and squirming around soon enough." He asked a few more personal questions about her condition, and then patted her shoulder.

"I'm going to recommend you stay in that bed until at least tomorrow, and that you take it easy for the next little while."

The rest of the day? Kate shook her head. The nap was nice, but she had things to do. "We're having company this evening. It's our turn to host the Advent party. I need to help Inge get ready."

"No, you don't. Inge and Martin and little Liesl have things well in hand. Anyway, if I let you out of that bed too soon, Oscar might have me tarred and feathered." He coiled his stethoscope. "I think you'll be just fine, but a little extra rest for a woman so close to her confinement is never a bad thing."

"I wish you'd talk to Oscar. He refuses to let me do much of anything now, but if you tell him I have to stay in bed until tomorrow, he'll probably insist I not get up at all until the baby's born."

Dr. Horlock chuckled as he went to the washstand and began to scrub his hands. "Expectant fathers can be like that. It seems like the bigger and tougher they are, the more they worry and fret."

Heat charged into Kate's cheeks. "Oscar isn't my husband."

The doctor stopped, his hands dripping water onto the hardwood floor. "Oh, that's right. I'm so sorry. I forgot." He reached for the towel on the back of the washstand. "It just seemed so familiar to me, the wife calm and steady and the husband pacing a groove into the floor. I'll have a word with him before I leave."

"Inge won't let you out of the house without some coffee and a pastry or two." Kate tried to cover her embarrassment with hospitality.

"I'm counting on that." He snapped the case shut. "Send for me if anything troubles you."

"Thank you, Doctor."

He opened the door, and Oscar brushed past him into the room as if he'd been hovering by the door. "What's the verdict?"

"She's fine, but I want her to rest. In bed until tomorrow, then in a nice comfy chair or settee for a good part of each day." Dr. Horlock spoke as he went down the stairs, his voice becoming fainter.

Oscar stood at the foot of the bed, looking down

on her, and she smoothed her hair again. "Oh, mercy, I didn't even take my hair down before I fell asleep. I must look like a back-brushed cat." She pulled the pins out, letting her messy hair fall over her shoulders. It would be a rat's nest if she didn't braid it.

Oscar's hands tightened on the footboard. "You look fine. Rest like the doctor says, and I'll be up to check on you later. And don't worry. I'll head into town and tell Mrs. Hale and Mrs. Tipford we're not hosting tonight."

Her hands stilled in her hair. "No, please. Inge and Liesl would be so sad. They've been planning this for weeks. I promise to stay up here, but please, let them have their party."

He appeared to be considering it, but he wasn't looking at her. He kept his gaze on the flowered wallpaper over her head.

"Ask Dr. Horlock if it's all right." She gripped the edge of the blanket. It meant so much to her to be able to give Inge at least a little joy this Christmas. She didn't want to be the cause of her sweet Grossmutter missing out on her celebration. And Liesl was practically bursting from her skin anticipating the arrival of guests. "I don't want anyone to be disappointed."

"You promise you'll stay in bed?"

"Yes." Though she would be the one disappointed to miss the guests and the fun. She had been looking forward to tonight, too. Not just the company, but seeing the joy on Liesl's face, the happiness shining from Inge's eyes.

He sighed, and his lips pressed together, as if he had come to a decision.

"Fine. I'm going to go talk to Dr. Horlock, and

you're going to go to sleep." He scrubbed the back of his neck with his palm. "You scared about ten years off my life today."

"I'm sorry. I will be more careful. The doctor says I'm fine, though. The baby is fine, too. Dr. Horlock said he could hear the baby's heartbeat, and he's sleeping right now—most of the time he's moving around a lot, so that's good." She rubbed her hand against her side where even now an elbow or knee thumped. "Ah, he's awake." She tried a small smile, but Oscar wasn't in a smiling mood yet.

"I'll go see the doc. You rest."

Kate napped off and on all afternoon, interrupted periodically by an excited Liesl climbing the stairs to tell her about the latest decoration or treat preparation.

"Miss Kate, I made a paper chain, and Grossvater made a row of paper stars. He folded the paper, and cut and cut and cut, and then, when he opened the paper, it was stars, holding hands." She clasped her own hands under her chin, marveling. "And we hung the tree branches we got today in the window."

Inge entered the room with a bowl of popped corn and the sewing kit. "I thought you two could string the popcorn up here together. Something nice and quiet. I hate that you are being left out of the fun."

So Liesl climbed up beside Kate, and Inge put the bowl of popcorn into her lap. Kate took the sewing box and threaded a needle with a length of white cotton. "You can pick out just the right pieces for me, and I'll poke them onto the thread."

When they had a string long enough, Kate coiled it into the bowl. "There, you can take that downstairs. It will look lovely."

"Miss Kate," Liesl said, sliding off the bed and reaching back for the bowl. "What do you want for Christmas?"

Pausing from replacing her sewing needle in its case, Kate looked up. "Me?" She'd been too busy to think about what she might want for Christmas. If she had her heart's desire, it would be to stay here in Minnesota, to be able to keep her farm. "I think what I would love best for Christmas is to see everyone in this house happy. For us to make some lovely memories to carry with us forever." She wound her thread and tucked it into the sewing basket. "What about you? Have you decided on just what you would like?" If she was still set on getting a baby, would the dollhouse Oscar was building be a disappointment? Or the apron Inge had sewn? Or the pink dress Kate had been working on in secret?

The little girl hugged the bowl against her middle, her hands barely reaching around the circumference. "Daddy says I can't have a baby. He says that's not how families work." She sighed, shaking her head. "He says just because we pray for something, doesn't mean we will get it. Sometimes Jesus has to say no."

Tears pricked Kate's eyes. Thus far, Jesus had said no to her wish to stay in Minnesota. It was so hard to trust that He knew best, that He only had what was best for her in mind. But she knew He was faithful. His Word promised that His love never changed, and He had never broken a promise.

She wished that what she knew and what she felt were reconciled more often. Though reminding herself of the truth often went a long way toward aligning her feelings.

Oscar carried her supper tray up to her that evening.

Kate scooched herself up against the pillows, thoroughly tired of being in bed. The oftener Liesl had bounced up the stairs to tell her of some new development for the party, the harder it had become to stay in her room. Everyone would be having such a lovely time, and she'd be all alone. Inside, she wanted to fuss about Oscar's and Dr. Horlock's restrictions. She felt fine, and she should be able to be downstairs with friends and family celebrating the season.

But when party time rolled around, she wasn't forgotten. Sounds of wagons and horses, laughter and singing came from the farmyard and porch, and the front door opened again and again. Somewhere Rolf barked, greeting each new arrival, and the smells of cinnamon and bread and *Kinderpunsch* drifted up the staircase.

And then footfalls on the steps. Mrs. Tipford tapped on the doorframe. "Kate, dear?"

"Come in." Kate smiled, so grateful for company. "Season's greetings."

"And to you. What's this I hear about you falling today?" The tiny woman tugged off her gloves, her cheeks and nose red with cold. She hadn't even waited to remove her wraps downstairs. "Are you all right?" Her brows nearly met over her nose, and she sat on the bedside, taking one of Kate's hands in hers, studying Kate's face.

"Yes, yes, I'm fine. It wasn't much of a spill, and I landed in the snow." Kate shrugged. "It's a lot of fuss over nothing. You'd think I'd taken a fall off the henhouse roof the way Oscar reacted. He even went for the doctor. It's rather embarrassing."

"Oh, my dear." Mrs. Tipford put her hand to her chest. "Of course he was concerned. After what happened to Gaelle." She shook her head, lowering her chin. "Surely he's told you."

"Oscar rarely speaks of her. I know she died, and a child, also."

"It was so sad. She was expecting, and a few weeks before she was due, she fell on the stairs. The fall caused her to go into labor early, and in spite of everything the doctor could do, she lost the baby. And later that night, she passed away, too." Mrs. Tipford touched her little finger to the corner of her eye to catch a tear. "It was so very sad, and Oscar was beside himself with grief. He blamed himself. He was outside in the barn when she fell, and she couldn't get up, and Liesl was so young... It was quite a while before he found her." She sat quietly for a moment, then shook herself, as if scattering the bad thoughts. "It's no wonder he was concerned for you."

Kate bit the inside of her bottom lip, her heart aching for Oscar. Here she'd been chafing over what she considered his bossiness, when he'd only been trying to protect her from the same tragedy that had befallen his wife.

"Anyway," Mrs. Tipford said, too brightly. "Everything looks lovely downstairs, and I don't know who is more pleased, Inge or Liesl."

"I'll get to see it all tomorrow. The doctor said I only have to stay in bed today and tonight. Tomorrow, I can go downstairs, though I suspect I'll only be allowed to sit in the rocker or rest on the settee." And she'd do it, too, so as not to cause Oscar more worry. He'd been through enough. Kate considered all the times she'd brushed aside his concerns, or thought she was just humoring him…like going into Mantorville to be checked out by the doctor, or promising not to use the stairs without his assistance, or not walking outside alone…and all the while, he'd been trying not to relive the worst thing that had ever happened to him.

Oscar stood on the porch, watching the last sleigh leave the yard. Light spilled from his front parlor window out onto the snow until Martin lowered the sash and drew the drapes. Inge must've passed a hundred cookies through the open window to their guests over the last hour.

He had wondered how many of their friends and neighbors would make the trip clear out to the farm, but the townsfolk had surprised him. They'd arrived with lanterns and treats and holiday cheer. The men and children had joined together to make a huge snowman in the yard. The snow sculpture now wore one of his old hats and a scarf, and cast a long shadow in the clear, moonlit night.

Stamping the snow off his boots, he returned inside. Warmth hit him in the face—the warmth of the stove as Inge lifted one of the lids to stir the coals, warmth from the fireplace in the parlor and warmth of…well, almost of family. He'd entertained in his house for the first time in more than two years. Never one to seek out group events, the ease with which the evening had passed surprised him.

Though there was one thing he'd noticed all night. He missed Kate. Several times he'd mounted the stairs to check on her, only to hear laughter and chatting as various women took turns keeping her company. Oscar hadn't intruded, but it had reassured him to hear her voice.

When she'd fallen that afternoon, everything had stopped. His mind. His heart. His ability to breathe. He wasn't even sure what he did or said, he was so frantic to get her to safety, to get the doctor to her.

And though Horlock said she would be fine, Oscar still wasn't at ease. Until that baby was safely delivered and deemed healthy, and Kate was back on her feet, he wouldn't be able to relax. Just thinking of everything that could go wrong made his muscles clench and his stomach resemble a ball of knotted twine.

But he'd missed being with her tonight. Over the past few days, every evening after Liesl went to sleep, they'd gone into the workshop to craft the dollhouse. Kate liked to talk while she worked, reminding him of Liesl, who was never quiet for long. But unlike Liesl, who could chatter on without input from him for long stretches, Kate asked him questions and for his opinion.

She was surprisingly well-read and up on state and national politics. And she seemed to remember in great detail everything Liesl had said or done during the day, and to relate it to him so vividly that he felt as if he had been there, too.

Martin sat in a chair before the fire, Liesl on his lap, her head on his shoulder. He was telling her a story. "And we would walk through the middle of town, holding up the stars we had made, singing all the Christmas songs we knew. The march always started at the low end of town and we worked our way up the hillside all the way to the church door. Then everyone went inside for the Christmas Eve service. I remember being so excited I could hardly sit still, because Christmas Day was only one more sleep away."

"Mrs. Tipford says we are going to have Star Singing this year, and I can make a star and sing and march through town with the other kids." Liesl's eyelids drooped.

The old man hugged her. "I look forward to hearing you sing. It will remind me of when I was a boy in Switzerland with all my brothers and sisters."

"Did you have lots?"

"It seemed like it once, but now there is only my brother Victor."

"I don't have any brothers or sisters." Liesl yawned. "I wish I did. I would be the big sister, and I would have someone to play with every day."

Oscar barely refrained from wincing as a shaft of regret shot through him. If everything had gone according to his plans, Liesl would have an almost two-year-old sister by this time, and who knew? Maybe another sibling on the way.

"Time for bed, Poppet. You've had a big day." Oscar lifted his daughter into his arms. "Thanks, Martin."

Martin levered himself up, working a kink out of his back. "She is a treasure. Good night, little one." He caressed Liesl's head with his work-worn hand.

Inge wiped the kitchen table with slow strokes. She must be exhausted, too. The house had been cleaned and decorated, food prepared and every guest welcomed eagerly. "Will you want coffee?"

"If I do, I can make it. You should rest." Oscar paused in the stairway door. "Thank you for making the party so nice tonight. Everyone I spoke to seemed to be enjoying themselves."

Even him. If anyone had asked him six weeks ago if he would ever host a party at his house, and if he did, would he have a good time, he would've answered both those questions with a resounding "no."

At the top of the stairs, he whispered to Liesl, "Do you want to see if Miss Kate is still awake so you can say good night to her?"

She nodded against his shoulder.

Tapping on Kate's half-open door, he considered again how things had changed. Where at first he was resentful at the intrusion into his home, defensive and uneasy about having strangers at his table, digging in his cupboards, sleeping under his roof, now it seemed natural.

And he would miss them when they were gone.

"Come in?"

He peeked around the door. She sat up against the pillows, a scrap of cloth in her hands, her needle poking in and out. When she looked up, the blue of her eyes was like a blow to the chest. Would he ever get used to that? Her hair lay in a thick braid over her shoulder, and she had the red shawl wrapped around herself.

When she spied Liesl, she tucked her sewing away into the basket. "Aw, are you tuckered out, sweetling?"

Liesl leaned away from him, and he set her onto the bed where she crawled up to snuggle against Kate's side. Kate held her close. "Thank you for helping Grossmutter with the party. I knew I could count on you to take my place. Tomorrow, after you've had a nice sleep, you can tell me all about it, all right?"

"Can you come downstairs tomorrow?" Liesl yawned again.

Kate glanced up at Oscar. "Yes, but I have to take things easy. The doctor says that would be best for the baby and me. You go get your rest now, and have sweet dreams." She didn't seem as reluctant to follow the doctor's orders as she had been earlier in the day. Did that mean something *had* happened as a result of her fall? Or did she finally realize what *could* have happened? The look she gave him was soft and kind without a trace of the frustration she'd shown before.

Oscar bent to pick Liesl up once more. "You should get your rest now, too. Is there anything you need before bedtime?"

"No, I'm working on a few little sewing projects." She inclined her head toward Liesl, which he took to mean she was working on the dollhouse project.

"I'll say good night, then. Leave your door open a bit, and I'll do the same down the hall. That way I'll hear you if you need anything in the night." He'd toyed with the idea of putting an old cowbell on the table beside her bed so she could ring it if she went into labor at night, but he had hesitated, not knowing how she would take that. But now he promised to bring a bell up from the barn tomorrow.

He wished the baby was safely here. He wouldn't sleep well until it was over.

Chapter Thirteen

"I'm sure sitting at the kitchen table won't tax my strength any more than sitting in the rocker in the parlor." Kate pressed a drinking glass top into a sheet of cookie dough, cutting out a perfect circle. Oscar stood in the workshop doorway, frowning at her. "All the interesting things are going on here in the kitchen, and I want to be a part of them."

Liesl stood on a chair beside the sideboard, playing with her Advent Nativity blocks. The collection had grown to twenty-three pieces now. With only two more days until Christmas, the sideboard was full of wooden pieces. The child continued to amaze Kate with her imagination. Was that because she was an only child, and there was no one else to come up with ideas for what to play?

"What are you making?" Oscar closed the workshop door. He'd been spending a lot of time in there the past week, though he'd said he was finished with all the Christmas orders. That dollhouse must be taking him longer than he thought. He'd told Liesl that the room was off-limits for the time being, and he hooked the latch up high as insurance against her forgetting.

"*Mairlanderli*. Lemon cookies. Grossmutter made up this batch of dough right before she left, but she didn't have time to roll them out and bake them. She said she would bring back more candied lemon peel from town. These are Grossvater's favorite cookies, so she makes a lot of them this time of year. If we still had all our cookie cutters, we would have diamonds and crescents and trees. But this glass works well." It still surprised Kate the extent of their losses in the fire. Things she had always taken for granted, things she didn't miss until she needed them, kept cropping up in her memory.

"I expect Martin and Inge will be late? Where is the Advent celebration tonight?"

"It's at the Hales'. Mrs. Hale will be singing a couple of selections from the *Messiah*. She has such a beautiful soprano. I'm sure it will be lovely."

"And tomorrow is the Star Singing." Liesl jumped off the chair, her braids bouncing. "I have my star all ready. Grossmutter helped me make it." She ran to the living room and brought back a paper star the size of a dinner plate. "Grossvater bent this wire into a star shape, and Grossmutter helped me cut out a paper star and paste it on the wire." She held the star over her head by the wire handle. *"Stille Nacht! Heil'ge Nacht! Alles schläft, einsam wacht."*

Kate grinned. Grossmutter had been hard at work here. "You won't sing 'Silent Night' in German tomorrow, will you?"

"No. Grossmutter says we'll sing it in American."

Kate's glance connected with Oscar's, and she almost laughed aloud. Oscar's moustache twitched, and he coughed.

"But I like the way it sounds in German. That's the way Grossmutter sings it when she's cooking or cleaning." Liesl waved her paper star. "When I grow up, I want to be like Grossmutter."

Kate cut out the last cookie. "So do I." She placed the cookies on the sheet. "Oscar, would you put these in the oven for me?"

He slid the tray into the hot oven, and Kate checked the clock on the wall. "Those will only take a few minutes. My trouble with baking is that I get distracted and forget something's in the oven. Liesl, you'll have to remind me. It's easier if I'm making *Tirggel*. Those bake up in about ninety seconds, so there's no time to forget."

"Will you make *Tirggel* this year? And what is *Tirggel*?" Oscar folded the kitchen towel he'd used to protect his hand from getting burned.

Kate shook her head. "No. We don't have the wooden mold you need. *Tirggel* is a honey and flour cookie. The dough is pressed very thin with a wooden mold that has a picture carved into it, sometimes with a Christmas theme, but sometimes, like ours, it's a landscape scene. Grossmutter's was a carving of her childhood home, the town and the mountains and, very tiny in the distance, the chalet where she grew up."

"You lost it in the fire?" Oscar asked.

"Yes. Grossmutter brought it out every year to make *Tirggel*. She would make them early in the month, because according to her, the harder they get, the better they taste. But I liked them warm out of the oven, too." Though she'd only been an Amaker for not quite two years, she felt as if she had adopted their family history. After all, her baby would be an Amaker and their history would be his or hers. Her father had passed away when she was fourteen, and her mother six months later, so the Amakers were the only family she had left.

The sound of horses and a wagon turning into the drive caught their attention. Rolf rose from the rug in front of the fireplace with a low woof. Oscar went to the window and drew aside the curtain. "Looks like Martin and Inge got home sooner than we thought. I'll go help with the horses." He shrugged into his big, black coat and grabbed his hat.

Liesl put her star back in the parlor as Kate pushed herself up from her chair and began dipping water into the coffeepot. They would be cold from their trip. Grossmutter came inside, tugging her kerchief from her hair and shaking snowflakes from her sleeves.

"Ah." She sniffed. "You are baking the *Mairland-erli*. They are done, I think."

"Oh, mercy." Kate grabbed the kitchen towel and opened the oven door. "See, Liesl. I told you I would forget." She pulled the baking sheet from the oven and set it on a trivet on the table. The cookies were nicely browned around the edges, and as she slipped a knife under the edge and peeked, she blew out a sigh. They weren't burned. "How was the party tonight? You're home earlier than I expected."

Grossmutter hung her coat on the hook by the door and came to stand by the stove. "It was very nice, but we decided that with the snow, we should not stay long. Mrs. Hale loved the cake you helped me make, Liesl."

Liesl beamed.

Kate reached for the coffeepot once more, but Grossmutter took it from her hands. "You want to be sitting down when Oscar comes back."

Shaking her head at the conspiracy to coddle her, she resumed her seat at the table. "I feel restless. It was nice at first, loafing, sleeping during the day, keeping my feet up and letting you all wait on me, but all day I've had the urge to work." She leaned back, trying to draw a good, deep breath, something that was more and more difficult to do these days. "I find myself wanting to scrub a floor or wash the windows. Which is silly, because I don't even like washing windows."

Grossmutter eyed her closely. "You are nesting. That is often a sign that the baby will come soon. Are you having any pains?"

"No, not labor pains, though I am uncomfortable and ready for this baby to get here." She piled the cookie-making paraphernalia into the mixing bowl. "It could be any time now, but I don't think I'm due for another week or so."

"Babies come when babies decide to come, and it doesn't matter if they are early or late, the last week is always the hardest on the mama." Grossmutter set the coffeepot on the stove to heat and dipped water from the warming reservoir into the dishpan. "Oh, Liesl, I brought something from town for you. Mrs. Hale gave every family a gift." She went to her coat and removed a little bundle from the pocket. "I thought we could hang it in the doorway between the kitchen and the parlor."

"What is it?" Liesl stood on tiptoe as Grossmutter bent down and unwrapped the package.

"It is called mistletoe. It was used in ancient times as a medicine, but now it is hung up at Christmastime, and when two people meet under the mistletoe, it is customary for them to share a kiss." She held up the bundle of green leaves with white berries. The sprig had been tied with a red ribbon.

The kitchen door opened, and Martin walked in, followed by Oscar. Oscar's eyes went to Kate, found her sitting in a chair and seemed satisfied.

"Look, Daddy. It's mistletoes." Liesl pointed. "Grossmutter says it makes people kiss."

Martin grinned and took the mistletoe, holding it over Inge's white hair and giving her a peck on the lips. "It looks like it works well enough." He handed it to Liesl. "Try it out."

She climbed onto a chair and held it up to Oscar, but it was still a foot or so from being over his head, so he lifted her up. She gave him a smacking kiss on the cheek, just over his beard.

Kate sighed, and when Oscar looked at her, she put on a smile. At the moment, she felt a bit lonely, the odd person out. The baby thumped low on her side, and she smiled. Soon, she'd have someone of her very own again.

Oscar hung the mistletoe in the doorway for Inge, going so far as to give her a quick kiss on the cheek and a wink when she stood beneath it. "Hard to believe Christmas is only two days away. If I'm going to get everything done that I need to, I'd better get back into the workshop. Martin, I could use some help if you would." He turned to Liesl. "Remember, no going into the shop."

"I know." She pursed her lips. "But I need more wood for my 'Ativity set." Checking the calendar on the wall where she had faithfully marked each passing day with a red *X*, she said, "Two more."

"Which pieces do you still need?" Kate asked. She had been amazed at Liesl's memory. No matter how many pieces she added, she knew each one, and they never changed.

"Joseph for tomorrow, and on Christmas, Baby Jesus."

"I'll bring you some new wood blocks. For now, why don't you help with the dishes, and maybe Miss Kate will read you a story or two before bedtime."

He took the coffee cup Grossmutter offered him, and Martin carried his cup and a plate of cookies into the workshop.

Kate looked at the calendar. Two days until Christmas, then how many until the baby came? And how many more days after that before they were on their way to Cincinnati, leaving everything they loved behind?

"I'm glad of your help." Oscar sipped the hot coffee. "I should've asked for it sooner. I'm not sure I'm going to be able to finish a project I took on, and just tonight, I learned of something else I'd like to make before Christmas morning."

Martin inclined his head to the cloth draping Liesl's gift, his brows lifted. At Oscar's nod, he raised one corner of the sheet. The dollhouse was complete and had been for more than a week. The furnishings had taken the longest, a little stove, table and chairs, a bed and dresser, a bench. Everything was simple and tailored for a four-year-old. As she grew older he could make more intricate furnishings.

Oscar picked up a little pillow from the small bed. "Kate made the mattress and little blankets, and the curtains and cushions and such."

"Liesl is going to love it." Martin examined one of the rugs, crocheted by Kate into a multicolored oval.

"I hope so. Kate made a little family for it, too." Oscar pointed to the kitchen where a man, a woman and a little girl sat. They were made of cloth and filled with sawdust, with yarn hair and ink eyes and mouths. The little girl wore a dress made out of a scrap of material left over from one of Liesl's new dresses. "I think Liesl will be happy with it."

Martin chuckled. "This reminds me of something my mother used to say back in Switzerland. We had a small cabin and there were many Amaker children. Sometimes my father would bemoan the fact that we didn't have a bigger house. But my mother always said, 'A small house can hold as much happiness as a big one.' I never forgot that." He scratched his beard, his eyes far away. "I told Johann that when he wanted to build the bigger house. Always moving, always dreaming, always planning something new. That was Johann." Martin seemed to come back from wherever his mind had wandered. "What is it that I can help you with?"

Oscar showed him the project he'd been working on for the past month and more, hoping Martin's reception of the idea would indicate what Kate might think of it on Christmas morning.

The older man nodded thoughtfully, stroking his beard, pushing his glasses up higher on his nose and bending to study the detail. "It is beautiful. Unique, but also like the original."

"Do you think she'll like it? It isn't very practical." With all the things the Amakers needed, spending so much time on something that wasn't necessary might seem foolish.

"Sometimes we need things that are beautiful to look at and serve no other purpose than the pleasure they give us. They make us feel better." Martin ran his hand over a satiny curve of wood.

His pronouncement quelled some of Oscar's doubts and increased his anticipation of Christmas morning. "There's something else that I need your help with, too. Kate told me that your wife made a kind of cookie that needs a wooden mold. The one she lost in the fire was a picture of her home in the Old Country? I thought maybe I could try my hand at carving one, if you would sketch out what the mold looks like and the picture."

Martin looked away, his back going stiff.

Oscar closed his eyes, tipping his head back. "I'm sorry, Martin. We don't have to make one." It was obviously upsetting to the old man.

Turning back, Martin shook his head, digging out his handkerchief and dabbing at his eyes. "No, son, it is just that you are so thoughtful. Inge has felt the loss of that *Tirggel* mold. It belonged to her mother. That you would make her a new one…" He blew his nose. "I am a sentimental old man these days. Anything will make me cry. I will help you. And Inge will love your gift."

"I thought you might like to be the one to give it to her." Oscar reached into the rack and chose a nice, straight-grained piece of white hard maple. It wouldn't be the easiest to carve, but hard maple didn't have a lot of oils or resins in it that might make food taste odd. And it would last a very long time.

"Perhaps it can be a gift from both of us." Martin picked up a pencil, and Oscar pointed him to the small stack of blank paper he kept for designing projects.

While Martin sketched and Oscar picked out the gouges and mallets he would need, Martin talked. "When I was in town, I received three letters. The postmaster brought them to me at Mrs. Hale's." He frowned. "I am not much of an artist. I will need to tell you what I have drawn, because I don't think you will know from how it looks."

"We can figure it out."

"I have not spoken of the letters to Inge or Kate. I wanted to talk with you about them and get your advice. The first letter was from Mr. Siddons. He has named a price for my farm and livestock." Martin drew a jagged line of what Oscar supposed were mountains on the paper, not looking up. "It was a very fair offer. More than I would have expected. Enough to pay off the debt on the farm, and enough to get us to Cincinnati with enough left over to perhaps rent a place of our own."

Oscar's heart grew heavy at the sadness in his voice. And the thought of losing his neighbor just as he was getting to know him. He regretted the years he'd spent keeping everyone away. Why was it that he only realized what he had when it was too late to do much about it?

"The second letter was from my brother. It seems he has needed to hire a janitor to replace the one that left. He cannot wait until we get there to have the factory clean, so that job is no longer available. But he has said I can fill the role of night watchman, patrolling the factory grounds from dusk to dawn. The pay is less, and the apartment will not be available now. But it is a job. With the money from the farm, we would manage to get by." He drew little boxes, which Oscar took to be the village, including one smaller one on the mountainside. In the front, he drew in a lake. "He has said that Inge can make a little money on the side by doing some cooking and cleaning at his house. He has a cook that lives in his house, but he must give her one day off a week, so Inge could cook for him on that day."

Oscar couldn't imagine Martin, bundled to the eyes, carrying a lantern, walking around a factory, testing locks. What kind of brother did he have that would be so cavalier about his family in need? And to have his elderly sister-in-law doing household chores for him when he was obviously in a position to hire staff? Oscar clamped down on what he wanted to say. "How big should this mold be?"

Martin indicated with his hand a rectangle about four inches by six. Oscar marked the lines with a pencil and straight edge and began sawing.

"The third letter..." Martin paused and drew the envelopes out of his pocket, sorting one out and opening it. "It was from a mercantile in Saint Paul where we sold some of our cheeses. The owner says his customers like the cheese very much, and that he would like to purchase all we can produce next year. He wishes to become the sole distributor of Amaker cheeses in the state. He is offering a very good price, one that, if I was able to keep the farm, I would agree to without hesitation. Johann dreamed of something like this someday. I wish he was alive to see it."

Oscar nodded. "I know how you feel. I had that same thought about tomorrow's Star Singing in town. Liesl is so excited, and I wish Gaelle could be here to enjoy it all." He waited for the familiar crush of regret and grief. But while the regret was there, the grief wasn't as sweeping and all-consuming as it had been.

"Time is strange. Time heals, there is no doubt about that." Martin laid his pencil down. "And yet, time is cruel, too. If so much time had not passed in my life, if I was a younger man, the bank would extend my loan and I could keep my farm. But I am not a young man, and I never will be again. I worry about leaving Inge and Kate alone with no one to provide for them." He rubbed his hands down his face. "I know that God loves my family even more than I do, and that He is not surprised by all that has happened to us. I know He will care for us…but it is hard not to worry."

"Or hard not to want to blame God. Knowing that God is all-powerful, knowing that He could prevent bad things from happening to us… Sometimes it's hard to reconcile that with the truth that God loves us and that His plans for us are for our good." Oscar picked up the sketch and began transferring the lines onto the wood. "I've been trying to teach Liesl that just because we want something or because we pray very hard for something, it doesn't mean that we will get it. Sometimes God has to say no."

"God does say 'no' sometimes. And He says 'yes' sometimes. But for me, the most difficult one is when He says 'wait.' I am not good at waiting." Martin gave a rueful smile. "I think the hardest part about waiting for God to answer my prayers is because I don't know if I am waiting for a 'yes' or a 'no' or for more 'wait.'"

"What are you going to do about your letters?"

With a shrug, Martin folded the pages and returned them to his pocket. "I am going to pray. One thing I do know. My faith grows best when it is tested."

"Martin, would you wait to answer them? Until after Christmas? Those things can wait for a few days, can't they? Put them aside for now and, as you say, pray about them. Enjoy the season here, and after Christmas, you can decide what is best to do." The burden the Amakers had been carrying for so long… surely they could lay it down for a few days. "Maybe not even tell Inge and Kate about them until you have to? That way they can enjoy Christmas without more worry, too?"

And Oscar realized that he was going to have to make some decisions about his life, too. The way he had been living over the past couple of years couldn't go on. Not for Liesl's sake, nor for his own. He needed to move on.

But was moving on the same as forgetting?

Chapter Fourteen

"I promise, I won't stir a step without you. I'll even stay in the wagon if you can drive up close enough that I can see the children." Kate put her hand on Oscar's arm. "Please. I don't want to miss this. And no one else here should, either. If I have to stay home, you won't let me stay alone, so who would have to remain with me?"

She took a deep breath, trying to keep her emotions…which were behaving like a deer trying to run on the ice…under control. For the past month she'd looked forward to attending the Star Singing, had helped Liesl learn the Christmas carols, had sewn her Christmas dress, which she wore now, twirling in circles to bell out the skirt. If Kate had to stay behind, and someone else had to stay with her… She blinked hard against the pricking high in her nose and the watering of her eyes.

"You need rest right now." His brow furrowed.

"I've never felt better. Maybe it's cabin fever, maybe it's 'nesting' like Inge said, but I feel restless, like I need to be doing something. And I've looked forward to this day for weeks."

He didn't look convinced. All the grown-ups waited for his verdict.

"Daddy, look," Liesl interrupted, pointing. "You're standing under the mistletoes." Her grin split her face. "Now you get to give Miss Kate a kiss."

Everyone in the room went still. Kate's eyes collided with Oscar's, and warmth spread up her neck into her face. She could read nothing in Oscar's expression, but his eyes darkened.

She swallowed, and her tongue darted out to moisten her suddenly dry lips. His gaze followed the motion like a hawk on a mouse.

"Go ahead, Daddy," Liesl prompted.

A small uptick at the corner of his mouth, as if a chuckle had almost worked its way out, caught her attention. He glanced up at the bundle hanging from the lintel, inches above his head, and rubbed his palm on the back of his neck.

"Kate?"

Kate matched his almost laugh with an embarrassed smile of her own. She nodded her permission. He would give her a quick peck on the cheek, and that would be it. But if that was so, why on earth was she wondering if his beard felt as soft as it looked, and if his lips would be firm and warm?

Then he had his hands on her upper arms, and as he bent his head, she held still, not knowing which cheek he would kiss…but he didn't opt for her cheek. His lips met hers, and in an instant, several of her questions were answered and a hundred more popped into her head.

His beard *was* as soft as it looked, and his lips *were* firm and warm against hers. She was too surprised to even close her eyes, and she had no idea how long the kiss lasted, but long enough for her to feel as if... should he loosen his grasp on her arms...she might spin right out into space.

Then he straightened, slanting a look at Liesl. "Fair enough?"

"Good job, Daddy." Liesl climbed up to check on her "'Ativity" scene on the sideboard. "Now Mary and Joseph are here. We just have to wait for Baby Jesus."

If Kate had thought her emotions were a skittery jumble before, she had been mistaken. A kite in a tornado had more control of itself. Kate didn't know where to look. Was her face as red as it felt? Here she was, as big as a barn with this baby, widowed less than a year, and all she could think about was how nice it was to be kissed by Oscar Rabb.

What was wrong with her?

She caught Inge's eye, and her grandmother-in-law's lips trembled and her eyes sparkled. Martin coughed, but he couldn't quite cover his laugh.

Oscar cleared his throat and drew her into the kitchen, away from the mistletoe. "You should stay home, you know."

Her heart dropped out of its rosy bemusement back to reality.

"But," he continued, "if you promise to be care-ful, to let me help you and to stay where I put you while we're in town, you can go." He held her gaze effortlessly.

Swoop! Her heart soared again, and not just because

she was going to get to go, but because of the warm look in his dark eyes, at the cloud of...awareness... that seemed to encircle them.

"Is it time to go yet, Daddy?" Liesl had been asking all day. Oscar turned, shoving his hands into his pockets.

"Not yet, Poppet. Why don't you help pack up the goodies Mrs. Amaker is taking tonight?"

When it was time to get ready to go, Kate burst out laughing. Oscar came down from upstairs with what looked like every blanket in the house in his arms. "What are you doing?"

"I don't want anyone to get cold, and these will make the ride more comfortable, too."

Martin came in from the front porch. "The horses are ready. It's a beautifully clear night, but it is going to be a cold one." He blew on his hands.

"See." Oscar handed Inge a couple of the heaviest quilts. "Warm these by the stove. I'll put the rest in the wagon."

Kate helped Liesl into her red and black plaid coat and tugged on her little mittens. "You need to keep your hat on, missy." She stretched the knitted cap over the pinned-up braids and tied the bobbles beneath Liesl's chin. "Do you have your star?"

"I'll get it." She scampered into the parlor.

"I don't know who is more excited, her or me." Kate reached for her burgundy cloak, but Oscar, coming back into the kitchen, took it from her hands and draped it over her shoulders, tying the strings under her chin.

"Are those bricks ready?" Oscar asked.

"Yes. I wrapped them in towels to keep them hot."

Martin hefted the laundry basket. "I'll go put them into the wagon."

Inge took one last turn around the house, making sure every candle and lamp was extinguished, and that the fire in the stove was well-banked with every door closed and the damper drawn down. They still had no idea how the fire had started at their house, but since that night, she took every precaution.

Oscar insisted on carrying Kate to the wagon and settling her into the deep bed of hay on the pile of blankets. Martin put a hot brick at her feet, and Inge covered her with one of the quilts she'd warmed in front of the stove.

"I feel like the princess in your storybook, Liesl."

Liesl climbed in and snuggled under the blanket with her, careful not to mar her paper star. Martin helped Inge into the back and took the seat up front with Oscar. With a clash of bells, the horses started.

Hundreds of stars shone overhead, and the sled runners squeaked on the snow. Over all, the cheerful jingle of the sleigh bells competed with the clop of the horses' hooves.

Kate wanted to treasure this moment in time, so she could remember it in the coming days and weeks when things were hard. She still couldn't quite wrap her mind around the thought that, in less than a month, they would be leaving this place, these people.

And she knew that leaving the people would be even harder than leaving the place. Wrapping her arm tighter around Liesl, she bit her lip to stay her tears.

They crossed the bridge into Berne, and Liesl could sit still no longer. She crawled across Kate's legs toward the front of the wagon to stand behind her father.

Lights shone from many windows, making blocks of golden orange on the snow and deepening the shadows to blue and purple.

"We're meeting in the churchyard, and the children will march around 'The Circle.'" Martin's breath plumed as he gave Oscar the instructions. "Then we meet back at the church for the service."

Kate shifted on the straw as her back complained. The ride had been fairly smooth, but in spite of the blankets and straw, it was difficult to find a comfortable position.

Wagons lined the side streets, but several men were directing folks to stay away from the parade route, to keep it clear. Oscar bent to talk to Bill Zank, who stood in the middle of Buchanan Street with his lantern.

"Sure, go ahead, then drive over by the church to tie up."

Oscar turned onto Jackson Street and stopped in front of Hale's Mercantile. He jumped down onto the snow and came around the back of the wagon.

"I'll drop you ladies off here." He pulled the cottar pins out of the tailgate and lowered it. "Liesl, you wait there. All the children are meeting Mrs. Tipford at the church to line up."

Gently, he helped Inge to the ground and offered her his arm for the few steps to the front porch of the store. Lamps burned on every porch post, and a crowd of townsfolk milled, waiting and talking. Oscar returned to the wagon and reached in for Kate.

"I can walk easily enough," she reminded him as he lifted her into his arms. He smelled of sawdust and winter air, and he held her firmly, his arms strong bands behind her shoulders and beneath her knees.

"I know, but then you'd deprive me of the chance to show off." He grinned, his face close to hers, and she remembered the wonder and thrill of his kiss.

"Right here," Mrs. Hale called from the porch. "I have a place all ready for her." People stepped aside, and Mrs. Hale stood beside a blanket-covered chair. She flitted and fluttered, twitching the blanket, moving the chair until it sat just so. "My dear, I was perfectly astonished when I saw you. I thought you'd surely stay home tonight."

Oscar bent and set Kate into the chair, holding her gaze. "Martin and I will be back soon."

"Thank you." She adjusted her cloak and skirts. "And thank you, Mrs. Hale. I'll be most comfortable."

"You're a brave woman. I don't think I put my nose out the door for two months before each of my children was born."

Inge carried one of the quilts and draped it around Kate's shoulders. "It can get cold, sitting."

Liesl waved from the back of the wagon as Oscar pulled away. Kate's heart swelled with love for the little girl, so exuberant and vivacious. How was she going to bear to leave her behind when the time came?

Neighbors and townsfolk greeted her and Inge. There were more people this year for the parade, it seemed.

"Oh, yes, the township has almost a thousand people living here now." Mrs. Hale rewrapped her scarf. "Did Martin get his letters? I can't remember the last time someone got three letters all at once, and from as far away as Saint Paul and Cincinnati. I half expected to see him at the post office with replies, especially to Mr. Siddons's letter."

Kate caught Inge's eye. Martin hadn't mentioned letters to her. Inge gave a tiny shake of her head. Inge put her hand on Kate's shoulder, squeezing. They would discuss this later, out of earshot of the eager Mrs. Hale.

Oscar and Martin arrived, and Inge threaded her arm through her husband's. Oscar came to stand beside Kate. "All right?"

"Yes." She shifted on the chair, pressing her hand against her middle. "Did Liesl find the right place?"

"She's practically floating across the snow. I left her to Mrs. Tipford's tender mercies." Oscar stood behind Kate's chair, his hands on her shoulders.

"Are you trying to make sure I stay where you put me?" She turned her head and smiled up at him.

"Something like that."

"Here they come!" a man up the street yelled.

"Silent night, holy night, all is calm, all is bright." Children's voices, high and pure, rose into the night, and the watchers grew quiet. Slowly, in pairs, with stars raised high, the children marched behind two of the older boys who carried lanterns on poles to light the way.

Kate found Liesl in the front, face bathed in light from the lantern, the white fur from her hood hiding her hat, her mittens gripping the handle of her star. She tilted her head slightly as they drew up opposite the store until she spied the people she was looking for. Breaking protocol, she waved to them, her smile a little sunbeam of pure joy.

"God rest ye merry, gentlemen, let nothing you

dismay." The children, nearly thirty in all, marched down the street, turning from Jackson onto Clay. Their voices carried through the clear night air, and as they marched, the onlookers joined in with the tune. Even a block over on Mill Street, Kate could hear when the song changed to "Hark! The Herald Angels Sing."

Kate shifted in her chair again. "Oscar, can you help me stand?"

He was at her side instantly. "What do you need?"

"Just to get to my feet. I think it would be easier. I've had a bit of a backache today, and this chair isn't helping."

He put out his arms for her to hold on to, and she slid to the edge of the seat and stood. "Maybe we need to head home."

"No, this is better. All bent over like that, it's hard to get enough air in my lungs sometimes." She smiled. "Should we start toward the church? If we go now, we'll be able to see them come around the corner."

Others had the same idea, and Oscar held Kate back until the porch steps were clear. The church was across the street from the north end of the mercantile, perhaps forty yards away.

"This time, I will walk."

"If you do, you'll have to put up with my arm around your waist."

"What waist?" She laughed. "But I will be grateful for your assistance."

His support along her lower back pushed away some of the ache. The board sidewalk extended to the street corner, and someone had cleared it of snow, so the early going wasn't too bad. When they crossed the street, Oscar slowed their pace to a crawl, and Kate concentrated on walking carefully across the packed and rutted snow.

To their right, the children turned back onto Buchanan, the lanterns swinging on the poles.

"She's having the time of her life." Oscar helped Kate onto the church steps. "I wonder if she will sleep at all tonight."

"Eventually, but the anticipation is good. It's good to have something for which to look forward." She paused, wincing. "My back is going to be glad when this baby is born. It's been achy off and on all day."

"Let's get you inside to a seat before the kids get here."

As they entered the small vestibule, they nearly collided with Martin. He had been backed up to the door by a tall, gray-haired man, and when Kate leaned to the side, she saw it was Mr. Siddons. What was he doing here on Christmas Eve?

"I'm telling you, Amaker. It's a fair price. I want the deal done by New Year's. I've got a crew of men coming over from Mankato, and they're going to see about moving that barn off the property to a place near West Concord. Just take the deal." Mr. Siddons was crowding Martin, looming over him.

Oscar put himself between Kate and the men and said, "Is there a problem here?"

His voice was low, but the strength in it sent a thrill through Kate.

"No problem," Mr. Siddons snapped. "Except that this old fool doesn't know a good offer when he hears one."

"Gentlemen, I would suggest we continue this discussion at a more appropriate time."

Mr. Siddons glared, but he stepped aside so the churchgoers could continue to file in. "I suggest you talk to Kleiner over at the bank, because I bought the note on your farm yesterday. Either you make the mortgage payment on the second of January, or I take the farm. If you're going to sell, you should sell now before I just take the property when you can't pay the mortgage. I'll get it sooner or later, so it might as well be sooner."

Kate gripped Oscar's arm. Mr. Siddons now held the note on their farm?

Oscar's hand came down over hers, and he squeezed. "Don't worry. We'll sort it out. For now, forget about it." He guided her past Siddons, indicating that Martin should go into the church ahead of them. As he drew abreast of Mr. Siddons, he said, "Come out to the farm on the second, and we'll settle the matter then. Until then, leave the Amakers alone."

Inge waited in a pew on the left-hand side, and Kate followed Martin in and sat down. She removed her mittens and scarf and untied her cloak. Oscar sat beside her, shedding his own outer garments, his face stern. The encounter in the vestibule had unsettled her, and she was glad Oscar had been there to take charge.

"Grossvater? What are we going to do?"

He patted her hand and shook his head. "You are not to worry about it. I am not going to worry, either. I promised Oscar that I would enjoy Christmas, and I want you to promise me that you will, too. Remember that not even a sparrow falls but that our Heavenly Father knows. And you're more valuable to Him than a sparrow."

Kate nodded, but it was hard to quell the disquiet in her heart.

The church was well-lit, with the reflectors behind the wall lamps spreading illumination to every corner and the pendant lamps shining on their long chains. The coal stove glowed cherry-red, and Pastor Tipford stood at the front with his hands clasped before him, rocking on his toes, a broad smile on his face.

The children lined up at the back door, their shoes scuffling on the hardwood, whispering and giggling and milling about as they all found their places. Mrs. Tipford entered, walking backward so she could see her little charges. Two-by-two they came up the aisle, holding their stars high, singing "The First Noel" in high, clear voices. Liesl lined up on the front row as they turned to face the congregation. Mrs. Hale pumped away on the little organ.

Kate looked from one face to the next, returning often to Liesl's, and a lump grew in her throat. This was her church. This was her place. These were the people who helped make her who and what she was.

How could she leave them? Leave all that was dear and familiar? How could she bear to say goodbye?

Liesl's head bobbed she sang with such gusto, her hair pinned up in braids crossed over her crown, her cheeks red from walking in the cold, her white pinafore snowy. When Kate was gone, hundreds of miles to the east, Liesl would grow up, go to school, learn and change and expand her horizons.

And Kate would miss all of it.

And Liesl wouldn't be the only one Kate missed as if a piece of her heart had been left behind.

Her leg brushed Oscar's as she tried to find a comfortable position on the hard pew, and his nearness sent awareness ricocheting through her. When she left Minnesota, she would also be leaving Oscar.

Oscar, who started out remote and cool to the idea of opening his home, but who had turned out to be kindness itself. He'd allowed every corner of his life to be invaded, and though he had tried to shield himself and his daughter from involvement, he'd become entangled in the Amakers' affairs from the very beginning.

She wore clothes he had given her, ate food at his table, sat by his fireside for warmth. She got to love and cherish his daughter, conspire with him to create a Christmas gift for her, watch him craft things out of wood and his imagination. She had worked alongside him, watched him, and somewhere along the way, she had fallen in love with him.

Closing her eyes, she concentrated on that thought.

She loved Oscar Rabb.

How could that be, when she loved Johann so very much? Her love for Johann had been a whirlwind. He'd caught her up in his excitement, pursued her with ardor, won her easily with his charm and vision and big ideas. They had met, courted and been married within the space of three months.

And Oscar was his complete opposite. Steady, thoughtful, guarded, careful. He made her heart feel sheltered and cherished, though he'd never displayed any romantic feelings for her. The kiss under the mistletoe didn't count, did it? Since he'd practically been forced into kissing her by his daughter.

Though he could've kissed her on the cheek instead of the lips.

She opened her eyes and realized that Oscar was looking at her with a frown. "Are you all right?" he whispered as the children filed off the platform to find their parents and Mr. Tipford took his place in the pulpit.

His eyes were close to hers, the same color as Liesl's, the rich brown of the walnut he used in his furniture making. Her breath caught somewhere high in her lungs.

She couldn't speak, so only nodded, and though she felt she could stare into his eyes forever, she forced herself to face forward. Paying attention to the sermon was beyond her ability at the moment, but she must at least appear to be listening.

Of course, she could never let on to him that she loved him. He would neither want nor accept her love. His heart still firmly belonged to Gaelle. He'd been in mourning for two years, and from what she could tell, he'd never contemplated taking another wife, even though that would've eased his burdens considerably.

Oscar turned and picked Liesl up when she returned to their pew, setting her in his lap so she could lean back against his chest. He put his arms around her and brushed his beard on the top of her head.

Kate shifted again, pressing her palms into the hard seat and squirming. Inge leaned forward and studied her, questions in her eyes. Kate shook her head, giving Inge a rueful smile, apologizing without words for being so fidgety.

The service finally ended, and they were on their way out of the church when Kate stopped on the steps, the pain in her back growing sharp, taking her breath. She winced, gripping the handrail and bending slightly at the waist.

"What's wrong? Did the baby kick you again?" Oscar handed Liesl over to Martin and took Kate's arm.

"No, it's just this backache." The pain eased some and she straightened. "It's been coming and going all afternoon."

Mrs. Frankel, coming through the church door with her baby in her arms, said, "All afternoon? Sounds like you might be starting your labor."

"Oh, no, it's just a backache." Kate closed her cloak collar against the cold night air. "I'm sure I would know if I was in labor. It doesn't feel anything like the doctor told me to expect."

"Honey, I've been through this a dozen times. Doctors are well and good, but they're men, and they don't know bees from a bull's foot about being in labor. The pains can come a lot of ways, and a backache is one of them. I'd advise you to get home right smart. And if you want, as soon as I get the children bedded down, I'll come over."

Patsy Frankel had a comforting brusqueness about her that calmed Kate. She was sure the older woman was wrong, but at the moment, getting back to the house and into bed sounded like a wonderful idea.

"Thank you. I'd like that."

Oscar stood still as if stuck to the porch boards. "You're saying her time's come?" His voice sounded hollow and dry.

"Most likely." Patsy checked to see that her little one was covered with the blanket. "George, round up the kids. It's time to go." She patted Kate's arm. "Don't you worry. First babies take an age. I'll be there as soon as I can."

Jerking like a statue suddenly come to life, Oscar shook himself. "Wait here and I'll bring the wagon around." He held out his hands. "Don't do anything until I get back."

He vaulted the porch railing and rounded the church. He would be back soon, so why was Kate feeling so scared and abandoned right now?

The baby was coming.

That was the only thought Oscar could muster as he urged the horses into a steady trot. Every few seconds, he checked back over his shoulder to where Kate lay on the straw. Inge patted her hand, and Kate protested that she wasn't sick. The pain wasn't bad, and they were all overreacting.

And the panic he'd been suppressing grew claws and hiked its way up his rib cage.

Martin leaned close. "Do you think I should ride into Mantorville for the doctor?"

"No, you should stay at the house and do whatever the women need—heat water or keep the fire stoked or… I don't know. I'll go for the doc." Oscar slapped the lines again. If he had known she was going to start the baby, there was no way he would've let her take so much as a single step out of the house tonight. What had he been thinking?

He'd been thinking of how blue her eyes were, and how, when she asked him for anything, something in his chest sort of burst from its bonds. He found himself wanting to do everything he could for her.

He had found himself thinking about that kiss. The first kiss he'd shared with a woman in two years.

Putting the brakes on that thought, he concentrated on getting them home quickly and safely.

"Daddy, is Miss Kate sick?" Liesl clung to the seat back.

"No, Poppet. She's not sick."

"Why do you need the doctor, then?"

How much should he tell her? "It seems it might be time for Miss Kate to get her baby, and doctors can be right helpful when it's time for a new baby."

Liesl's face brightened. "Oh, good. I've been praying forever."

They turned onto the farm road, crossed the bridge and swung into the yard. Rolf greeted them with a deep woof, coming up off his place on the porch. Martin went to help Inge, and Oscar plucked Liesl up and set her on the porch. "Go on inside and hang up your coat. I'll bring Miss Kate."

He rounded the back of the wagon. Kate had her head down, and he reached out with his gloved hand to touch her chin and lift her face. "How are you doing?"

"I'd be lying if I said I wasn't a little bit scared." Her pupils were so big her eyes looked dark.

"Me, too, but you're going to do great. I'll get you settled in the house and head out for the doctor. And Mrs. Frankel will be here soon. She's done this plenty of times."

Her lips trembled, but she nodded.

"Are you having any pain now?" He didn't want to jostle her or try to pick her up if she was hurting.

"No."

"Then put your arms around my neck, and we'll have you inside in a flash." He gave her a wink that belied how jittery his insides were behaving.

Inge had the lamps lit, and Martin was stirring up the fire when Oscar came in, heading straight for the stairs. The minute he had Kate in her room with Inge coming along behind, he headed back out the door.

Martin met Oscar on the porch with a lantern. "Do you want to take the team, or do you want to saddle a horse?"

"I'll take the team, just in case the doc wants to ride back with me."

"Take your time. It is very dark, and the roads might be bad." He fastened the lantern to the wagon seat beside Oscar to help light his way.

"Right." Oscar knew he wouldn't be able to take his time. But he wouldn't be foolhardy, either, because an injured horse or broken wagon wouldn't help Kate, either.

The road to Mantorville was rutted and well-traveled, which helped him see where to go. A few clouds had drifted in from the north, muting the stars.

Thankfully, Dr. Horlock was at home, though Oscar felt bad taking him from his family on Christmas Eve night.

"Don't worry," the doctor said as he wrapped well against the cold. "Babies seem to like to come on holidays and at night. My family is used to the hours I keep."

Dr. Horlock told Oscar to go ahead while he followed on his saddle horse. "That way you won't have to bring me back later, especially if this is false labor."

A couple miles from Mantorville, the doctor caught up with Oscar and passed him, and when Oscar arrived back at the house, Martin met him at the door.

"How's it going?"

"Fine, I suppose. Mrs. Frankel is here, and the doctor. I'll put the horses away for you. You have to be cold. The fire's roaring in there, and I've boiled enough water to fill a lake." He smiled, but his voice was tense.

"Where's Liesl?"

"She's in the kitchen. Didn't want to go to bed until you got back."

Oscar bounded up the steps and into the kitchen, a blast of heat smacking him in the face. Liesl stood on her chair by the sideboard, moving the wood blocks on the tablecloth.

"Hey, Poppet." Oscar unwound his scarf, pulling it and his hat off together. "I think it's time for bed."

She pursed her lips. "But will the baby come soon? I want to see him."

He picked her up, tossing her as high as the ceiling would allow. "It takes a long time to get a baby, and you need your sleep. Anyway, it's Christmas Eve, and if you want to wake up to your presents, you need to get to bed." He set her on the chair, then turned around and squatted. Liesl climbed onto his back for the ride upstairs. "You keep calling the baby 'him.' You do know that it could be a girl, right?"

She laid her head on his shoulder, her arms around his neck. "Yes, but I think it will be a boy. I asked Jesus for a boy baby."

"I'm just praying that he or she will get here safely, and that everyone will be healthy." Oscar helped Liesl with her bedtime routine. He left the hall lamp burning and her door half-open. "Good night, Poppet. Sweet dreams, and I will see you in the morning. You did a beautiful job with the singing, and I was very proud of you."

As he passed Kate's room on his way back downstairs, he paused. When the door opened, he started. Dr. Horlock came into the hall, wiping his hands on a towel, and as he closed the door, Oscar glimpsed Kate's dark hair on the pillow, and Mrs. Frankel bending over her.

"How is she?"

"She's doing well. It sounds like she went into labor early in the afternoon, but didn't realize it. Attributed it to backache. It happens that way with some women. But she'll be a while yet." He indicated for Oscar to precede him down the steps. "Time for some coffee. And Mrs. Amaker says there are enough cookies and treats in the house to feed an army of doctors."

Oscar nodded. "I am beginning to learn that the way Mrs. Amaker shows her love and care is through sweets. I don't know how I haven't gained ten pounds in the last couple months."

Dr. Horlock took a chair at the table, leaning back, relaxed, but Oscar couldn't sit still. He paced from the front window to the workshop door, into the parlor and back to the stove. Martin came in from the barn, brows raised to see the doctor in the kitchen.

"Is it over, then?"

"No. It will be a while yet. The women will call

me when I'm needed." Dr. Horlock sampled a square of *Brunsli*.

"You don't think that fall she took last week did her any harm, do you?" Oscar leaned on his palms on the back of one of the kitchen chairs. "Or being out tonight?"

The doctor shook his head. "I was recently going through the medical records that my predecessor left when I took over his practice. Kate's situation is nothing like what happened to your wife." He glanced up. "I'm sorry about that. But there is no reason to think history is going to repeat itself here. Kate is in fine health, the baby has been quite active and she has suffered no ill effects from the little tumble she took. I imagine that in a few hours the house will be filled with some rather loud squalling, and you'll wish for some peace and quiet."

It all reminded Oscar so much of that night, two years ago, when he'd paced the kitchen, waiting and waiting for the sound of a baby's cry. The house seemed to close in around him. His heart thundered in his ears.

"Oscar, maybe we should go into the workroom." Martin took his elbow. "We have a few things to be finishing before morning. It will be good to keep our hands and minds busy. Herr Doctor, you are welcome to join us."

"If you don't mind, I think I'll stretch out on the settee in the parlor for a while. It's going to be a late night." He rose, stretched and sauntered into the parlor.

Oscar's hands fisted. How could the doctor be so casual?

"Come, Oscar." Martin nudged him into the work-room and brought one of the lamps from the table.

It was just as well that there was no intricate work that needed to be done. Oscar felt as if his mind was wrapped in cotton wool. Martin gave him a carved piece and a bit of sandpaper, but over and over, Oscar's hands fell to his lap and his mind refused to focus on the work.

How had he come to be in this place in his life? He, who had vowed never to open his heart to anyone else, to never be this vulnerable to hurt again? Then Kate Amaker had dropped into his life and everything had changed.

"It's hard, isn't it?" Martin asked.

"What?" Oscar blinked.

"To wait. When we care so much about the outcome." Martin set down the piece he was working on. "The past two months have been very difficult, waiting. Waiting to see what God would have us do. Waiting to hear from my brother, waiting for a door to open so that we could stay in Minnesota. Now waiting for the baby. But through it all, there is the certainty that God is big enough to take care of us, no matter where we are or what happens to us. Things don't always work out the way we would hope, but if our expectation is always that God will reveal Himself, and that what He does is for His glory and our good, it makes the waiting easier."

Steps sounded, coming down from upstairs, and Oscar ducked into the kitchen. Mrs. Frankel went to the stove and poured water into a basin. "Doctor, it's about time."

Dr. Horlock rose from the couch, wide awake, and headed up the stairs.

"Is she all right?" Oscar asked Mrs. Frankel.

"She's doing just fine. Won't be long now." She tossed a couple of clean towels over her arm and picked up the steaming basin.

From that point on, Oscar couldn't even pretend to work. He paced. He stared out the window into the darkness. And he faced up to the truth he'd been avoiding for the past month.

He loved Kate Amaker, and he didn't want her to leave.

After what seemed a couple of lifetimes, a baby's cry drifted down from upstairs, and Oscar sagged into one of the kitchen chairs, his head in his hands.

Chapter Fifteen

Kate had an entirely new perception of what it meant to be tired, and yet, she was too excited to sleep. Inge helped her sit up, stacking more pillows behind her back.

"Well done, Kate." Mrs. Frankel laid the blanket-wrapped bundle in her arms. "All clean and ready to meet Mama."

Blinking away the tears that clouded her eyes, she looked down into the face of her son. Round cheeks, button nose, cap of dark hair. His tiny hand opened and closed, impossibly small fingers, each with a perfect miniscule nail.

"I'd guess he'll go about seven and a half pounds." Dr. Horlock rolled down his sleeves and buttoned the cuffs. "Strong little heart, and as you've heard, a very sturdy cry. I don't envy you when he gets wound up in the middle of the night telling you he's hungry." He grinned. "Mrs. Frankel, you are welcome to assist me on any delivery. I've never seen a better midwife."

"Practice makes perfect, both the having and the

delivering. I imagine I've assisted at more than half the births in this county over the past fifteen years."

Inge leaned over and kissed the baby's head. "You did a beautiful job. Thank you, Kate. This little one gives me hope. It has been a long time since I had hope. Can Martin see him?"

"Yes." Kate couldn't even look up she was so captivated. "I can't wait to introduce them."

"Come along, Doctor." Pasty Frankel finished straightening up the room. "We've earned some rest, and they don't need us hanging about."

"Right. And I know where there are some excellent cookies downstairs." He followed her out of the bedroom, and in minutes, Martin was in the doorway.

One look at the baby, and he was digging for his handkerchief. "Bless you, Kate. He's a handsome boy."

"Would you like to hold him?" Kate's heart threatened to overflow at the sight of his tears.

Nodding, Martin sat on the side of the bed. He took the baby into his arms, and Inge rounded the bed to stand beside him, her hand on his shoulder.

"I wish Johann could see his son. He would be so proud." Inge cupped the little head in her hand.

Kate nodded. "He would already be making big plans for the two of them, wouldn't he?"

"We must be making plans, too." Martin looked up. "But not tonight. Tonight we will rejoice in God's goodness to us." He raised the baby in his arms and kissed him on the head. To Kate it seemed like a benediction spread over her son.

"Kate?"

Oscar stood in the doorway, his hands shoved into his pockets.

His hair stood on end as if he'd rammed his fingers through it many times, and one of his shirttails hung out.

He'd never looked better to her.

"Come in."

Stopping after only a couple of steps, he said, "I don't want to intrude."

"No, come and meet your latest houseguest."

Martin rose from the side of the bed and held the baby out. Oscar looked to Kate for permission, and at her nod, he took the baby in his arms.

Another rush of tears came to her eyes. What was it about a strong man holding a newborn that made her insides melt? Or was it *this* strong man holding *her* newborn? Even as he cradled her son protectively, she felt protected. He had cared for her family and given her a safe place to have her baby. How could she ever thank him?

Oscar met her eyes, and something powerful passed between them. Her breath grew shallow.

"Inge, it is very late, and I think you should rest." Martin threaded his wife's arm through his.

"Yes, I am tired. Kate, I will leave my door open a crack. You will call me if you need me?" Inge went with Martin to the door, leaving Oscar holding the baby.

Oscar pulled the rocking chair up beside the bed and sat down. "I don't even know…is this a boy or a girl?" He rocked gently. "Liesl prayed for a boy, but I have a feeling it won't matter once she lays eyes on this baby."

Kate smiled, resting her head against the pillows. "It's a boy."

"What are you going to call him?"

A tinge of sadness nudged her joy. "Johann. After his father. Johann Martin Amaker, but I think I will call him Joe. Maybe Joey for now, and Joe when he's older."

"Kate." Oscar looked up quickly, so many words crowding into his eyes. "Don't go."

She frowned, puzzled. "I'm sorry?"

He looked as if the words had surprised him, too. His Adam's apple lurched, and he shifted the baby to snuggle against his chest.

"I don't want you to go to Cincinnati."

She shook her head. "I don't want to go, either, but I don't know that I have much choice in the matter." Though she'd give almost anything to stay, they hadn't found a way to make it feasible. "In a week the farm will be sold, and in less than a month, we'll be on our way to Ohio."

Oscar shook his head. "No. There is a way you can stay." He slid off the rocker to his knees beside the bed, still cradling Joey to him. "Stay here with me and Liesl. Marry me. I know I'm not Johann. I'll never be adventurous and exciting, but… I'm steady and strong. I'll take care of you, and I'll treat Joey like he was my own."

Kate put her fingertips to her lips. He was asking her to marry him? The man who hadn't wanted her in his house in the first place, the man who had kept everyone at bay and didn't want any reminders of past hurts? His eyes bored into hers. Her heart leaped, but…part of her held back. He hadn't said the one thing she would need to hear to make her say yes.

"And Martin and Inge, too. I wouldn't dream of asking you to stay and sending them away. I realized a while ago what it has done for Liesl to have them in her life, to have that sense of more family than just me." His eyes pleaded with her.

They had been good for Liesl. He wanted her to stay for his daughter?

"And you've all been good for me, too. You've brought me back into the community, into living again."

Which made her happy, but it wasn't enough. How could she say yes when he'd given no indication of how he felt about *her*?

"Kate, please. I've done something very foolish." A sigh surged through his chest, lifting Joey as he inhaled. "I've fallen in love with you. If you leave, I don't know that I can bear it. I know it hasn't been long since Johann's death, and the loss of your house, and a new baby, but I can't help it. I love you."

There it was. His heart, laid bare.

"Oh, Oscar." Tears welled and overflowed, and she reached for his hand. "You mean it?"

He clasped her fingers. "I never meant to fall in love again. I didn't even think I could, and then, before I knew it, I was a goner." He sat on the side of the bed and leaned forward, resting his brow against hers. "Please say you care about me at least a little bit."

Her hands came up and cupped his beard. "Oscar, I do love you. It was breaking my heart to think of leaving you and Liesl."

Then his lips were on hers, gentle and sweet. Not a

public, awkward kiss under the mistletoe, but a kiss of shared love, of an entwined future, a kiss of promise.

Joey snuffled and squirmed, letting out a squeak, and Oscar sat back, a rueful smile on his face. "And so it begins." He laid the baby in his arms again. "Don't you know you're horning in on something pretty special here, young man?"

"What will Liesl think?" Kate asked.

"That her daddy is a very smart man," Oscar boasted. "Now, little mama, you need to get some rest. You've had a hard day. And tomorrow...actually, later today, we'll have a lot to talk about and settle. But for now, you need to sleep."

"I don't want to go to sleep. I don't want to miss a minute of this." But waves of tiredness washed over her, and her eyelids grew heavy.

"Don't worry. Joey and I will be right here getting acquainted." He reached over and turned the lamp wick down to barely a flicker and settled back in the rocker.

Kate eased down in the bed, turning carefully to her side so she could watch them, drinking in the sight of the man she loved holding her son.

"Oscar?" she whispered.

"Yes?" He looked up.

"Merry Christmas."

Kate eased herself out of the bed and donned her dressing gown. "You take the baby, and I'll follow behind."

"I think you should stay in bed." Oscar frowned. He still looked rumpled and short of sleep, probably because he'd spent the remainder of the night in the rocking chair watching over her and Joey, stepping out only when Joey demanded to be fed. Inge had come across the hall to check on them, but the baby had no trouble getting the hang of eating. The minute he was done, Oscar had been back to hold him while she slept.

"I wouldn't miss Christmas morning with our family for the world." It felt so wonderful to say that. "Is Liesl still sleeping?"

"No, she's waiting downstairs. With Inge and Martin." Oscar took her elbow with one hand, holding Joey with the other. "I'll go first down the stairs, and you keep your hand on my shoulder."

"Just like old times. You do realize that very soon I will be able to go up and down stairs all by myself." She squeezed his arm. "Do Martin and Inge know? Does Liesl?"

"No, I thought we'd tell them together." He stepped down onto the first stair. "Easy, now, and go slowly."

They reached the kitchen, and Liesl ran to her, braid's flying. "Miss Kate!"

"Easy," Oscar cautioned. "Hug her gently."

Kate embraced Liesl. "Merry Christmas, sweetling."

"Can I see him?"

"Absolutely. How about if we go into the parlor and you can hold him?" The pocket doors to the parlor were completely closed, something she hadn't seen before.

"What's going on here?"

"Christmas surprises. Martin and Inge and I have been very busy this morning." Oscar grinned. "Breakfast first?"

"I'm famished, but I don't know if I could stand the suspense." Kate inhaled the aroma of fresh coffee and baked goods. "Perhaps we could have a quick snack and then a full breakfast later?"

Inge sliced hot, fresh *Zopf*, spreading it with thick, creamy butter. "This will tide you over, but you need to eat well. You have Joey to think about now."

Liesl tugged on her father's arm. "I can't see."

He crouched and folded back the edge of the blanket. Liesl's lips formed an "O" and she touched the soft little fist beside Joey's cheek.

"This is Joey. He's as perfect as a shiny new nickel, isn't he?"

She nodded. "Is he sleeping? Why doesn't he open his eyes?"

"Babies sleep a lot, and he's tuckered out. Being born is hard work for a baby." Oscar straightened.

"It's no picnic for the mama, either." Kate laughed. At Oscar's concerned frown, she shook her head. "I'm fine."

He sent her a look that made her feel all glowing and warm. For the moment, they had a secret, and she was content to keep it to herself, but soon, they would share it and hopefully everyone would be happy.

Liesl could hardly be persuaded to leave Joey's side to eat her breakfast.

"He'll be here when you're done," Oscar promised.

Liesl ate quickly, and when she was finished, she came back to gaze at Joey. She didn't seem at all jealous that her father was holding him. "He's beautiful."

"That he is. And born on Christmas Day, too."

"Oh, yes." Liesl left Joey long enough to push her chair up to the sideboard. With great formality, she placed the last wood block in the center of the pieces. "Now the Baby Jesus is here. Because it is Christmas."

"That it is, Poppet." Oscar handed Joey to Kate and picked his daughter up, kissing her on the cheek. "Merry Christmas. Are you ready for your surprises?"

"Yes!"

Oscar slid open the pocket doors, and Liesl let out a squeal. "Oh, Daddy. Look!" She pointed. A small evergreen tree stood in the corner of the room, festooned with paper chains and popcorn strings.

"When did you do all this?" Kate asked.

"Martin and Inge were up very early today. We put the finishing touches on things when you were feeding Joey." Oscar nodded to Grossvater and Grossmutter. "I couldn't have done any of this without them."

The Advent window still wore its swags of pine branches, and the room smelled wonderfully of forest. A fire crackled in the fireplace. And a blue cloth covered something on the mantel, but when Kate raised her eyebrows to Oscar, he shook his head. "Patience."

They all sat, and Kate helped Liesl hold the baby. Oscar reached for his Bible and spread it on his knees. "We'll start with the Christmas story." And with a strong, steady voice, he read from Luke 2. When he was finished, Martin led them in a prayer of thanksgiving.

"Liesl," Oscar said. "You wait here, while we go get your present, all right?" He and Martin went out of the room. Kate took Joey back from Liesl.

Martin and Oscar came into the parlor carrying the dollhouse between them.

Liesl's eyes grew round, and she breathed, "Oh, Daddy."

The men set the dollhouse on the floor, and she went down on her knees beside it.

"Merry Christmas, Liesl." Oscar came to sit beside Kate, and he put his arm around her shoulders. She glanced up at him, but no one was looking at them. Martin and Inge were watching Liesl, and the little girl was totally engrossed with her present. She lifted each piece of furniture, turning it in her hands before placing it back exactly where she had gotten it.

"Look, it's me." She touched the girl doll. "And Daddy." Easily recognizable by his beard. "And Rolf!" Snatching up the carved dog, she held it up. "It looks just like him."

Kate leaned into Oscar's side. "All that work was worth it." She'd marveled at his ability to carve such an accurate representation of the Bernese mountain dog, but when he'd painted it in black, white and brown, it had almost sprung to life. Every piece of the dollhouse had been fashioned with love, and the reward was seeing Liesl's happiness and wonder.

"And here's Kate, and baby Joey, and Grossmutter, and Grossvater." Liesl lifted each little doll from the kitchen chairs.

Inge had a small apron she had made for Liesl, who insisted on putting it on right away over her pinafore. Inge had also used some leftover white fabric to make a set of handkerchiefs for Oscar. She'd hemmed the squares with a red, blanket stitch and embroidered his initials in one corner.

"To say thank you for your hospitality. It is not enough, but we do thank you."

"And this is for you, my dear." Martin handed a small package to Inge. "Oscar helped me make it."

Inge squeezed his hand and unwrapped the brown paper. "Martin." Her lips trembled, and she hugged the *Tirggel* mold. "It is my home in the Emmental."

The old couple embraced, and she kissed his lined cheek. "Thank you, Martin. And thank you, Oscar. You have blessed us so much."

"And now for your gift, Kate. I hope you like it." Oscar went to the mantel and carefully raised the blue cloth.

"Oh, Kate, look." Inge gasped.

Kate let out a slow breath, and stood carefully. "Oh, my." She swallowed, turning to look up at Oscar. "But how? When?"

He shrugged, taking her hand. "I finished up my Christmas orders a while ago. Every night when I went into the workshop, I was carving on these. Martin helped with the sanding and letting me know what pieces to make."

She passed Joey to Inge and went back to the fireplace. Arrayed along the mantel were piece after carved piece of a Nativity set. Camels, donkeys, sheep, magi and shepherds. A star hung from the top of the crèche over Mary and Joseph and the Baby Jesus.

"Do you like it?" Oscar asked from behind her, his hands coming to rest on her shoulders.

"Like it?" She spun and put her arms around his neck. "It's beautiful." Tears sprang to her eyes, and she buried her face in his chest. He rested his chin on her hair and stroked her back. When she stopped crying, he gave her one of his new handkerchiefs.

"You might as well break it in," he teased. "Now, how about if we give Inge and Martin our Christmas gift? And Liesl, too?"

She nodded, wiping at her tears, and he moved to her side, putting his arm around her waist.

"Liesl, Martin, Inge." He looked down at Kate, sending a thrill through her at the warmth in his eyes. "Kate has agreed to marry me. Soon."

A trickle of anxiety rippled through Kate. What would Martin and Inge say? After all, it had been less than a year since their grandson, her husband, had died.

"This means that you can stay here." Oscar gestured toward Martin and Inge. "There's no need to go to Cincinnati. You can use the rest of the money you made from selling the cheeses to pay the loan on the farm, and I'd like to chip in the balance to pay off the note entirely. You can continue to live here with us, and we'll run the two farms together if that's what you want."

A spark of hope lit Martin's expression, but doubt hesitated there, too. "Kate, is this what you want? Are you sure? We don't want you doing this because you feel you need to."

Inge nodded, lightly rocking Joey. "You must not think you have to do this."

"Oh, you dear people. Of course I want this." She leaned into Oscar's side. "I love Oscar, and he loves me, too."

Liesl stood up from the dollhouse. "Does this mean we get to keep you?"

Kate held out her hand, and Liesl came to her, looking up. "Would you like that? For Grossvater and Grossmutter and Joey and me to stay here for always?"

"Yes! But, Daddy, I thought you said I couldn't have my Christmas wish. That Jesus had to say no."

Oscar leaned down and picked her up. "I thought you wanted a baby for Christmas."

She shook her head. "I did, but you said I couldn't have one, so I changed my wish." She nodded, serious. "I prayed every night."

"And what did you pray for?" he asked.

"I prayed for a family for Christmas."

He hugged her tight, reaching out and drawing Kate into the embrace.

She rested her head on his shoulder and smiled into Liesl's eyes. "You know what? I wished for the very same thing. Merry Christmas, sweetling."

* * * * *

*If you liked this story,
pick up these other heartwarming books
from Erica Vetsch:
HIS PRAIRIE SWEETHEART
THE BOUNTY HUNTER'S BABY*

Available now from Love Inspired Historical!

Find more great reads at www.LoveInspired.com

Dear Reader,

I love Christmas, don't you? I especially love Christmas traditions, those special things we do once a year, those things we anticipate all year long. For the Vetsch family it is making peanut brittle, watching the 1951 Alastair Sim version of *Scrooge*, waffles on Christmas Day and reading the Christmas story from Luke 2 before we open gifts.

In *A Child's Christmas Wish*, the Christmas activities center around Swiss traditions—especially dear to me, as my husband's family is Swiss. In Switzerland, Advent calendars are a big part of the festivities. Parents desire to instill both patience and anticipation in their children through the countdown to Christmas Day. I love this practice, because isn't anticipation of Christmas a huge part of the holiday season?

I hope you enjoy *A Child's Christmas Wish*, and that you will celebrate this season with a few traditions of your own!

Merry Christmas!
Erica Vetsch

HIS FRONTIER CHRISTMAS FAMILY
Frontier Bachelors • by Regina Scott

Newly appointed as guardian of his late friend's siblings and baby daughter, preacher Levi Wallin opens his home to them and their elder sister, Callie Murphy—a woman he can't help but fall for at Christmastime.

ONCE UPON A TEXAS CHRISTMAS
Texas Grooms • by Winnie Griggs

After arriving in Texas to revamp a hotel during the holiday season, Seth Reynolds clashes with the young woman assigned to help him. But when Seth starts to care for feisty Abigail Fulton, will he have to choose between business and love?

WOULD-BE MISTLETOE WIFE
Boom Town Brides • by Christine Johnson

Worried she might lose her teaching job when funding is cut for the boarding school, widow Louise Smythe must consider marriage. But the only prospective groom in town is lighthouse-keeper Jesse Hammond, and he wants children—something she may never be able to provide.

THE GIFT OF TWINS
Little Falls Legacy by Gabrielle Meyer

When twin five-year-old boys are left on Reverend Benjamin Lahaye's doorstep, he and schoolteacher Emmy Wilkes work together to care for the children. But can their temporary makeshift family become permanent?

Get 2 Free Books,

Plus 2 Free Gifts—

just for trying the Reader Service!

Love Inspired HISTORICAL

*All Miranda Morgan wants for Christmas is to be a good
mom to the twins she's been named guardian of—but their
brooding cowboy godfather, Simon West, isn't sure she's
ready. Can they learn to trust in each other and become a
real family for the holidays?*

Read on for a sneak peek of
TEXAS CHRISTMAS TWINS
by **Deb Kastner**,
part of the **CHRISTMAS TWINS** miniseries.

"I brought you up here because I have a couple of dogs I'd
especially like to introduce to Harper and Hudson," he said.

She flashed him a surprised look. He couldn't possibly
think that with all she had going on, she'd want to adopt a
couple of dogs, or even one.

"I appreciate what you do here," she said, trying to buffer
her next words. "But I want to make it clear up front that I
have no intention of adopting a dog. They're cute and all,
but I've already got my hands full with the twins as it is."

"Oh, no," Simon said, raising his free hand, palm out.
"You misunderstand me. I'm not pulling some sneaky stunt
on you to try to get you to adopt a dog. It's just that—well,
maybe it would be easier to show you than to try to explain."

"Zig! Zag! Come here, boys." Two identical small white
dogs dashed to Simon's side, their full attention on him.

Miranda looked from one dog to the other and a light
bulb went off in her head.

"Twins!" she exclaimed.

Simon laughed.

"Not exactly. They're littermates."

He helped an overexcited Harper pet one of the dogs and, taking Simon's lead, Miranda helped Hudson scratch the ears of the other.

"Soft fur, see, Harper?" Simon said. "This is a doggy."

"Gentle, gentle," Miranda added when Hudson tried to grab a handful of the white dog's fur.

"Zig and Zag are Westies—West Highland white terriers."

Zig licked Hudson's fist and he giggled. Both dogs seemed to like the babies, and the twins were clearly taken with the dogs.

But she'd meant what she'd said earlier—no dogs allowed. At the moment, suffering cuteness overload, she even had to give herself a stern mental reminder.

She cast her eyes up to make sure Simon understood her very emphatic message, but he was busy helping Harper interact with Zag.

When he finally looked up, their eyes met and locked. A slow smile spread across his lips and appreciation filled his gaze. For a moment, Miranda experienced something she hadn't felt this strongly since, well, since high school—the reel of her stomach in time with a quickened pulse and a shortness of breath.

Either she was having an asthma attack, or else—

She was absolutely not going to go there.

Don't miss
TEXAS CHRISTMAS TWINS
by Deb Kastner, available December 2017 wherever
Love Inspired® books and ebooks are sold.

www.LoveInspired.com

LIEXP1117

Love Inspired®

Inspirational Romance to Warm Your Heart and Soul

Join our social communities to connect with other readers who share your love!

Sign up for the Love Inspired newsletter at **www.LoveInspired.com** to be the first to find out about upcoming titles, special promotions and exclusive content.

CONNECT WITH US AT:

Harlequin.com/Community

 Facebook.com/LoveInspiredBooks

 Twitter.com/LoveInspiredBks

LISOCIAL2017